TURNING SAMOAN

A NOVEL

TURNING SAMOAN

A NOVEL

DENNIS CHUTE

GREAT PLAINS
PUBLICATIONS

Great Plains Publications
3 –161 Stafford Street
Winnipeg, MB R3M 2W9
www.greatplains.mb.ca

Great Plains Publications gratefully acknowledges the financial support provided for its publishing program by the Government of Canada through the Book Publishing Industry Development Program (BPIDP); the Canada Council for the Arts; the Manitoba Department of Culture, Heritage and Citizenship; and the Manitoba Arts Council.

Design & Typography by Gallant Design Ltd.
Printed in Canada by Kromar Printing

CANADIAN CATALOGUING IN PUBLICATION DATA

Main entry under title:
Turning Samoan

ISBN 1-894283-29-5

I.   Title.
PS8555.H883T87   2001   C813'.6   C2001-910922-9

For Janet, my long suffering wife, who wanted to be a Samoan woman and gave me the idea for this book. For my parents, my patrons. And for Joan Osborne, whose album Relish, which I play obsessively while doing rewrites, encouraged me to think about words in a whole new way.

CHAPTER 1

Maria doesn't mean to be bad. She didn't start out bad. No single traumatic event reshaped her life. Time has just rotted her to the core.

The city is nearly silent as Maria lies down in the middle of the road. The warm, late May sun has already heated the pavement to a comfortable temperature. Wearing a summer-weight, white cotton dress Maria feels the heat rising up off the pavement, warming her back. It would be easy to fall asleep in the middle of the road, with the birds singing and the bright sun overhead.

Her husband, Draj, thought up this scam shortly after they'd come to Canada. Well, Maria thought it up, but Draj likes to take the credit. Maria hoped Draj would want to be the star, to lie in the road and pretend to be hurt. If he got run over it was fine with her. But lying in the road seems like dangerous work to Draj, so Maria is the one who ends up doing it while her husband and his brothers extort money from the drivers who think they've hit her.

The *gaujo* in Canada are so...gullible. Gullible, that was a good word she learned in ESL class. After fourteen years in England Maria thought she spoke English pretty well, but in Toronto the immigration officials hadn't been able to understand her thick Yorkshire accent. Neither had the social worker in Edmonton. So assuming she didn't know how to speak English, they had signed her up for ESL classes at their expense.

Out doing the shopping and the extortion and everywhere else Maria can't help hearing more useful words. Often it's just one word like "pickup" or "weed" that she adds to her vocabulary. But sometimes it's an entire phrase she falls in love with, like "up your tailpipe, imbecile."

Maria is learning other things in Canada besides new words. You can survive having icicles hanging from your nose. Your man isn't supposed to beat you unless you want him to. Also, Canadian women are obsessed with careers and orgasms and they all want to be thin with big breasts. Being herself thin and big-breasted — and therefore a constant target — Maria isn't sure it is a state women should strive to achieve.

At the laundromat they play classic country music on the radio and Maria knows that the women with their somebody done somebody wrong songs are singing about her life. There are also magazines at the laundromat and Maria devours them. These magazines talk about getting a man, keeping a man, women's liberation and TV stars. Maria spends a lot of time watching TV at the Sony Store in Londonderry Mall. The staff let her choose whatever channel she wants, and she sees women who have "thrown off the shackles of male oppression." Maria really likes this phrase.

But best of all are those rare occasions when Draj and Marko send Maria to Hub Cigar Store to buy the vile Panamanian cigars they like to celebrate with when they extort money successfully. Hub has more than a thousand magazines on sale. Maria likes them all. Even the ones she's never had time to read. She loves the ones about UFO abductions and other conspiracies.

Maria has decided to liberate herself. The first step, the TV and magazines tell her, is to gain financial independence. That proves easier than she expected.

Maria begins every morning with the same ritual. After she has made Draj his breakfast and before he can run off for the day with his worthless brothers, she sits down at the kitchen table and says, "I needs money, Draj." And then she squeezes his left bicep, as hard as she can. He just laughs.

"What for you need money?" Every day Draj asks this.

"Groceries," Maria says on Monday.

"New running shoes for Marko," Maria says on Tuesday.

"Laundromat," Maria says on Wednesday.

"Take Nana, get her hair done," Maria says on Thursday.

"Booze," Maria says on Friday, knowing Draj and Marko, Nana, and even Yannis drink themselves blind every Friday night. After Draj passes out Friday evening, Maria goes through his wallet and takes what she wants. Draj is too hung over Saturday morning for their usual conversation. Sunday they spend the day extorting money.

Each evening, before bed, Draj makes her account to him for every penny spent on groceries or laundry or shoes or the hairdresser. For Maria this isn't a big problem. She uses the skills she learned in India as a little girl to confuse poor Draj, counting the same loonie four or five times. Each week Maria manages to pocket sixty or seventy dollars. She has a bank account her husband and his family know nothing about. But there is only a few thousand dollars in it and Maria knows that isn't nearly enough. Not to get away from the Raklos forever.

Tuesday evenings, when the Raklo family goes to the Purple Onion, Maria goes to a movie theatre. At first Draj used to drag her along to the Onion but Maria flirted with every man there until it drove Draj crazy. When they'd get home he would tear off her dress and take his big leather belt, the one he'd bought especially with the studs, and he'd whip her with it. Her half naked, with the whole family watching, he'd beat her until she screamed, begged him to stop, promised to be good, until the pain was unbearable, until she couldn't even feel her back anymore.

Wednesday mornings were agony, her back would be so stiff and crusted up that Maria had to roll out of bed, she couldn't sit up. Lying face down on the floor, she'd arch her back slowly, like a cat, breaking the scabs, regaining mobility. Taking a deep breath, she'd use the dresser to pull herself upright. Then she'd cry for a few minutes, put on her dress and go out to the kitchen and make breakfast as if nothing had ever happened. The welts never healed from week to week, but it was worth it to her. She knew *Draj* would eventually start making her stay home, not let her near the men at the Purple Onion, and she was right.

Tuesday nights now belong to Maria. The magazines say that's the second step, make time for yourself. Right from the beginning Maria cherishes her Tuesday nights. At first she uses the skills she learned as a child to entertain people. Maria picks the popular movies, the ones where the line snakes out of the theatre and down the street, or she works the cineplexes where no one seems to guard the lobby and people mill about. Maria just stands there making cigarettes disappear up her nose and come out her ear.

Soon people stop to watch, not sure whether she is performing or grossing them out. Once she has an audience, Maria takes out one of her ruby silk scarves and ties a knot in it. Gold threads woven into the fabric reflect the theatre's neon lights. She hands the scarf to someone in the crowd, has them tie a knot in it and pass it on to someone else who also ties a knot, and so on, until the scarf is twisted and gnarled and people's fingers can't force it into any tighter confusion. Then she picks out a cute little kid and places the scarf in his hands.

Maria has her assistant scrunch the scarf up in a ball and hold it tightly in his small hands, hidden as best he can. She tells him he is magic, carefully forming each word so that both he and the audience understand her. She gets her little helper to say the magic words, *gilli, gilli, gilli.* When he opens his hands and tugs at the seemingly still intractable chain of knots, the scarf not only unravels, it is amazingly uncreased. Then she passes the hat, a lime-green bowler hat that makes nearly everyone assume she is Irish, what with the accent and all. After each new trick she passes the hat again.

Maria always ends a performance with a few card tricks. It's what she does best, cards dance for her. Her favourite trick involves the invisible deck. Kids are so good at make-believe. She pretends to be shuffling a giant deck of invisible cards, then she asks for a volunteer, she picks the cutest little boy in the audience and she has him pick one of her imaginary cards. He has to look at it and then tell an adult he's with what the card he sees is, the child whispering to the parent. Then Maria takes a real deck, never been opened, has a little girl in the audience shuffle that deck and pick a single card out of it, then the girl gives her parents the rest of the cards. Maria never touches this deck at all. Then the little boy tells the audience what card he picked, the three of clubs, say. The little girl holds up her card and sure enough it's the three of clubs. That one always pulls in the big money and applause. Maria really likes the applause.

Her good looks also attract a lot of attention from single, middle-aged men and packs of teenage boys. She is quite adept at deflecting their advances with humour and grace. But one guy keeps showing up at whatever theatre Maria is working. At first he doesn't say anything. Just stares. Not at her face but at her hands. Maria tries to ignore him.

Then one night he says, "My name's Bob. Do you play poker?" To Maria all *gaujo* look alike but even she recognizes that this guy is more average than most. Average height, average weight, hair an average mousy brown. After that night she always thinks of him as Average Bob. Her new sideline of helping Bob cheat at poker turns out to be a much more lucrative Tuesday night activity than doing magic.

Some of the money she makes goes into spoiling the Raklos. Maria buys fifteen-year-old Yannis books. He orders her around like a servant, get this, take that, but he reads anything and everything and will read it aloud for her pleasure. She buys nineteen-year-old Marko porno magazines and awful Turkish cigarettes. The porno is to keep him from making clumsy passes at her. The dung smell of the cigarettes reminds Maria of home. She buys Draj cheap jewellery, rings mostly. Anything shiny and gold distracts him from all but her worst transgressions. Nana Raklo is tougher. Sometimes Maria pays for a perm, and sometimes it's tea at the Russian Tea Room, and sometimes it's a new pair of heels. With Nana nothing makes up for the fact she isn't producing more little Raklos.

"You're such useless jackasses that if you were stuck on a small raft in the middle of a lake you wouldn't be able to find water to drink," Maria yells at the men, as she lies in the middle of the road. "You're missing so much brains you'd starve at a buffet, if some woman didn't tell you to eat."

"You've got the easy job, sister," Marko says. "All you have to do is lie there. We do all the real work."

"We shake the money out of people's pockets. You're not going to get some mean mother-trucker to give you money," Draj says.

"Like you do. It's hard to shake someone down when you're running fast as your chubby little legs will take you in the other direction."

When Draj and Nana finally realize Maria isn't ever going to get pregnant they take her to a doctor, a specialist, who doesn't really understand what they want to know. She assures them that there is nothing wrong with Maria and that she'll get pregnant when God wishes. Then she says they should check out Draj, see if he is the problem.

The Raklos are out of there so fast they forget Maria, who's been sitting in the waiting room while they talk to the doctor. Maria doesn't notice them leaving. She is seeing her future in a magazine. A picture of a huge, beautiful, brown woman. The woman looks like she is six feet tall. Her body is armoured with mounds of solid flesh. She is standing in front of a mountain. She *is* a mountain. She is the most powerful woman Maria has ever seen. The caption under the photo identifies her as a "typical Samoan woman."

Maria realizes if she looks like this no man will ever take her money, and if they try she will mash their heads like ripe watermelons between her huge hands. Men won't be able to demand sex whenever they feel like it. And she'll never be cold, not with all that fat to keep her warm, and in Canada that will be a very good thing. From then on, every night, after the Raklos are asleep, she tries to conjure up a spell to turn herself into that woman in the magazine. She'd torn the picture out that day at the doctor's office and at night she clutches it to her chest and quietly works her way through all the incantations she can remember her grandmother and mother using when she was a little girl. Nothing ever happens but Maria knows for sure that if she just keeps reciting the magic for long enough she'll be transformed.

There is never any traffic this early on Sunday morning. Lying there waiting for the first traffic of the day Maria tries to will herself to grow and turn dark brown. When she grows bored with that she practices her English by reciting children's stories to herself, softly enough the men can't hear. In ESL classes the instructor, Mr. Martin, had Maria read to the whole class, hoping it would help her pronunciation problems. When she left, Mr. Martin gave her a handful of books: *Cat in the Hat, Green Eggs and Ham, Winnie the Pooh*, and *Wind in the Willows* and told her to keep working on her accent.

Maria knows she is the best thing that ever happened to the Raklos. They were Rom just like the gypsies she lived with in England. But her adoptive family, the Leeses, called them garbage-eating donkeys. When the Raklos parked their rusting motor caravan next to the Lees *kumpania's* wagons the Lees men would stay up all night to keep watch.

After she left India, Maria spent her years in England *dukkering*, telling fortunes, and she was good enough that the Rom she travelled the Yorkshire dales with called her Yokki Juva and compared her to those great artists Triffeni Scamp and Cineralla Purrun. They had been dead for more than a century but were forever alive to the Rom. Maria was sure then that one day she'd be telling fortunes for the lords of the manor just like Triffeni and Cineralla.

She did something, she never knew what, some violation of the superstitions that ruled their lives, their *Mokkado*, and the old man, Shaggy Lees, the chief of the *kumpania*, shunned her. Even then Maria didn't realize how suddenly her life would crash. The *kumpania* wanted rid of her but saw no reason they shouldn't profit from her expulsion. She wasn't of their blood, just a poor beggar girl who didn't understand their ways.

So they sold her to the marriage broker, Anya Heron, for a hundred pounds. Anya thought that Maria was fourteen rather than twenty-seven. By the time she worked out that the Lees had conned her, they were long gone. She was stuck with Maria, who was too old, not a virgin, and mouthy to boot. Anya dragged Maria around the countryside, becoming increasingly annoyed with her. Then they bumped into the Raklos on Clapham Commons.

Discovering Maria was available for the right dowry, the Raklos decided they had to have her. Nana Raklo scraped together every farthing and gee-gaw she had to make a dowry for her oldest boy, Draj. Anya took the modest package, claiming it didn't even cover the cost of feeding Maria. Maria herself never knew what price the Raklos paid for her. However small the dowry, Nana Raklo remained convinced that she spent too much money on Maria.

Maria has tried to make the best out of the situation, teaching the Raklos how to pick pockets. They just aren't good criminal material. Draj, dumb and greedy, is always getting caught. Twice in Canada he has been caught with his hand literally in someone's pocket, trying to steal their spare change.

Nana is too sure she knows everything but all she knows is *Mokkado*, how to look great in a strict and bound way, and boss her sons around. Marko is a drunk with shaky hands, and is too good-natured. He'll bump into a promising victim and strike up a conversation, often still standing around chatting when the guy realizes his wallet has been stolen. Yannis is bright and kind and worries about his eternal soul, which limits his effectiveness.

Maria has tried gently to guide them toward criminal success but it has been like leading a team of mules, each wanting to go their own way, all determined to resist her guidance. Still, in the year since the marriage, the Raklos have gone from living in poverty in a rusted-out motor home to a two-bedroom apartment and a full refrigerator. And the financial rewards from falling in front of cars is rapidly pushing them into the middle class.

So Maria lies in the road in Edmonton, Alberta, Canada, looking cute and sweet and innocent, hoping not to get run over while earning a living for her family.

In the distance, Maria hears the first vehicle of the morning starting down Queen Elizabeth Hill. Looking up, she sees the moon still sharing the sky with the sun. *O chonut asal amen*, the moon smiles, she thinks. It smiles on me. A big foolish grin.

CHAPTER · 2

While Maria is carelessly daydreaming, Willie Jakes is working on his psyche. He is on his way to pump some serious iron and that requires a serious attitude. Willie throws things; the discus, the shot, the hammer, the caber, boulders. As part of his training four days a week he lifts weights. Two of those days he goes to the gym on campus and does heavy weights.

Another day he tosses stones around, big stones from the river. He digs them out with his fingers, out of the mud of the river, and then he hauls them up to his chest, rolling them up his belly, covering himself with river clay. Willie tosses them up into the sky, as high as he can, as though he is trying to toss them over a high wall. People going by on the trails beside the river stop and stare at the huge, half-naked, tattooed man, tossing boulders from the river up into the air.

One day a week he goes to the Kinsmen Centre and does aerobic weight training for a couple of hours. He runs from exercise to exercise, three hundred and fifty pounds of brown mass, rumbling and quivering across the gym. The only practical time to be doing such a thing is early Sunday morning when the place is deserted. Willie wonders what God thinks about him training on the Sabbath. Overall he guesses God is pleased. Willie does his workout with true religious fervour.

This morning Willie is driving Truck. Truck is his labour of love. Originally a 1951 International one-ton flatbed, Truck is now a piece of trash art. As parts have rusted off and fallen out of Truck, Willie has replaced them with things he's found dumpster diving, at the dump, and, when absolutely necessary, parts he's liberated from scrap yards. Some of the additions he's painted, some are now covered with stickers and stamps he's found on his dumpster route. Willie doesn't drive Truck, he babies it. So when he starts down the hill toward the Kinsmen Centre his foot is already on the brake.

Even so he doesn't see the girl until it's too late. Willie stands on the brakes so hard his bum comes right up off the four-by-fours that pass for a bench seat. His first thought is, Truck, what have you done. He doesn't feel any impact but he is sure he has just run over somebody. Forcing the door of the truck open, Willie races around to the front and discovers he hasn't actually hit anyone. He has stopped about four inches short of running over an exotic young woman in a gossamer white cotton dress.

As soon as Maria sees the big man who looks so much like the woman she wants to be, she realizes he is a sign. She is amazed. Her body shudders, uncontrollably. God has finally gotten around to dealing with her numerous prayers. Clearly the giant has been sent to show her the way.

Astounded as she is, Maria keeps her eyes closed. Seeing with her eyes shut isn't hard for Maria. To look convincingly unconscious or asleep while doing it is far harder. Maria first mastered the sleeping sight in order to appear to be in a trance while watching her audience, telling their fortunes. She was ten, still safe in India, and already a natural-born liar.

Not that Maria was always lying when she told fortunes, but she gave her audiences what they wanted. And they wanted a little Maslet girl who went into trances and danced like a dervish and spoke in strange tongues and conjured and finally divined their futures. Otherwise they just didn't believe her and, worse, they didn't pay her. Of course their futures were always filled with better: better jobs, better children, better houses. The trick was to make sure that it wasn't so much better than the here and now that they didn't believe you. Performing on the streets of Delhi, most of the people she met believed in magic and fortune tellers but they were pragmatists at heart and used to working their way slowly around the wheel of life.

In India telling fortunes was just a stage act, for entertainment only. But in England, Grandma Nose, the gypsy witch she lived with for almost fifteen years, taught her *dukkering*, the gypsy way of telling fortunes. You have to visualize a tableau, a painting in your head, a painting of your subject's life.

Other people's fortunes appear to Maria as Renoir paintings of picnics. She always wants to go on a picnic, not that the Rom do that. But whenever their caravan passes *gaujo* having a picnic Maria longs to leap off the back and go join them. She chose Renoir because of The Bathers, and Venus Victrix. Maria wants to look like a Renoir nude, round, succulent. Instead she has what her first boyfriend called "a tight little bod."

Everything Maria sees at a picnic means something. The ants are bad fortune, the eggs are children, yet unborn. Maria didn't start off knowing what everything meant. She has gotten better at telling fortunes as she has aged, lived, and learned to recognize more of the things at the picnic. The salt shaker represents sex, a wicker basket means the person's happiness is fragile. Where the picnic takes place is important as well. Maria had to learn to look at the surrounding countryside. Now sometimes she sees a river rising dangerously close by, a picnic deep in the woods and hard to get to, or in a meadow filled with flowers. In her late teens Maria discovered the weather was critical, some picnics get rained out or the wind blows them away, while others take place under benevolent, cloudless skies.

Because telling fortunes frightens her it also excites her. It gives her the ability to make people happy and sad and she likes having the power to decide which she'll make them. If she doesn't like the person, she only picks up the bad things from the blanket of their future. If she likes them then she tells them only the good things. Nobody ever gets an entire reading from Maria, no matter how many times they pay her, and this, she knows, is vital to keeping the power.

When she looks at the huge brown man hovering over her, she has a sudden vision — the strangest picnic she has ever seen. It is on the beach and the happy blue sea washes in and out, gently lapping on the sand. There are trees she's never seen and vegetables and fruit she's seen at Save-On Foods but never dared to buy lest the men beat her. And everywhere there is a rock, the same rock, as much as she moves her viewpoint it moves with her, so it always fills much of the picture. The massive rock goes forward and backward in time; it is, it always has been, and it always will be. Maria finds it impossible to make any sense of this man's picnic and that reassures her. Surely if God is going to send her a big brown man with purple tattoos as a sign, She will have made sure that the man has an extraordinary future.

The crisis over, his heart beginning to beat again, Willie looks around. Early on a summer Sunday his is the only vehicle anywhere in sight but just a few yards away a group of scruffy, swarthy men stand around wringing their hands. When they realize Willie is looking at them they turn and run away. Willie doesn't find this particularly strange. People often run away when he looks at them.

Willie knows what people think when they first meet him. He's actually asked people he knows well what they first thought and they all say the same thing. "My God, a big mean cannibal!"

Willie fantasizes about going around with a sign on his chest that says, "pacifist vegetarian." The Samoans of Falemusu have been vegetarians, most of the time, since they first settled the island, more than a thousand years ago. They've never been cannibals. Even as a child Willie hated mutton and has always been allergic to dog, which, along with corned beef and Spam make up the meaty portion of the diet on Falemusu. Willie loves corned beef, but hates the version that you get in North America, all lean and firm. The corned beef of his youth was ninety percent fat and you could spread it like peanut butter. When they first moved to Los Angeles and the price of Spam suddenly went from nine dollars to under two dollars he and Maam lived on a diet of fried Spam, until neither of them could ever look at a tin of the pink gunk again without being sick.

Pacifism has been a difficult but conscious choice for Willie. It keeps his blood from getting all riled up. When he lets himself get angry the anger lasts for days. His stomach hurts and his head pounds. He likes going through life on neutral. But he never seems to get a chance to explain this to most people he meets since they just turn and run the other way as fast as they can.

Regretting his reduced social circle isn't fixing the current problem, Willie figures. He is stalling, hoping the girl will wake up or someone will come along and take her off his hands. When it becomes apparent neither is going to happen, Willie kneels beside her and, with careful and practiced hands, checks for any sign of injury. Every time he touches her, a small jolt of electric current runs through Maria. It takes all of her self-control not to shiver. Finding no injuries, Willie slides his hands underneath her back and lifts her straight up. He carries her over to Truck and lays her gently in the bed of the pickup.

When he lifts her, Maria can feel just how strong he is. It is as if he is lifting her and throwing her up into the sky, all the way up to the sun. And that's when Maria, for the first time in her life, enters into a true unconscious trance. In the arms of God's messenger, her personal totem.

Driving even more cautiously than normal, Willie transports the girl to the University of Alberta Hospital. He parks in the emergency bay and honks Truck's horn. It sounds like a drunk goose and eventually brings doctors and nurses shuffling out to see what all the racket is about. They are like zombies from *Night of the Living Dead*. Willie knows they have all been without sleep for far too many hours. He remembers sleep deprivation as the worst part of being an intern.

The medical staff take Maria off on a stretcher and, having asked him if he is next of kin and listened to his story, they lose all interest in him. He hops back into Truck and heads back towards the Kinsmen Fieldhouse. For the rest of the day Willie has the sense memory of her weight and warmth resting on his forearms.

Maria spends the rest of Sunday convincing doctors that she is well enough to be left alone but sick enough she needs to be left in the hospital. She also prays very hard that the big brown man will come and find her. She has important plans for him.

CHAPTER · 3

Willie has taken Monday morning off from his studies. He always feels vaguely guilty when he doesn't put in his self-imposed hours of study, not quite able to accept that Ph.D. candidates in the English department set their own schedules and that even the most obnoxious of supervisors don't expect them to punch a clock. It is due to all those years of medical training where people counted on him to be where he was supposed to be when he was supposed to be there.

Rationally, Willie knows that Mark Twain can wait a day. But he likes to think of himself as a serious scholar and that means discipline. Stopping to rescue a damsel in distress is fine but he has to get back to his real task.

He is sitting in the girl's room. None of the chairs can support his bulk so he is sitting on the window ledge, in the corner farthest from her bed, lest when she awakes he scare the living daylights out of her. He is patient. His instinct says she'll wake soon and then he can satisfy his curiosity and get on with his life. Then the men he saw near the girl the previous morning creep into her room. Willie waits to see what will happen, impassive, immobile, hidden in the shadows, just like his uncles taught him.

The oldest of the three men goes up to the girl and begins shaking her. He is whispering a yell at her. All Willie gets out of the man's tirade is that her name is Maria and these three men all assume she is faking. Maria sleeps on. When her interrogator lifts her by her upper arms, she hangs limp, her head tilted back. He draws back his hand and while he supports her with one hand he slaps her across the face with the other. Willie stands and crosses the room like a fluid rock.

"I don't think you should do that," he says, resting his large left hand on the man's right shoulder. The man turns and looks at Willie's chest and then up to his face. But he doesn't put the girl down. Willie increases the pressure on the man's shoulder, begins to squeeze the soft tissue. The slappy man's eyes bug out.

The other two men begin backing out of the room, leaving behind a boozy vapour of garlic. Eventually the remaining man realizes that Willie wants Maria returned to the bed, and he eases her upper body down most gently. He then bolts for the door, crouched down in a duck-walk to avoid Willie's massive hand.

At the last second Willie grabs him by the collar and swings him back and forth like a pendulum. The man gurgles and chokes while Willie debates roughing him up a little, having no use for those who practise violence against the defenceless. His gentle disposition gets the better of him and he lets the man's feet return to the ground while keeping a grip on his shirt.

Willie has time to assess his captive's features as the man desperately tries to speed away, his feet spinning like bald tires on ice. He has a thick brow and dark, curly hair. His eyes are almost black and his skin is a pasty shade of olive. His nose is beak-like but badly dented, and he is determined. Despite the obvious futility he continues running in place.

Nothing he says in response to Willie's questions is vaguely comprehensible to Willie except for the repeated use of words ending in "uck." It seems to Willie he is being called a fridge-trucker and told to bucking luck off and it irritates him that he can't understand this man well enough to scare some answers out of him. Finally he lets his captive go, suddenly, just to see what will happen. Free at last but badly off balance, the man gathers speed quickly and races, out of control, at the door. Just then an unsuspecting technician pushing a steel cart laden with gloves and tubes and needles enters the room.

Willie watches in amazement as the man collides with the cart. In the midst of his flight he could have elected to jump over top of the cart. He could have dodged. He could have stopped. But instead he tries to dive through the cart. Willie feels this is a foolish decision. People often make foolish decisions when Willie wants to talk with them. He is quickly proved right as the man ends up stuck in the cart. Above the man is the flat surface where the technician has placed her supplies. Below him is a second flat aluminum surface that has remained unadorned. His feet stick out one end and his head the other.

The cart itself ends up out in the hallway. Willie follows it. He thinks the situation is ideal for ensuring that Maria will not receive any more unpleasant visits. The other two men are still lurking down the hall, and that worries him. He grabs the handle of the cart and pulls it back towards himself, gives it a gentle push while still holding on to the handle and then repeats the process three times, each time faster than the last. Near the end of each push he gives the cart a little wobble to judge its stability. On the fifth push he fires the cart down the hall, aiming right at the two men who stand frozen in place as their comrade races towards them, still stuck in his cart, which is now spinning round and round. The spinning cart cuts the two men down.

Willie shouts "strike" and then steps back into the room. He is just in time to see Maria racing to get back into bed, the open back of her hospital gown flapping invitingly in the breeze. As he approaches her bed she wiggles down under the covers. He reaches down and pulls the covers back. Maria is smiling up at him. Then she starts to giggle. Her giggle is so maniacal and contagious, he can't help joining her.

Willie knows he should be leaving, that his little impromptu throwing party will eventually attract the attention of security. Last he saw of the technician, she was running off looking for reinforcements. On the other hand, he feels both chivalrous and immensely curious.

Willie smiles at the elfin girl and says, "Hi, Maria."

"Is my name Maria?" She looks puzzled.

"The men I chased out of here called you Maria," Willie says. He has squatted down beside her bed so as not to intimidate her.

"Well, they'd know. They're my husbands."

"All of them?"

"All of them. Believe me, together they don't make one good man."

"I should have let them stay?" Willie asks, vaguely troubled by the concept of multiple husbands and more troubled by the idea that he might have chased off somebody Maria wanted to see.

"You did just right, big brown man," Maria says reaching out to pat Willie's massive right forearm.

"My name's Willie Jakes."

They shake hands very solemnly.

"Please tell me how you got so big, Mr. Willie?" Maria asks. A simple question that Willie nearly takes to be a joke. But he wants to spend as much time with this girl as he can. So he gives her the most complete answer he can imagine.

"My Maam's nearly as big as me. Then I was a large baby. And my Maam she wanted me to grow up to be as big as her and my uncles so she fed me a lot when I was little. Taro and yams and coconut and I ate and ate.

"I could barely crawl the first time I tried to lift something. I can remember it, or maybe Maam's just told me the story so many times, I tried to lift the kitchen table. It had these big, heavy, square, wooden legs and I'd crawl over to the table from wherever in the house my mother set me down and put one hand on each side and try to squeeze the life right out of one of those wooden legs. Then I'd try to stand up, still keeping my grip on the table leg. I got slivers that Maam would have to pull out and the table never budged."

"Then one day when I stood up the table lifted just enough that it tipped my Maam's cake batter over and it poured onto the floor. She just laughed and laughed. After that she'd leave me outside in the garden amongst the trees and at first I tried to tear them out of the ground. One of my uncles gave me a rock to play with, a big boulder for a baby to be moving around."

"Why do they give you a rock?" Maria asks.

"To my people, I come from Samoa, rocks are magic."

"What sort of magic, Mr. Willie, please?"

"Do you go to church?"

"As I can."

"And do you know what an altar is?"

Maria shakes her head, so Willie explains. "An altar is that long wooden table the minister stands at to do all the religious stuff, blessing the wine, and the Eucharist, praying to God Himself."

"What's a youcrist?"

"The wafer, the cookie, the thing that you eat, it's supposed to be the body of Christ, or the minister makes it the body of Christ, something like that. When I was little, the Catholic nuns left my village and the Protestant missionaries set up shop and I've always been a little confused about these things. But a rock, that I understand. Sometimes we use a big one as a table to do magic on, bless babies, sacrifice a pig to God. You see we think God is inside rocks. Sometimes we carry little rocks around so that we can always have a piece of God nearby."

"Is it all rocks, God is in?"

"No. It's only the rarest ones."

"Like diamonds?"

"No. The rocks God is in, they don't look different from any other rocks."

"So how do you know which rock is magic, Mr. Willie?"

"You have to listen to it. If you know how to listen, like my uncle Duncan does, then you can hear God inside the rock. I don't think I know how. I've listened to a lot of rocks but I haven't heard anything, let alone God talking to me."

Maria smiles with such warmth that Willie's heart skips. "I know things too, big man, and one of the things I knew about you before you ever spoke was that you knew how to listen to rocks. You just haven't found one of the magic ones yet. But tell me what the rock your uncle gave you had to do with you being so big."

"Well, I carted that rock around everywhere. I could barely walk, but I'd hug that rock and totter around the yard, so my uncle gave me a bigger one. Whenever it got so I could carry the rock without any problem, my uncle or one of my older cousins gave me an even bigger one. When I was older I found out that each of those rocks came from the landslide, where half a mountain fell on my father. My Samoan relatives figured my Dad's spirit was in those rocks. The only thing I brought with me when my Maam and I came to the United States was a rock from the landslide, just a little one."

Willie reaches into his pocket and brings out a small, black stone worn smooth by years of handling. He places it in his left palm and holds the palm out to Maria. She gingerly takes the rock and closes her right hand around it. Minutes pass in silence.

"I don't get it. You a big brown man, but your father, he was a thin white man. He was some sort of doctor?" Willie is momentarily stunned, wondering how this total stranger could feel a rock and suddenly know so much about him.

"Yes, he was a doctor, Maria. A white doctor who was fascinated by diseases that kill people where it's warm. He was trying to get to a remote village where there was some horrible bleeding fever when the mountain fell on him. I don't know if he was going to help or to study, but the mountain fell on him anyway."

They get interrupted by the police who want to know what is going on. The policemen know that Willie is a troublemaker. Reaching this judgement only takes them one quick look. They want to arrest Willie, or at least try, but the victims have disappeared. They have to content themselves with escorting Willie off the hospital grounds. He goes quietly.

Just before they lead Willie out of the room Maria grins and says, "I'll see you later, Mr. Willie."

CHAPTER · 4

After his visit with Maria, Willie doesn't feel right. He wants to sneak right back into the hospital and spend the rest of the day with her, hide under her bed just before visiting hours end, spend the night with her. He ends up sending her flowers. He can't decide what to say on the card, so he writes nothing.

Willie knows he needs to calm down, re-center himself. For this he has a ritual. Willie has a ritual for everything important.

In Capilano Park, on the far east side of the city, there are three massive boulders. They were dumped on the middle of the main trail through the park, spaced just a little apart, like three giant, prehistoric teeth, to prevent off-roaders and other yahoos from driving their vehicles into the park. Each boulder, by itself, is too big to be displaced by someone driving into it with a four-by-four or a pickup.

Willie has made it his mission in life to move them.

By himself. No mechanical help. Just his own muscle power.

The middle one, at least.

A man needs to know when his reach is exceeding his grasp.

Centering himself, Willie looks like he's just resting against the lichen-covered boulder. But every muscle is straining as he leans back against the rock face, pushing on it. When nobody is looking he turns and tries to shove the rock. He isn't re-centred until he's exhausted himself.

After Maria, he was looking forward to struggling with an immovable object. But on this day his concentration is repeatedly broken by someone nearby playing the same song over and over again. He can't make out most of the words but the refrain sounds like, "What if God were a slob just like you and me?" Willie can't get past that idea to reach his inner sanctuary. He heads off to work still not quite right, displeased, unsatisfied, unsettled.

When Willie first started on his Ph.D. all he had was a little cubicle, a desk not as wide across as his shoulders, and a surplus chair that collapsed under his weight. Then he helped the Dean find his missing daughter. It hadn't been hard, he'd known exactly where to look. Everyone in the Faculty of Arts knew, they just didn't want to be the one who told the Dean. Dr. Richards had the reputation of being a man who shot the messenger.

Susy Richards was living with a Devil's Rebel. They couldn't even claim to be a major bike gang, more sort of biker wannabes. The Devil's Rebels rode around on their sad Harleys trying to find someone to frighten, usually with very little success. They sold drugs, mostly marijuana since no supplier would trust them with the real thing, and broke kneecaps for an aging bookie named Keno Reno.

The Devil's Rebels leader was a dropout from dental school named Jerome Morgan. Jerome had watched a few too many Marilyn Manson videos and had a serious cross-dressing problem. He was into biker leather, with a very feminine corset and a white painted face. His pet ferret occasionally poked his head out from between Jerome's giant fake boobs. Further adding to the effect, the ferret, whose name Willie never did get, hadn't been de-scented. Jerome liked to call himself "Fetish." He was Susy Richards' main squeeze.

Generally speaking Willie is a tolerant guy. But Susy was fourteen and Jerome had the annoying habit of referring to Willie as the Pillsbury Doughboy, the Michelin Man, lardo and fat fenders. Willie was raised to believe it was impolite to speak to someone who was elocuting passionately, so he stood outside the Commercial Bar on Whyte Avenue, where he'd finally run Jerome and Susy to earth, while Fetish heaped abuse on him in an annoyingly nasal whine. Finally Jerome had made the mistake of tugging on one of Willie's substantial ears and saying "Who was your Dad, Dumbo?"

That was when Willie turned his back on the harangue, bent down and grabbed the two wheels of Jerome's Harley. Once he had a firm grip Willie stood up and slowly raised his arms until he was holding the bike at chest height. Then he turned so he was facing Jerome, who was busy sputtering some nonsense about putting his bike down. With one mighty exhalation

Willie brought the two tires together, neatly folding the bike in two. Then he dropped the mangled mess at Jerome's feet, instant modern metal sculpture.

"I think you'd better come with me, Ms. Richards," he'd said. And she did. And Willie got his office, the very next time a professor retired, which was quite a while later.

In the office he has books, one copy of every book written by or about Mark Twain, and a number of books about the Southern United States between the time of the Civil War and the First World War. He also has books about the various places Twain travelled, and biographies of the people he met. They are all neatly stacked in steel bookcases he bought at an auction of surplus army equipment. Everyone else was bidding up the weapons and uniforms while Willie got a deal on solid steel bookcases, a General-sized desk and three file cabinets.

In one file cabinet he keeps all the journal articles about Twain, about his contemporaries, and copies of all Twain's correspondence. In the second he keeps all the various drafts of his thesis. Homosexuality on the Mississippi, The Racist Twain, Father of Feminism, Twain's Black Dogs, Twain the Mystery Writer, they are all there, every draft, every word. Willie isn't sure what the third cabinet is for yet. He's only had it for six years and he doesn't want to just fill it up with odds and ends.

One time he'd tried keeping all the memos that circulated in the department and then all those e-mails in that third cabinet, but it just didn't feel right to him. One day he'd taken everything from that file cabinet out into the parking lot and burned it. Roasted some marshmallows, got some use out of it. Nobody seems to send him memos anymore, which is too bad since they'd added an interesting flavour to the marshmallows. Ever since then the third cabinet has been empty.

Willie knows the basis of his Ph.D. is in that room somewhere, a single little fact hiding out amongst all the others. He's developed his own unique ways of looking for it. Some days Willie takes a book off the shelf and tosses it in the air. He catches it by an open page and reads and hopes for inspiration. Other days he reaches into his Twain cabinet and grabs a handful of files and starts reading. The last two hours of each work day he forces himself to work on the thesis, sitting at his computer. Two thousand words, it is never the same thesis twice but it is two thousands words every day and they all go in the thesis cabinet. Willie never leaves a messy desk behind.

Still feeling unsettled, Willie re-reads everything he has on Twain's years in San Francisco. He keeps a note pad beside him as he reads, writing every stray idea that flies into his head, noting every lead to follow up. Maybe he'll take a trip to San Francisco, go by Salt Lake City, stop and visit with Maam. The day's thesis entry turns out to be about the possibility that Twain had a completely *sub rosa* affair with a Chinese laundry girl.

After he's finished his two thousand words for the day Willie hikes the two miles out to where he's parked Truck. Willie refuses to pay for parking. When he first started on his Ph.D. it was only half a mile he had to walk. But with the boom in the number of students, the all-day, free, unlimited parking has slowly been swallowed up and he's had to park farther and farther away. The length of his daily walks is a slap in the face to Willie, forever reminding him of how long he's been working on his thesis. On the afternoon of Willie's first conversation with Maria, Truck is reluctant to start, needs all of Willie's exhortations as well as his skill with the choke. It's like Truck doesn't want to go home.

Home is temporarily the Maple Village Trailer Park. Willie hopes it is temporary. Not that he dislikes the trailer he lives in, he's specially converted the thirty-foot extra-wide to accommodate a man of his size and he has no intention of giving it up. But this spring Willie had a little extra money and he bought a piece of land, mostly forest, bog, and lake. Now he wants to move the trailer onto it. But, of course, there are reams of development permits required, and he has to clear the land, dig a well, and arrange to have power brought in and that all takes even more money, and he has to save enough to pay his taxes.

Willie knows something is weird at his trailer before he finishes parking the truck. He seems to be throwing a party for his neighbours. Willie likes his neighbours and they like him. They are long past being concerned by his size and tattoos and he's become an indispensable part of their community, able to fix anything that breaks, always ready to lend a hand, or a massive shoulder to cry on, or lend them a few bucks. On the other hand he can't remember inviting them to hang out in his postage stamp backyard, drinking. But Mrs. Mitchell, Jimmy Dean, the Franluck twins, Dingo Albee, his part-time boss, and a number of people he hasn't met are doing just that. There are nearly forty people Willie guesses, since they are in constant motion he can't be sure.

The party has a very friendly and efficient hostess, who is busy grilling lamb on Willie's ancient oil drum grill, and plantains, and yams, and taro, and mixing drinks, and yattering away in semi-English, and charming everyone. Up until he sees Maria, Willie has been hoping that the whole thing is some kind of spontaneous block party. Actually he isn't too concerned about the party. He doesn't drink and he doesn't eat meat, so neither the booze or the lamb are his. On the other hand Maria looks like she's moved right in and made herself at home.

Willie tries to part the crowd, but everyone wants to tell him what a great party it is, and what a swell gal Maria is, and how happy they are for him that he's finally found someone. When he finally makes his way to Maria, she hands him a plate stacked mountainously high with grilled vegetables and a large mug of tropical fruit punch.

"What are you doing here?" he asks.

"I came for you to teach me how I get to be Samoan, like we started in the hospital."

Willie decides to ignore her comment, for now. He finds the vegetables fabulous, grilled soft and sweet, basted in some sort of nut sauce.

By the time Willie finishes eating, Maria is leading a very uncoordinated Conga line. Maria has moved Willie's Bosc sound system outside. She's gone through his music collection and picked anything with a beat, from the Macarena tape he hates, a gag gift, to the Boss. With the system cranked to max, the whole trailer court is shaking. Maria is dancing up a storm. Her complete lack of style, a hilarious bump and grind combined with bits of dances like the Twist and the Funky Chicken, has broken down people's reserve and nearly everyone is dancing. Anyone who seems hesitant she drags out on to the grass, dances with them, dances for them, moves their arms and legs until they finally give in and dance. Willie is her last victim.

When the Conga line passes the sound system he reaches out and turns it down. He's in the middle of the pack. When Maria, leading the line, passes the sound system she turns the volume back up.

As the night progresses, booze flows and people forget themselves. Wendy and Wilma Franluck are the first to make complete fools of themselves. They are retired librarians who work as substitutes in various local school libraries. Both are wearing yellow, green, and red floral print dresses.

Willie can't tell them apart so all he can say for sure is that one of them is doing gymnastics on the railing of his patio, eight feet off the ground. As her routine gets more aggressive her dress becomes a problem, endangering both her limbs and her modesty. In back flips, cartwheels, and forward somersaults it falls around her ears and over her head, revealing her red lace undies and blinding her. Not to be outdone her twin shucks her dress and climbs up on the railing. The crowd gets the idea just in time and gathers in front of her as she leaps out into space, into the improvised mosh pit that carries her in near naked imperial glory around Willie's backyard.

Things deteriorate from there.

Maria wants Willie to carry her around the yard. Just him. Nobody doubts for an instant that he is strong enough. But all his neighbours know he's far too reserved.

Maria is determined. Willie is trying to talk to Dingo over the din of the music when she sneaks up behind him and begins scaling his back like she was climbing a telephone post. Before he can grab her she's sitting on his neck, her bare legs dangling down his chest, her hands in his hair, tugging.

"Giddy up, horsey," she commands. He takes a few halting steps. "You've got to be able to go faster than that," she says, kicking him in the chest.

Willie starts a shambling run around the yard, dodging the other guests. Most are now too inebriated to get out of the way of a charging Samoan. Maria climbs up onto Willie's shoulders, so she's standing erect as he runs. The crowd cheers the strange sight.

"If I were still in the outback I'd think I was seeing a mirage," Dingo, who has known Willie the longest, says to Mrs. Mitchell, who thinks of herself as Willie's substitute mother. Or at least dispenser of romantic advice to the most lovelorn man she's ever met. A little boy really, with a glass heart.

Later the two of them watch Willie and Maria dance a very slow waltz, glued to each other.

"What a lovely couple they make," Mrs. Mitchell says.

"Maybe," Dingo says, "maybe, but there is something, I don't know, not right."

"He's nuts about her!"

"That's it exactly. He's being bulldozed by her. But I don't get the feeling she feels the same about him," Dingo says.

"Well, I don't care. After all this time alone, maybe he *needs* a woman to take the reins."

They are interrupted when Maria comes running up to Dingo to get him to dance a tango with her. She can't get Willie drunk enough.

In the next hour or so the temperature drops ten degrees. The embers of the party die out suddenly. Dingo Albee, the last guest, comes over to Maria and gives her a hug.

"Great party," he says. Then he stumbles off home. Maria comes and sits beside Willie on his back patio deck. She's found a sweater for him and a blanket for her.

"You aren't mad, are you, Mr. Willie?" She asks curling up against him. He puts a massive arm around her.

"No, Maria. I'm not mad but I am surprised. How did you get out of the hospital and find me here?"

"I think I'm better so I leave that place, and I find this." Maria hands Willie his wallet. "I wanted to thank you so I think party." Looking inside his now nearly empty wallet Willie realizes where the lamb and booze came from, or at least who paid for it.

They sit there in silence listening to the chorus of crickets and frogs. Mosquitoes buzz around them and occasionally Willie reaches out and catches one, crushing it in his hand. They show no interest in biting Maria.

"I don't think you can just decide to be Samoan, Maria. Samoans are very family people. The family is everything, and the families are often huge, three or four hundred people. My family would do anything for me and I'd do anything for them. And our families keep growing, we have lots of kids, we Samoans. But the families grow for another reason, we adopt people. Not children-adults, like you. Come to the door of our hut, say I want to be part of your family, we'll welcome you with open arms, instant family. You should know though that we will also expect you to support us, your money is our money, your things are our things.

"Lots of white people, from Europe, from the U.S. and even from Canada, they think Samoa is paradise. They come around and just settle right into a Samoan family. They eat, sleep, and make love Samoan style. We welcome them with open arms because they are our major cash crop. My point is that none of these people, no matter how long they stay has ever turned Samoan. Believe me that would be big news in the islands. Everyone would know."

"Why don't they turn Samoan?"

"It doesn't work like that. I'm Samoan because my Maam is Samoan, because I was raised Samoan."

"But your Dad was white. If you'd been raised in England would you be English?"

"No. I think I got all my race genes from my Maam. I'd have turned out Samoan wherever I'd been raised."

"What's a jean?"

"You know, like DNA."

Maria shakes her head.

"Inside us, inside every cell of us, is stuff that decides what that cell is going to be, what we are going to be. That stuff is called DNA. Little pieces of DNA that decide something in particular are called genes. So we have a gene for hair colour, and a gene for eye colour, and so forth. But some things, like race, are much more complicated. Different races have different eye colours and hair colours and hair textures, and different shapes of noses and lips, and of course different skin colours and that's a lot of little genes doing something very specific. And they all make me Samoan and you whatever you are."

"I'm Maslet and Romni and Canadian."

"Canadian isn't a race."

"Why not?"

"To be a race you've all got to be alike."

"So are all Samoans as tall as you, Mr. Willie?"

"No."

"As round?"

"No."

"As dark?"

"No."

"Got marks on them?"

"No."

"Have hair as thick and black?"

"No." Willie smiled.

"Have such big, bright tooth?"

"Teeth, no."

"Are they all men?"

"No."

"If I get a whole bunch of big brown men in a little room, how do I know who Samoan and who not? You tell me?"

"You can't absolutely know, no one can. But they could tell you."

"What if they didn't know? Maybe they raised yellow or blue, or in New York."

"Well, then we couldn't be sure."

"Can't we take some of this DNA stuff and find out?"

"No. We can take the DNA and test it for sure, but no one knows which genes make someone Samoan."

"So I might have Samoan jeans."

"No. It doesn't work that way. The only genes you have are ones you got from your parents and your parents weren't Samoan were they?"

"No, they were Maslet."

"Then you are Maslet."

"But I'm not like my parents. My mother breasts weren't the first thing you met when she came around a corner, and my Dad had a nose with a huge hook and look at me, straight nose."

"Well your parents' genes combine in unpredictable ways but cows don't give birth to horses and Maslets don't give birth to Samoans."

"But Mr. Willie, can't people be really different from their parents? I read at the laundromat that people are apes, that our old people are monkeys."

"We evolved, it was a long series of mutations."

"What's that last thing?"

"It's pronounced Mew, like the sound a cat makes."

"Mew."

"The rest of it is tay."

"Tay."

"Tay shun."

"Tay shun. Mew tay shun."

"That's it. A mutation is a little change from your parents' genes. And sometimes that little change makes you better able to get along in this world than your parents were, and you survive and pass that change on to your children and so on, until monkeys become people."

"Maybe my jeans mewtayshunned and I'm Samoan."

"We say mutated and if they had, your parents would have had themselves a Samoan baby. You grew up to be a Maslet girl."

"You said you were Samoan because you grew up in Samoa. I grew up in India. Maybe all my mewtated genes need is for me to live Samoan for a little while. Please."

"We can try but I don't think you should hold out any hope."

"All right," Maria says and gives Willie a hug.

Falling asleep in Willie's massive guest bed, Maria tells her jeans over and over that they better be mewtated.

CHAPTER · 5

The next morning Maria begins her seduction of Willie Jakes, though things don't go exactly as planned.

She doesn't want to just climb naked into bed with him. Men need a semi-modest seduction, that way they can think sex is their idea. Willie is sound asleep when she creeps into his room dressed in her t-shirt and panties.

Maria had stopped at the Raklo's on the way to Willie's trailer to pack up all her things. She knew the Raklos wouldn't be there. They were at their regular appointment with the social worker, Jan Erickson. The Raklos need her to sign their welfare documents. No visit to social worker, no welfare, so the Raklos never miss a visit. It didn't take Maria long to gather up her few things.

None of her old wardrobe is right for seducing a strange new man. She's been working very hard at not seducing Draj. Twice he bought her lingerie fit for a lady of bad reputation. Maria thinks he probably stole the dirty little nothings from one of the prostitutes he visits whenever he gets a few dollars ahead. Maria wore each outfit once and then managed to lose it. But that leaves her with few tools to use in her campaign to conquer Willie.

What she wants now is one of Willie's t-shirts. Maria doesn't know why but a woman dressed in a man's t-shirt is a turn-on. She's seen it in the movies.

She finds one of Willie's t-shirts easily enough. He is extremely neat and organized and keeps everything tucked away, not like those pig Raklo boys. T-shirts are in the third drawer she opens. Maria quickly slips out of her t-shirt and panties and pulls Willie's t-shirt over her head. As soon as she puts her arms down it falls to the floor. As big as her breasts are, they aren't big enough to hold up Willie's shirt. Holding the shirt up to the pale light coming through the drapes Maria realizes she could quite possibly crawl through the neck opening. She tries many ways of wearing the t-shirt before settling on one in which the neck opening rests on the outer edge of her left shoulder. The t-shirt itself is bunched up and pinned under her right arm pit. The one sleeve dangles, a useless appendage. Worn like that the shirt hangs down below Maria's knees.

When she is finally ready to climb into bed with him Maria discovers that Willie is wide awake, and having trouble not giggling. The bed is also a major surprise. Maria has never been in a waterbed before. She's seen them in the store, but that was no preparation for Willie's. His constrained giggles have created a surge of waves. Poor Maria has to grab the frame of the bed and hang on for dear life lest she is swept overboard. Which of course just makes Willie laugh harder.

Finally Willie calms down enough to speak.

"Good morning, Maria. Take off that tent and let me look at you."

Ah, Maria thinks, it's working. She struggles out of the t-shirt, and lies back on the bed. Reclining there, looking up at the ceiling, naked on top of Willie's duvet, gently rocking in the swell, Maria feels as aroused as she's ever been.

"Roll over," Willie says.

Once Maria has done so Willie climbs naked out of bed, which leaves Maria temporarily body surfing. He crosses the room and pulls open the drapes, flooding the room with bright sunlight. Then he pads back across the room and sits on the edge of the bed. Watching him, Maria can't take her eyes off his penis. Like the rest of him, it is huge. Like the rest of him, it is tattooed, covered in what looks like a climbing vine.

Willie puts his hand on her shoulders and leans down like he plans to kiss her in the small of the back. Gradually Maria realizes he is staring at her back. His fingers tentatively poke and prod.

"How long have you had that?"

"What?"

"You have a patch of very dark skin in the small of your back. It's about the size of my fist."

"I don't know I had anything there. Can I see? Do you have the mirror?"

"There's a full-length mirror in your room on the closet door." Maria leaps from the bed and runs back to her room. She has to contort and twist but sure enough there is a dark brown patch on her light brown skin, just above her right buttock.

Willie comes into the room, dressed now in what Maria thinks of as half a sari. His massive chest and stomach are bare. She is still preening in the mirror, checking for other spots.

"See, Mr. Willie," she says. "I'm turning Samoan already."

On his way to work, Willie spends a little time thinking about the new development in his love life. Not that he's in love. But Maria does seem to be inserting herself in his life. As he shifts gears on Truck, Willie wonders why.

On the seat beside Willie, Maria is thinking her own thoughts. She has invited herself along because seducing Willie is part of the plan. But, to her discomfort, she finds she also likes the way Willie treats her, and explains things to her, and politely pretends not to stare at her. Her plan is becoming complicated.

Willie had wanted to go alone, but Maria swears she'll stay out of the way and not be a bother, except she says brother. On the drive into town Willie beats out time to his own personal rhythm, his huge left hand thumping the side of Truck, which produces a variety of different sounds as the metal crinkles and pops. He tells Maria what a bother is and why brother isn't a perfectly acceptable synonym, and what a synonym is and why you might want to use them from time to time to make your speech more interesting. It isn't easy since Maria has a dozen questions for every statement Willie makes.

Dawdling in traffic, Willie realizes he is running late for work at the detective agency and that bothers him. Not that he is worried about his job security. Dingo Albee, his boss, is undoubtedly still sleeping off his hangover from the night before, and even if he isn't, they are mates and Willie can do nothing to change that, because, as Dingo is fond of pointing out, mates are forever. Willie is concerned because he believes that punctuality is vitally important to a fruitful life. If you aren't where you said you were going to be how can God know where to find you? Well, of course, He can find you but it would require some effort on His part and you don't want to go around antagonizing God, especially when He might have more important things to be doing. As they enter the city limits Maria begins composing a list of all the synonymic words she knows, checking in each instance with Willie to see if she is right.

"Food, eats, grub, and chow," Maria says.

"Sustenance, cuisine, and manna," Willie says.

"What do all those words mean, I know they mean food somehow, but how?" Maria asks.

"Sustenance is anything that maintains health, but especially food," Willie says.

"I read these magazines in the laundromat. They say much of what we eat isn't good for us. Does that mean that a Big Mac isn't sustenance?"

"I guess not. Cuisine comes from a Latin word, *coquina* which means kitchen or cookery but we use it to refer mostly to food that comes from one place or group of people. The Rom have a cuisine of their own, and so do Samoans. Manna is a little tougher. According to the Bible, Moses and a lot of other Jews were trapped in Egypt, effectively slaves. Then Moses led them to the Promised Land, what we call Israel now. But in between was a great big chunk of desert with no food at all. Well, God fed them by raining food out of the sky, and they called that food manna. These days if someone says they are eating manna, they mean that the food is fit for the gods. Manna is also what we call the stuff plants secrete to feed aphids and other little bugs so that they will pollinate the plant."

"So manna is either aphid food or God food. English is a very strange language," Maria says.

"Isn't it just," Willie agrees and they travel a little way in silence.

"I'm never going to be able to talk good," Maria says, and gives a little sigh.

"Your English is already far better than it was yesterday in the hospital," Willie says. "I can understand you much easier."

"That's 'cause of the woman who came to see me after you go. She was a social worker. Worked with, what did she call me, it were this strange word. I try and say it, okay?"

"Okay."

"*Fascinoma.* I think that's how she taught me."

"That's probably it all right. Do you know what it means?" Willie asks.

"The doctors can't figure out what's wrong with me. They think I must be wrong in my head but they can't figure out how. So they send Mrs. Johnson to see me, maybe I'll talk to her, tell her what's going on.

"I asked her why I'd do that?"

"What did she say?" Willie asks.

"That it's on account of how she's one too, a *fascinoma*. Mrs. Johnson has terrible pain, muscle pain so bad sometimes she just has to scream, so weak she can't stand up without help and they can't find anything wrong with her either. She laughs and says she's spent so much time in the hospital they finally made her part of the staff.

"I asked her if she was painful right then, and she tells me all the time. Then she corrects my English. I want to keep her mind off the pain so I let her teach me more English. That's what she did, before she got the pain, teaches little kids English, mainly immigrants like me. We spent three hours with her teaching me, instead of me telling her why I was there.

"First thing she shows me is that I have to say my consonants. She tell me that English isn't just vowels despite what the Yorkshiremen think. I had to say them over and over again, and now some of them I can pronounce really good if I think about it hard.

"Anyway, Mrs. Johnson got better. After she leaves, I'm so bored I check out and come to find you."

"Let's try some more synonyms, you know some more?" Willie asks.

"Cunt, crotch, snatch, fuck box, and twat," Maria says.

"Those are all synonyms Maria, but they aren't ones you should use."

"Why not."

"Well, in Canada and the United States the people are really uptight about their bodies. Certain words you just don't say."

"So what can I call my cunt?"

"You could try vulva or better yet pudendum."

"Why are those better?" Maria asks.

"In most countries there is a class war going on. The rich are terrified the poor are going to rise up and massacre them. There really wouldn't be much the rich and powerful could do to stop it, there are just too many poor and downtrodden. One of the many ways the rich keep the poor under control is by robbing the poor of the power of speech."

"I'm not with you," Maria says.

"The rich and powerful love to say that the language the poor are using isn't really English, it isn't grammatically correct, it isn't spelled right. In the case of strong words that have very clear meanings and are simple to spell like cunt, fuck, screw, suck, and cock, the upper classes replace those words with words that are harder to say and harder to spell and harder for the poor to use. Now the upper classes can tell when they are meeting a class climber because when the upwardly mobile talk about sex they use 'dirty' words, not the Latinized words that the socially adept use.

"Vulva is a Latin word that means the covering of the womb. It's hard to think of any reason to object to that. But it covers all the important parts, the labia, the clitoris, the opening of the vagina. I'll tell you a little story that will explain why vulva is considered acceptable.

"A few years ago this female artist, Judy Chicago, created a piece of art that many people had a hard time talking about. It was a dining room table with many place settings, and each dinner plate was like a beautiful and unique flower opening. Well, each one was modelled on a different woman's external genitalia. A lot of newspapers suddenly had to figure out what they were going to call women's genitals. They settled on vulva and suddenly that was the acceptable term."

A car cut them off and Maria leans out the window. "Fucking vulva," she screams.

"Volvo," Willie points out as he brakes. "Besides, I'm not certain you should use any of those words."

"Why not?" Maria asks.

Willie is still trying to explain to Maria the concept of polite company and proper language when they arrive at the office of International Investigative Services. It is in the centre of the city in the Thompson Building. A magnificent four-storey brick building from the early part of the century, the Thompson once dominated Edmonton's skyline. Now it is completely surrounded by the modern office towers built during the boom times of the seventies and eighties. It is perpetually in the shade of its neighbours and its bricks are slowly being eaten by the acid from diesel exhaust.

The ground floor of the Thompson is home to various restaurants that change every time the building is sold and new owners decide to raise the rents. Each time the ground floor sits empty for six months and then the new owners go back to the old rents and new restaurants move in, negotiating special deals; now the new owners are losing money and they put the building up for sale, again. In the meantime the building's other tenants, mainly artists and galleries, suffer a severe reduction in service with each new owner looking for some way to improve the bottom line. The bathrooms on his floor bother Willie so much that at least once a week he cleans them himself.

"I still don't get it. How come I can't use these words, Mr. Willie?" Maria asks as they walk from the nearest parkade to the office along Rice Howard Way with its cobblestone paving blocks. "I learned them from watching movies and TV and from you."

"There are people who won't watch those shows because the actors use those words, Maria. You can't go wrong if you speak properly, and that's why I don't use even vulva and pudendum. The people who use 'fuck' every second word, they are going to think you are very educated or stuck up if you use don't use any sort of vulgarity, but the chances are they won't hold that against you once they get to know you. On the other hand, you say 'fuck box' in front of someone who doesn't ever speak of sex in public and they aren't going to take the time to get to know you because obviously you aren't their sort of person."

"Do I want to get to know people like that, Mr. Willie?"

Willie isn't quite sure how to answer that question. By then they are climbing the marble steps to the fourth floor where International, as all the staff call it, has its offices. The receptionist, Mary Beth, looks up from her Gameboy long enough to ask Willie if he has time to see a client, one who has been waiting all morning for Dingo. Since it is not yet ten o'clock Willie discounts the "all morning," though he understands the sentiment. Dingo's drinking binges are getting worse and they are getting in the way of business. Willie knows that all the other staff members expect him to speak to Dingo, since they are mates, and thus Dingo won't be quite as likely to tear Willie's head off.

Willie has a better plan. He is going to cure Dingo of alcoholism. Willie has a guaranteed cure, a drug called *kava kava* that his uncles have sent him. The problem is figuring out how to get Dingo to take it since it tastes like someone has dissolved pig manure in horse sweat.

CHAPTER · 6

The waiting client turns out to be a man. He stands as Willie and Maria enter the conference room.

"My name is Roger Flanman." He is a built like a pencil. His bald head even looks a bit like an eraser.

"Willie Jakes, I'm the senior investigator here," Willie says, directing the pencil into one of the burgundy plush leather, wing-backed chairs that surround the conference table. Maria takes a chair in the far corner of the room. Roger Flanman pays no attention to her. Maria doesn't like that, but she remembers her promise to be good.

"I was told to speak to a Dingo Albee," the pencil says.

"And may I ask who recommended our services?"

"Inspector Gillato." Willie picks up the phone that is kept on the bookcase beside the table and phones the police department. When it starts to ring Willie puts it on speaker phone.

"Inspector Spencer," a gravelly voice answers.

"Andrew, it's Willie Jakes, is Tony around?"

"Yeah. Hang on just a second and I'll get him."

"Hi, Willie. What can I do for you?"

"You had a guy come in and you recommended Dingo."

"Yup. I think his name was Flanman."

"Well Dingo is indisposed and Mr. Flanman is sitting here wondering if he can trust me and if I'm competent."

"We're on speaker phone aren't we, Willie? It isn't just that you're calling from the bottom of a mine shaft."

"No, we're on speaker phone."

"Well in that case, hello again Mr. Flanman. Can you trust Willie Jakes? With your life, your wife, or your cash, but I'd keep my daughters locked up. Is he competent? Willie is relentless, obsessively persistent, and he knows the business as well as any private detective I've ever dealt with, and that includes Dingo. If he can keep Dingo sober the two of them are a dynamite team. Does that help you, Mr. Flanman?"

The pencil leans forward. "You know what I need, Inspector. I made it completely clear. Now I find the detective you recommended doesn't exactly keep regular office hours and may have a drinking problem. Is this monster any better than your last recommendation?"

"Mr. Flanman, when I recommended Dingo I figured he'd pass you right along to Willie to do the grunt work while Dingo provided the higher cognitive functions. Given your request is a little quixotic, I thought you needed a firm that doesn't denigrate the unusual client. In other words, no other reputable firm is going to hear you out, let alone take your case. There are lots of seedy, fly-by-night operators who'll gladly take your case and your money. You can make up your own mind what you want to do.

"Willie, best of luck and you owe me lunch. Talk to you soon."

The eraser turns red.

"Mr. Flanman, maybe you'd better try explaining exactly what it is you need us to do," Willie says using the calming voice he learned on psych rounds.

"I want you to find Kennedy's brain."

"I assume we are referring to John."

"Do you know anything about Kennedy's assassination and why people are still looking for his brain?"

"I'm not exactly a conspiracy buff, Mr. Flanman, but I know the gist of the story. A lot of people don't think Lee Harvey Oswald acted alone, or maybe at all, in the assassination of President Kennedy. There are all sorts of different theories about what happened. Some of which could probably be at least disproved if we had Kennedy's brain, which was preserved after the autopsy but which subsequently disappeared."

"Very good, Mr. Jakes. Maybe you are the right man for the job after all. You have any idea what people think happened to it post autopsy?"

"Just what I remember reading in *Cause of Death*, which was a little vague."

"Vague is the right word, Mr. Jakes. Let me back up for a minute and explain how I got interested in Kennedy's brain. I deal in unusual objects, Mr. Jakes, Hitler's hand-embroidered hankies, Jeffrey Dahmer's dinnerware. It's a very good living.

"Still, sometime I get depressed handling all that detritus. And the buyers, most of them seem perfectly normal when they walk in the door, and then they want to know if I have any human skin lampshades from the Mengele collection...

"I've reached the point in my career where I want to make a mark. In the novelty collectible business, that means finding something that everyone wants but that's important historically as well, like the original, Betsy Ross sewn Stars and Stripes, or the plans for the Wright brothers' first plane, or the desk they used at Malta, or the quill pen the United States Constitution was written with, well I'm sure you get the idea."

"I take it that you think Kennedy's brain would be such an object, make your career?" Willie asks.

"Exactly so. The ultimate object. It might, as you point out, settle the whole conspiracy issue. The best part: at auction it would sell for millions of dollars, and I'd have the money and my fifteen minutes of fame as well. It's the American Dream, Mr. Jakes, truly it is."

Roger gets up and begins to pace. "Two months ago a man walks into my shop, in the Village in New York. I keep the shop because occasionally someone wanders in with something wonderfully horrible, a shrunken head, a Gestapo uniform, that sort of thing. They aren't truly top drawer, but they are valuable and I can turn them over as fast as I can get them. This neanderthal who walked into my shop had the look of third string Mafia about him, not bright enough to be a made man, but mean enough to be used to collect.

"Terry Sugwah. That's how he pronounced his name. I never did get a proper spelling. He claimed he knew where Kennedy's brain was.

"I'm not a conspiracy buff, never was, never will be. I wasn't quite sure what he meant or why he'd think I would be interested in such a thing. He explained it to me very patiently. Once I worked past his Bronx accent and atrociously misapplied vocabulary I began to appreciate why I might be very interested indeed.

"He claimed to be what he looked like, a minor hanger-on of the criminal enterprise. Anything for hire. Sugwah said that as a teenager he'd been a gofer for a minor capo in the crime family of Meyer Lansky. He'd run messages back and forth between the mob and the CIA, at least he'd worked out afterwards that was what he'd been doing. Back then he was more interested in liquor and women than the business. He'd made runs from New York and Washington, to Miami and the other way around as well. He'd been on the periphery of the Bay of Pigs and the attempts to assassinate Castro. He seemed, frankly, inordinately proud of his bit part in history.

"Then one day in '64 or maybe '65 he'd gotten a call from his boss to catch the next train to Washington and meet a man in the station who had a package for him to deliver. The man he met had tried very hard to disguise himself. He was wearing an overcoat, heavy wool, almost to his feet, pulled-up collar, a fedora pulled down almost to his eyes, and huge sunglasses. The sunglasses weren't too odd, it was the middle of a steamy hot August, with most of Washington empty. The rest was simply ridiculous. This fellow was carrying a box about the size of an orange crate."

Willie raises a hand to interrupt but the pencil pushes on.

"The man told Sugwah to take the package back to New York where another man would take it from him at the station, said if Sugwah opened it he was a dead man. He gave the package to Sugwah along with a ticket back to New York and then stood there, sweat pouring down his face until he saw Sugwah get on the train and start back to New York.

"Except no one was waiting for him, so he phoned his capo and was told to wait for further instructions. The instructions were simple, he was to throw the package away. Mr. Sugwah admitted to not being the brightest light on the Christmas tree but after all that trouble he was not about to throw the thing out."

Roger pauses. "Can you guess what was in the box?"

Willie scratches his head. "Kennedy's stomach?"

"Wiseguy. He opened the package at home and discovered it was a brain. Some of it cut up, a bit mangled, but a brain. He leapt to the obvious conclusion, that it was evidence in a homicide, evidence that was supposed to go missing. Well, you never know when such a thing will turn out to be a valuable asset. So he stuck it in a closet and over time forgot about it.

"The years passed and he got married, had children, went semi-legit in the vending machine business. He told me he had it all, nice home, great wife, good kids, BMW, a mistress on the side. A slightly askew Norman Rockwell life. Then one Saturday while he's re-stocking the Pepsi, chocolate bars, and condoms in his machines his wife has a garage sale. Sells his favourite sweatshirt, his collection of bent golf clubs, and the brain.

"He's naturally upset, more about the sweatshirt than anything else. But about two weeks later he's in a bookstore and he sees a picture that changes everything. He sees the man who gave him the brain." Roger pauses for dramatic effect. Maria twitches nervously, waiting for Willie to ask the obvious question, biting her tongue. Willie sits passively as the silence grows and grows.

"Bobby Kennedy," Roger finally blurts. "That's who Terry says gave him the brain. He also said it took him several hours before the penny dropped and he realized his wife had sold a priceless piece of Americana for $1.25.

"So he starts on this quest to track the brain down. Only having sat patiently on the top shelf in a closet for over thirty years, suddenly the brain is passing from hand to hand like a stick of dynamite, which Terry guesses it pretty much is. He's tracked it to this reclusive Montana militiaman, an anarchist who lives in the middle of nowhere and won't return Terry's calls. But Terry's learned that the fellow is a bit of a collector of "nasty" things. And that's where I come in."

"And he still had it?" Willie asks.

"Frank Jackson? I flew straight out to Butte only to find he's lost it in a poker game. But for the right price Frank was prepared to tell me who he lost it to and how he lost it. It cost me fifty dollars and a Charles Ng serial killer card but I got the story."

"And that story was?" Willie asks.

"To hear Frank tell it, the only way he ever lost the brain was because the other player was cheating. It was a private game, just a few business colleagues of Frank's, Canadians who sell him explosives and guns. But as the game went on and they had too much to drink they let some strangers join in."

"Where did this private game take place?" Willie asks.

"In Burnaby, a place called the Lumbermen's Club, in the North Burnaby Inn," Roger says.

"That doesn't surprise me," Willie says, "but it makes me suspicious."

"Why?" Roger asks.

"Did you actually go to the Lumbermen's Club, Mr. Flanman?" Willie asks.

"No, I didn't see any need. Why?"

"The North Burnaby Inn is a dive, Mr. Flanman. It's on East Hasting Street in Vancouver, not Burnaby at all. It's in a working class suburb called The Heights. You can rent a room for $500 a month, or twenty bucks an hour. It's home to the Showroom Club, which is the kind of place that takes the exotic out of exotic dancing, and the Lumbermen's Club which is where B.C.'s high rollers, problem gamblers, and criminals of all kinds meet to play high stakes poker. It's a pretty good bet that if Frank lost your brain there he lost to a crook, and getting it back could prove dangerous. People that play poker at the Lumbermen's Club have a habit of ending up missing or dead. Some didn't pay off their gambling debts, some were caught cheating by unsympathetic victims, but some just asked too many questions, made the other players nervous."

"Frank says the person he lost the brain to is Mr. Average, middle-aged, brown hair, blue or green eyes, average height, average weight, good quality suit, though worn. On top of the brain, Mr. Average took fifty thousand dollars off the table. He told Frank his name was Bob and he came from Edmonton."

"And what did you do next?" Willie asks. Maria suspects he isn't feeling as patient as he seems. She guesses that when Willie starts to pause between each word that his blood is on full boil. She can't figure out what it was Roger has said or done wrong that has Willie fuming, not for the life of her.

"I went home and told Terry we were dead as shooting gallery ducks. If you were conning someone who has his own private army and is in town to buy guns and explosives you'd not give your own name or home town, would you?"

"What did Mr. Sugwah say?" Maria asks, speaking for the first time. Roger peers at her, as if seeing her for the first time.

"Just his luck. And we left it there. Except the next morning his wife found Terry floating face down in his bathtub, fully clothed.

"I come into the office and there are two messages for me. The first is Terry telling me he's talked with some people in Edmonton and there is a man who plays high stakes poker there who calls himself Bobby Nevada and fits the general description. All average. Then the call from Terry's wife telling me he's been murdered.

"Not being too sure what happened to Terry I thought maybe I'd be safer taking a little trip. For a month I've been here doing the rounds of the casinos and private poker matches, playing as little as possible and losing less and looking for this Bobby Nevada, Average Bob. I'm getting nowhere and so I've come to you. I want you to find Bob, find out if he has the brain. If so, will he sell it. If he will I want you to set up a meeting, just him and me. Do you think you can do this?"

"I doubt it, but if you want to pay our fee we'll do our best," Willie says.

"What is your fee, Mr. Jakes?"

"Five hundred a day plus expenses and a five thousand dollar retainer, Mr. Flanman."

"That seems a bit steep, especially with no guarantees."

"We'll have at least three people working on it and this isn't likely to be a nine-to-five case. If we are really lucky we'll manage to make about twenty dollars an hour for our time and trouble and minimally we'll eliminate some obvious possibilities for you."

"You mean I missed something obvious, Mr. Jakes?"

"Actually a number of things, but you've done remarkably well for an amateur."

"You feel that a professional can do more?"

"Yes, Mr. Flanman I do. That's why people pay us. We know tricks — as Dingo says, we're initiates."

"I'll tell you what, Mr. Jakes. If you'll let me look over your shoulder, learn your tricks, I'll pay your exorbitant fee, and if you find the brain you get a ten thousand dollar bonus. Deal?"

"Deal, Mr. Flanman. Provided you don't mind if we start by checking out your story."

"Not at all, Mr. Jakes. I'll write you out a cheque, give you the name of my bank and you can start with that."

By the time Dingo comes in Willie has, with a little help from Maria, confirmed nearly all the critical details in Mr. Flanman's story, though he knows that simply because the facts are true doesn't mean the story is. Willie has a hard time explaining to Dingo why he's entered into such a "lemon-headed deal."

Dingo is a player and poker is his passion. Unfortunately he knows dozens of players who are average in appearance and dozens named Bob and quite a number of average-looking Bobs. And those are just among the guys who play in the poker lounges at the casinos. Then there are all the private games, from high stakes to penny ante, that the serious players frequent.

Dingo goes into the conference room to meet Mr. Flanman.

One of the things that Willie loves about Dingo, one of the reasons they are mates, is that Dingo genuinely likes people and they like him. Gnome-like, wizened, and leathery from years in the antipodean outback prospecting for diamonds, he goes through life with a smile on his face and makes friends of complete strangers. Willie figures that Mr. Flanman will be a good test of the Albee charm.

It takes a while for Dingo to thaw Roger Flanman but within half an hour they are talking like old friends. Dingo is soon regaling him with tales of crazy nights, wired on amphetamines, playing poker with thousands of dollars on the table. And Mr. Flanman is entranced.

CHAPTER · 7

Willie and Maria go out for lunch at the Blue Willow. Over a double helping of lemon chicken Maria stuns Willie.

"They like men, Dingo and this Roger. They like each other kind of men."

"What do you mean? They hit it off. Of course they like each other."

"You told me 'be polite little gypsy girl' now I don't know how to say it."

"So just say it."

"They want to have sex together."

"You think they're homosexuals!"

"Homosexals, exactly. The Rom, we say a man like that kisses ivory."

Willie hesitates. "I've known Dingo for years. I've never seen him with a man and he's never hit on me."

"No man with a mind that works would come on to you, big fellah. You are all man and all for women. But Roger isn't like you, he has sex with men and he isn't scary either."

"Dingo isn't scared of me and he isn't a homosexual."

"Trust me, Mr. Willie. Those two, they want each other. Wouldn't surprise me if they were doing it on that big table when we get back. And no, Dingo isn't afraid of you. He's afraid of what you think about him."

Maria delicately licks some sauce from her chicken. "Want to know how I knew Roger was a homosexal?"

"That's homosexual," Willie says emphasizing each sound.

"Homosexual. Want to know how I knew?"

"Yes, I want to know how you know he's gay."

"He was ignoring me, Willie."

"So just because some guy isn't panting over you he must be gay?"

"Look at me, Mr. Willie, men look at me, they can't help themselves. I think sometimes just walking down the street I'm giving men origamis."

"Orgasms."

"That's the word. In England the women said 'e blew me head oeuf 'e did'."

"You don't suffer from a lack of confidence, do you?"

"It's not my fault that my genes decided to make me a babe. But it isn't just that Roger was ignoring me. I couldn't get no rise out of him no matter what I did. I batted my eyes, I flicked my hair, I touched myself, all my best tricks. Nothing."

"Did it ever occur to you, babearama, that maybe you just aren't his type?" Willie asks as he scrapes all the leftover lemon sauce into a big pile on his plate and begins to scoop it into his mouth with a spoon.

"Mr. Willie, that's pure fat," Maria says horrified, slapping at the hand with the spoon.

"If you are ever going to be a Samoan woman you've got to learn to love fat," Willie says. He stops his own feeding to tempt her with a spoonful of her own. As he moves the spoon towards her mouth, Maria opens wide. She expects to be repulsed but the sauce slides down her throat.

"All men are my type," Maria says. "I'm the universal woman, I smell like sex."

Willie puts his spoon down and begins sniffing and snorting like a pig. Actually he has to admit she does kind of smell like sex.

"Besides, in case his nose was broken or something I asked him if he'd like to go back to his hotel room and have intercourse."

"You asked Roger, the pencil, if he'd like to fuck you."

"Please Willie, you told me I should never use words like that." She sounds like a proper Victorian lady.

All Willie can do is spray food out his mouth as he giggles.

"You think I'm making it up."

"No Maria, not even for a second. I just think you're amazing. And what did he say?"

"Sorry sweetie, my gate swings the other way."

Willie is reduced to sticking his tongue out, devoid of any witty retort.

"What did you think of Roger Flanman?" Maria asks.

"I don't trust the guy. I think he's hinky," Willie says.

"What's hinky mean?" Maria asks.

"Weird, strange, dangerous. My thinking is that if I agree to let Mr. Flanman look over my shoulder I don't have to worry about what else he is doing. Listening to him I kind of thought that maybe Mr. Flanman liked whips and chains and hurting people. Did you notice how he licked his lips as he described human lamp shades? He's either kinky, which in this context means sexually weird, or hinky, or having us on."

"Is what that second detective said true? The stuff about you."

"That I'm obsessive-compulsive. That's what they told me in medical school. I'll start working on something and I just can't stop, I've got to finish it, got to do it perfectly."

"Is that why your trailer is so neat, all your clothes folded up nice and put away?"

"That's one of my compulsions. If everything isn't put away exactly right I can't go to sleep. Sometimes I have to get up out of bed two or three times to check the trailer and make sure everything is right. And what's worse is I have to make the bed each time."

"Is that part of being Samoan? 'Cause if it is I don't think I can ever be Samoan."

"God no! Samoans are the most easygoing people you'll ever meet, they don't worry about stuff, obsess over things. In some ways I'm like that. I take people the way I find them, don't get frustrated, just put one foot in front of the other, all good things, but then I'll get into some weird compulsion. One time in medical school I decided I had to wash my hands every time I touched a doorknob. Metal objects are breeding grounds for germs. So I'd touch a doorknob and have to race off and find a sink where I could wash my hands. Everywhere I went in the hospital I carried a box of surgical gloves and I'd put on a new pair every time I came to a door I had to open. There weren't that many or it would have taken me all day to get from one side of the hospital to the other. They used me as the example for all the other doctors of how to prevent infections from spreading in hospitals. That's why I stopped being a doctor, I was just getting stranger and stranger."

Willie settles back in his chair. "Forget any idea you've got that I'm a normal Samoan. I was born on a little island almost halfway between American Samoa and Western Samoa called Falemusu. Neither country wants to claim the island because the people there have a big reputation for being trouble on the hoof. Western Samoa has a long history with New Zealand and the people are very poor and very self-reliant. Life is still pretty traditional. Falemusu is like that, but we think of ourselves as Americans, as part of American Samoa.

"But even on that island of individualists I was thought a strange child, far too independent and anxious to go my way and most of all far too neat. I was always running around picking up garbage and taking it away and burning it. At night I'd sneak out to the lagoon and sweep all the tracks out of the sand. Adults would deliberately litter, throw beer cans in the bay, just to see if I'd spend my whole day diving over and over in order to retrieve them. I would and they'd entertain themselves for hours watching me. So I'm not in any way a normal Samoan. Considering my Dad and all my time here, I'm not even a true *musu-musu*, which is what we islanders call ourselves."

"So you have changed from a Samoan to a big brown white man," Maria says, squinting her eyes. To which Willie has no response.

After lunch they pick up Truck and drive over to the university. On the way Willie tells Maria what a Ph.D. is and what a Ph.D. student does. She asks how one gets to be a Ph.D. student and so Willie tells her.

Maria shakes her head. "You went to school for twelve years, and then you went four years, and then you went two years, and now you are going five more. Let me count." Maria starts with her fingers, and then takes off her sandals and wiggles her toes, then she returns to her fingers. "Twenty-three years. That's how long you go to school."

"Don't forget I went to medical school as well. That was another six." More fingers are used.

"Twenty-nine years. All that education and you not learn how to tell your best friend is homosexual. What other good stuff didn't you learn? Me, I learned stuff, good stuff. I know how to do magic and pick pockets and tell fortunes and I'm a great treat in bed. You know how to play with rocks and read books. What an education."

Willie picks up his mail before heading to his office on the third floor of the Humanities building. Maria takes one look at his office and says wow. It is like a tropical forest, hot, humid and all full of plants. It reminds Maria of England, if England was ever hot. To keep her occupied while he tries to get some work done, Willie lets Maria open the mail.

He hasn't bothered with mail in days. Mail is handled by the Samoan side of his personality. That's how Willie sees his life, as a battle, and sometimes an armed truce between the Samoan side of his personality, the part he got from his Maam, and the anal retentive WASP side that he got from Dad. He thinks about what Maria said at lunch. Is he a big brown white man? If a native Indian gets assimilated, other natives call him an apple. Red on the outside, white in the middle. What does that make me, Willie wonders, a coconut?

Willie stares at Maria as she rips envelopes. He thinks Maria looks great sitting in a chair she's liberated from the study carrels just down the hall. She's wearing a light blue summer dress and she has taken one of the blue and yellow irises from the bowl of cut flowers in the department office and stuck it in her hair. She looks like pictures he's seen of Maam when she was a little girl.

Maria, fully aware of just how distracting she is being, carefully sorts Willie's mail, according to her rather unusual understanding of the vibrations given off by truly important communications. She makes four piles: throw it in the wastebasket — by far the biggest pile — read it if you are bored, read soon, and read now. There is only one thing in the read now pile. It is a new biography of Mark Twain called *Dangerous Water: A Biography of the Boy Who Became Mark Twain* by Ron Powers.

When Willie checks the piles he discovers that most of the mail from the department, all the memos and notifications are in the toss in the garbage pile. He ceremoniously hands that mail to Maria, who, giggling, tosses it in the garbage can beside his desk. The boring mail includes conference calls for conferences he'll never attend and calls for papers he'll never write and gossipy department news — who's retired, who's gotten married, who's gotten hired, who's gotten what grant. Willie puts that stuff in his in basket to read later so that he can hold his own when gossiping with the department secretaries. The read soon mail, which Willie reads right then, includes a notice from the University telling him that he has to pay another fifty dollars to keep his registration current, an overdue notice from the library, and a handwritten note from Bob Struter, his Ph.D. supervisor, wanting to know if Willie is making any progress on finding a new thesis topic.

Maria wants to know what a thesis topic is and where Willie lost the old one.

"As I told you earlier, to get a Ph.D. you have to do original research. You have to select a problem and research it and solve it. Then you have to write a sort of book about it, called a thesis."

"It's like being a detective."

"Well, yes and no. The two are a lot alike but being a detective is easier because people bring the problems to you. In your Ph.D. you have to find the problem. For me that's been the hard part. I want to write something about Mark Twain because my Grandpa met him. I've read everything Twain ever wrote, and just about everything ever written about him.

"But I can't get a topic, find a problem that works."

"How don't they work?" Maria asks.

"Well, sometimes I pick a problem I think is really neat and then I learn someone has already solved it. And their solution is the same as mine, and that's a no-no for a Ph.D. It's supposed to be unique. Other times I can't find a solution at all, and I've spent a lot of time working on those but have finally had to admit they aren't soluble."

"What sort of problems were these?" Maria asks. She's found asking questions is a good way of keeping a man interested in you.

"The big one was why he called himself Mark Twain."

"He wasn't Mark Twain?"

"His real name was Samuel Clemens. But he wrote under the name Mark Twain. That isn't that unusual, lots of authors use a pseudonym, a made-up name. Maybe they think what they write will offend someone they don't want to upset, or maybe they want to hide their earnings from a spouse or creditors, or maybe they write all kinds of different books and they want to help keep their readers from getting confused so they use a different name for each kind of book. There are lots of good reasons why they might use a pen name."

"So what was it about Mark Twain that's different? He didn't have any of those reasons?"

"No, he probably had a number of those reasons but he didn't stop with just using a pen name. He became that pen name. He made up this larger than life alter ego, other self, named Mark Twain and then he pretended to actually be him. Like there was a real Mark Twain and a real Sam Clemens and they were different people. He pretended so hard that he sort of became Twain. By the time he died no one really thought of him as Sam Clemens anymore. No other author before or since has ever carried using a pen name so far."

"You wanted to figure out why, that was your thesis topic?"

"You got it, Maria. In a way all my topics have been some sort of an attempt to understand why Sam Clemens became Mark Twain. And I keep failing, or come up with the same explanations other people already have, and when I read theirs I can't help realizing how lame they are. All of which takes me back to square one. I've actually started trying to find a thesis topic by dumb luck. I believe with all my heart that somewhere in this office, in all these books and papers, the answer is waiting for me. So I take out a book or a paper and toss it in the air and catch it as it falls and read the passage it's fallen open to and try to build that into a thesis topic. That's how desperate I am."

"I help you big fellah. I take this book, *Dangerous Water*, and I'm going to throw it up in the air and you'll catch it and there will be your thesis topic. You look like you don't trust me. Remember I can do magic, this will work."

Without any further warning Maria picks up the book, the only thing in the read now pile, and throws it up and over Willie's head toward the window. Willie has to spin and lunge to catch it just before it hits the floor. His fingers close on the outside jacket of the book. His massive thumb sticks into the early pages of the book. He is scared to look. Maria comes around the desk and gently takes the book, being careful to put her thumb where Willie's has been. Then she goes back around the desk and sits down to read. Her lips move, but Willie can't tell what she is saying.

"'John was a volunteer in her Uncle's fire company,' that's what it says where your thumb print is." She hands Willie the book, sure enough he's left a thumb print over the passage.

"What do you suppose that means?"

"Who was John?" Maria asks.

"He was Mark Twain's father."

"Why would you have a company to start fires?"

"A fire company doesn't start fires, it puts them out."

"Oh."

"And that still leaves my question. What does it mean? Are you sure it's important?"

Maria takes the book back and holds the relevant passage up to her forehead. Willie is surprised to find himself holding his breath while she ponders.

"It's very important," she says.

Willie lets out a massive sigh. "So all I have to do is figure out why it's important."

On the way out of the building, in the stairwell, they meet Willie's thesis supervisor, Bob Struter. Willie can't help his response. He cringes inwardly, thinking Maria will say the wrong thing.

She doesn't get off to a good start.

"Aren't you going to introduce us?" Dr. Struter asks Willie, looking at Maria. Maria sees a tall, stooped fellow with a mischievous grin. Maria knows imps come in all sorts and sizes.

"This is Dr. Struter, my supervisor," Willie says to Maria. "Dr. Struter, this is Maria Raklo."

"What he really wants to say is: Maria, this is that obnoxious, pedantic, overbearing guy whose mother lives under a porch and eats bones. The one who holds my future hostage. My principal tormentor and inquisitor," Dr. Struter says.

Maria nods. "He really wants to tell you that this is Maria, my girlfriend. The sexiest woman I've ever met. My soul mate. The missing half of me. The woman who in a few short days has already figured out how to drive me nuts."

Struter blinks. "Speaking of torment. Willie, you know I have to ask. Have you got a thesis topic yet?"

Willie just shakes his head dejectedly.

"I've decided to take early retirement," Dr. Struter announces. "Dean Richards wants your Ph.D. complete before I go."

"How long?" Willie asks in a state of shock.

"I'm just on my way to see Richards now. From today we have three months."

"Three months," Willie stammers. He has to sit down on the stairs. He'd assumed that he and Dr. Struter would go on forever, Willie proposing, Struter disposing.

Dr. Struter leaves them there. Maria pats Willie on the shoulder.

"Don't worry," she says. "You and I, together, we'll find your thesis topic."

CHAPTER · 8

Willie and Maria have an early supper at the Bottleneck in HUB Mall. Maria wants to know all about HUB. She loves the idea of it being a student residence and a shopping mall all at the same time. She keeps looking up at the roof and marvelling at how it is all windows, that she can look right up and see the sun.

Maria has never had Korean food but wants to try it. She has *bulgogi* and Willie has *falafels*. While she eats, she wonders if over-education is at the root of Willie's problems. She knows he has problems, she just hasn't figured out what all of them are. But it is obvious to her that he is educating himself right out of remembering who he is.

Meanwhile, Willie is still worrying about his thesis. Over the meal they try to work out what the passage might mean. Willie can't believe how eagerly he's accepted Maria's pronouncement about the importance of the passage. He feels that when she read it out loud something went click in his brain. But he can't sort out what caused the phenomenon.

Maria finally asks him if he trusts her.

"Why?" Willie asks.

"Do you?"

"Yes, Maria, I do. I just met you and I know you lie and steal but I still trust you, I think."

"Well, you're an obsessive-compulsive and I still trust you."

"Why did you want to know if I trust you?"

"Cause, big fellah, if you do, then I can do magic. More magic, more serious magic than the book. Magic that will help you understand this Twain writer and get your Ph.D. Do you believe in magic, Mr. Willie?"

"I've never really thought about it. When I was little my uncles were trying to train me to be a medicine man. That's sort of a magician and a priest and a doctor all rolled into one. They could sure do amazing things."

"Like what?"

"Well, they could make a monster big fire and let it burn down until they had red hot coals and then they'd dance on the coals. They'd also swallow fire. They'd put tar around a tree branch they'd pruned down till it was not much thicker than a finger and then they'd set the tar on fire. First they'd lick the fire, then they'd kiss it, and finally they'd ram the burning stick down their throats. When they pulled it out it would still be burning."

Willie smiles at Maria. "They saw visions as well. All my Maam's brothers saw visions. They tell me that I saw visions when I was little. That's why they thought I should be a medicine man."

"What happened? Why aren't you one?"

"My Maam, she became a Mormon."

"What's a Mormon?"

"Mormons are what you call members of the Church of Jesus Christ of the Latter Day Saints. They believe that there were modern disciples of Jesus in America late in the cowboy era and that their leader Joseph Smith talked directly to God. The result of their conversations was the Book of Mormon, which is their religion's addition to the Bible. The original Mormons believed in polygamy and everyone still tithes ten percent of everything they earn to the church."

"What is this tithe?"

"Tithing means they give part of what they make to the church as a form of religious observance."

"What a great scam. Way better than lying in the road."

"I don't think true believers look on it as a scam. The church needs money to operate and to spread the word of God. It's like Catholics giving to the collection plate and paying for masses. Every religion has some way of getting funds from the faithful."

"Were you ever a Mormon, Mr. Willie?"

"Well, my Maam tried to make me one but it didn't take. By that time I'd been a Catholic, a Methodist, and an animist. Mormonism held very little attraction for me."

"What's an animist?"

"Animists believe that God is in all living things and that you can reach him by praying to any animate object, anything that lives and breathes. In Samoa my family had extended the concept to rocks, but they were also fond of trees, and for reasons I never did learn, fish."

"They prayed to fish?"

"Yeah. My grandpa he'd go out in the bay and catch these brilliantly coloured fish and pull them up to the side of the boat. Then he'd have long conversations with them. After which he'd cut them loose. He claimed one fish he'd caught over a hundred times but I don't know how he'd have known that.

"Your question was do I believe in magic. The answer is that I think there is magic in the world. I'm just not sure we can really tap into it or use it in any meaningful way."

"One of these days, Mr. Willie, you are going to find a rock that talks to you and then you'll believe. For now you leave the magic to me. I'll find that dashed elusive thesis for you."

"Thanks, Maria. I appreciate your efforts. I have to ask, where did you learn to say dashed elusive."

"In ESL class we read the Scarlet Pimpernel. Please just don't be forgetting to help me turn Samoan. Now I want to show you something. It's hard to figure out, but I got it from the paper I was reading while you and Roger Flanman were talking." Maria hands Willie a clipping.

Left-Handed DNA Is No Fluke, Study Finds
Philip J. Hilts
The New Times News

This is a twice told tale of the unexpected.

The first time scientists actually saw the molecule of life, DNA, in 1979, it was not the curving helix James Watson and Francis Crick deciphered more than 25 years before.

Their observations based on chemical testing were of a molecule, curving gracefully to the right. What the crystallization of the molecule revealed in 1979, though, was an odd, zigzagging, left-turning spiral molecule. It was named left-handed DNA, or z-DNA, and molecular biologists dismissed it as fluke, probably just molecular junk.

Further research demonstrated that the right-handed version of DNA was the usual one, and history and the biotechnology industry moved forward.

But Dr. Alexander Rich, a molecular biologist at the Massachusetts Institute of Technology who first saw the left-handed DNA, never let go of it. He and others puzzled over it year after year, wondering whether it had a role in life's chemical process or was just a laboratory artifact.

Now their work has apparently paid off. Rich and his colleagues, Thomas Schwartz, Mark Rould, Ky Lowenhaupt, and Alan Herbert, have demonstrated that z-DNA is more than an oddity. In research described in a recent issue of the journal Science, *they found that nature does make and use a left-handed DNA, and its role in regulating the chemistry of life might be quite important.*

It was originally thought that DNA was just passive, a code to be read. But now, with this and other examples being studied, it appears that DNA is active, and can change its own written message as it is being read. The shape of DNA, whether it is right-handed or left-handed, helps determine how its message is read.

The story of its behaviour is intricate. In the classical description, DNA is a book of code, and it tells cells what substances to make to carry out daily life. There is a specialized molecule, called RNA polymerase, that "reads" the DNA code as it slides along segments of DNA.

This reader molecule passes on the information and begins the creation of the all-important proteins that the body can use for purposes like building cells and burning energy.

But Dr. Rich and his team say there is another possibility. In some cases — perhaps fewer than 10 percent, but the figure is not known — the reading of DNA itself changes the DNA's shape. It relaxes the strand and permits it to flip over into the left-handed variety.

When that happens, they say, another molecule comes into play. This "editor" molecule, RNA adenosine deaminase, according to the theory, can change DNA coding as it is being read, and is very attracted to the left-handed DNA.

When the left version appears, the editor molecule jumps in, attaches itself to the z-DNA and alters the message being read out. As a result, there turns out to be more than one way to read a DNA message, the regular and the edited version.

In life, proteins produced by cells with edited DNA turn out to be important. One of them is used as one of the key receptor molecules in the brain, Rich said. Without it animals tend to develop epilepsy and often die. Another edited molecule is a receptor for serotonin, the molecule whose level is increased by anti-depressants like Prozac.

The edited version of the molecule gives a more muted response to serotonin, and thus allows mixed, more finely tuned, reactions rather than only those with the unedited version.

This also suggests that z-DNA may be another useful control mechanism in biotechnology. In practical terms, this means that cells, or scientists at biotechnology firms making use of DNA, have another tool to control what DNA does.

"That's very interesting Maria, but what's your point?"

"Mr. Willie, don't you see, if we really work at it maybe we can edit my DNA so it becomes Samoan."

"Maria, we need to get back to the office and meet Dingo, but remind me to sit you down and teach you the basics of molecular biology."

"Yes, massah." Maria laughs, thinking to herself: There's more to me than big knockers, Mr. Smartass Samoan.

Roger and Dingo are visiting one of Dingo's favourite haunts, the Beverly Crest Tavern. When they get there, it's just a few regulars whittling away at an afternoon empty of excitement. Dingo gets a couple of draft from the bar and rents a pool table. The inside of the tavern, except for the addition of satellite bingo TVs and VLTs hasn't changed in thirty years.

"Play?" He asks Roger.

"Not in a long time," Roger answers.

"Until I see how good you are, I'll give you two balls," Dingo says.

"I suppose I might find uses for two of your balls," Roger replies.

They turn out to be evenly matched.

"I think I'll take those two balls back," Dingo says.

"I'm not sure I'm through with your balls," Roger says.

The Beverly Crest isn't the sort of place one engages in gay double entendres. Even on a slow afternoon. Dingo knows that. Knows the men at the bar are listening.

"Let's order some food," Dingo says.

"They've got food here?" Roger asks. "Good food? It doesn't look the kind of establishment in which one should put much faith in the quality of the food."

"Honest, they have a great kitchen, do tons of catering and a great buffet on Sundays. People come from out of town to eat here," Dingo tells him. He doesn't tell him he's cruising for a bruising.

"Well, nonetheless, let's not tax them too much," Roger says.

They settle on steak sandwiches with stuffed mushroom caps.

Over the food, which they eat standing up between pool shots, Dingo says, "Tell me about yourself."

"I've always been a trader. In elementary school I didn't play marbles, I traded them. Once, I traded some cheap cat's eyes for two steelies and sold them for $3 to a kid who didn't want to trade but desperately wanted steelies. It gave me my first erection, that cash," Roger says. Roger's a bit loud, and the acoustics are good in the tavern, the fake wood panelling absorbs almost nothing, bouncing the sound on around the bar.

"I'll get us a couple more draft," Dingo says. The bartender leans over as Dingo picks up his drafts and says, "Ding, I'd keep your friend a little under wraps. The locals are getting antsy." "I'll try," Dingo says. Planning no such thing.

He hands Roger a new glass of draft and says, "Tell me more."

"In junior high school I moved into comics and trading cards. It was in a high school economics class that I discovered a talent for commodities trading. The teacher was a retired stock broker and he set up a simulated training session for us. In a week I made $50,000 trading commodities." From the bar a voice says, "Bullshit." Roger ignores it and continues.

"I never made it to college. At eighteen I started apprenticing on the floor of the Chicago Commodities Exchange.

"It was in Chicago I'd finally realized I was odd. The traders would be sitting around drinking coffee, waiting for the trading floor to open, swapping tales of their sexual exploits. Mine always made the other traders, jaded to the core, nervous, uncomfortable."

"What sort of stories did you tell?" asks Dingo, expecting to be titillated, planning to finally light a fire under the six or seven drunks at the bar.

"I and a trader from another company, he was trying to be like a father figure to me, teaching me the ropes, we went out for a night on the town. We went into Little Japan, to what he called a Geisha house. We started with a bath. He and I together in this big steam bath. These Japanese girls all wrapped up in their kimonos, God they must have been hot, lathering and rinsing our bodies, all of our bodies. Gord, the guy I'm with, has this big erection, I'm staring at it, looking down at myself and nothing is happening."

Dingo climbs up on a bar stool, puts down his cue, tries hard to imagine the scene. Nobody at the bar or at the one table of drinkers is making a sound.

"After the bath we get all rigged up in kimonos of our own and bare feet and kneel on this mat at a little table and they serve us sushi and saki. A wonderful, wonderful meal. Then a different girl comes and gets me and takes me away. Paul calls out, 'Have lots of fun, I'm paying enough!'

"She takes me into a private room, doffs her kimono and underneath she's wearing a red silk teddy. Then she takes off my kimono and has me lie naked, face down on this strange table. There is a donut of leather at the head end that my face goes in. Then she starts rubbing me all over. It feels delightful, but not sexual. The next thing I know she's stripped and is rubbing her breasts up and down my back. By now even I have the idea, I'm supposed to be getting aroused. I'm not.

"The geisha rolls me over and starts licking my nether regions. Abstractly, I'm admiring her technique, but nothing, really. She tried her hands, rubs them with some magic potion and then rubs me. Still no luck. Well, suddenly she picks up this little hand ringer, a little bell and rings it. Makes a tiny tinkling sound you can barely hear. Out of nowhere this old woman appears wearing a magnificent silk kimono, purple and pink with cranes on it. She and my geisha confer." Roger pauses to take another sip of beer.

"So what happened next," Dingo almost begs him to continue. He can sense the tension in the rest of the audience.

"The old lady came over to me and reached down and grabbed my limpness and started to stroke. I know she's way better at it than my girl but even she can't raise a signal. The old lady takes my girl over to the side of the room and they have a more extended conversation. Then they both bow and leave the room."

"Come on, there has got to be more to the story than that," Dingo says.

"Much more," Roger says, grinning wickedly at Dingo. "I'm just about to get up when a new woman enters the room. She's bigger and coarser. Not a fine-boned little Japanese girl at all. She is carrying a large black lacquered box. She drags me off the table. I think, great, I'm being thrown out. Then she takes out some ropes from the box. Ties up my wrists. I'm completely stunned.

"When she takes off her kimono her body is muscled, muscled like a man's. She's all woman but she has these bulging braided muscles. Once she's naked she takes this whip out of the box. By now I've got it figured out, the geishas take it really personal if you don't get a hardon. This woman punishes you for their loss of face. 'Wait,' I say, thinking I can talk my way out of it. Then she starts to whip me.

"She gives me a hell of a working over. She didn't get naked for sexual reasons, it's just she didn't want to get sweat all over her nice kimono. Ten minutes of vigorous whipping and sweat is pouring off her and I'm enthusiastic. She crouches down exposing herself all bright red, I'm supposed to do it like a bull, and I'm happy to oblige. But between desire and execution my enthusiasm evaporates.

"But this woman doesn't give up easily. She forces me back on to the table and ties me to it at my wrists and ankles. I'm face up and wondering what comes next. My second girl doesn't disappoint. She starts biting me. She bites me all over, my chest, my stomach, my kneecaps, the soles of my feet. At first they are love bites, I'm barely aware of them. But then she starts really putting her massive jaws into the job. I'm screaming in pain and loving every minute of it. She begins to alternate the bites with some very skilful licking and sucking on the reluctant member of the company. It's great fun but somehow we can't quite get me over the psychological hump, so to speak.

"She goes back to her box and takes out a set of what look like straight razors with ornate handles. She debates for sometime before choosing one. That one she strokes gently with a fur cloth she also has in the box. Then she takes a little vase of sake and pours it over the blade of the razor. She sets the razor on fire, holding it, burning, in her hand.

"Feeling the razor is finally ready she brings it over to the table. She stroked the inside of my thighs with the back edge of the blade. It's dull. She rubs the blade on my belly. I can't help it, my stomach muscles clench. Then she grabs my foreskin hard and makes a diagonal slice in it. Blood is pouring everywhere before my brain registers how much it hurts. Then I'm pulling wildly against the ties that hold me to the table, bucking and screaming in horror and exploding, all over her, all over the room."

Dingo realizes he's panting, covers it up by draining his draft.

"That's the story I told. After that I never did have a chance of fitting in. But I really didn't care. I'd found three things I loved: trading, making money, and pain. I'd also found the perfect place to indulge my passions for all three, Chicago. But eventually burning the candle at both ends took its toll. I crashed and burned.

"At thirty I was burnt out. Burnt out, but a millionaire. I still wanted to trade but not pork bellies and soy bean futures. I guess what I'm saying is I wanted to trade real things."

"Pork bellies and soybeans aren't real things?"

"Yes, but the trader never sees them. I wanted something I could touch. I bought a little comic book shop and slowly diversified into collectible comics. One day a customer came looking for a complete collection of Playboy magazines. It took me nearly a year. I had to travel all over the country, trading, bidding at auctions and estate sales, following many wild geese, but I finally built a complete set. In the end I lost about a hundred dollars a magazine once all my expenses were built in, but I had a time."

"How did you end up dealing in...whatever you call it?" Dingo asks.

"There was no money in comics. Not much in pornography. I made some dealing rare erotic manuscripts. Just not enough.

"I'd developed a certain lifestyle, expectations. I started specializing in the bizarre, the obscene, and the grotesque for the money. Learned about it perusing a Soldier of Fortune magazine on a slow day at the comic shop. I'll say this. It's been a really good business."

They almost get out of the tavern without an altercation. But one rig pig with time on his hands can't let it go. As they pass his stool at the bar he sticks a leg out, stopping Roger from going any further. "I don't believe any of that crap," he says.

"Let's go," Dingo says.

"This gentleman has questioned my veracity," Roger says.

"So show him the scars on your penis and let's get out of here," Dingo says.

"Fag," the rig pig says as he lunges at Roger. Dingo taps him expertly on the back of the head with the edge of a stool. He collapses in a neat pile at Roger's feet.

"Homosexual panic," Roger says.

"Excuse for a brawl," Dingo says as the bar erupts in violence, only a small portion of it directed at Dingo and Roger.

The two of them are back safe and sound at the office when Maria and Willie arrive.

Willie wants to know what the plan is. Dingo says its' quite simple. He and Roger will head to the Baccarat Casino downtown. There is always a game there and Dingo knows all the players. He'll play a little, with Roger's money of course, and gossip a lot.

"Players love to dish," Dingo says. "It's part of the culture, and they love to tell tales of great poker scams. They'd kill any mechanic they caught but they idolize them at a distance."

"What's a mechanic?" Maria asks.

"A first class professional cheater, someone who can make the cards come out anyway they like. Some of them mark cards that go through their hands so that they know what you're holding and what's going to come up. Others will stick a new deck in play, one they've already marked. Some slip a new card into the game. Then there is dealing off the bottom of the deck. Here, let me show you," Dingo says.

He reaches into his pocket and takes out a deck of cards. "I carry these around so I can keep my fingers nimble." He shuffles the deck and then holds it upside down, everyone can see the bottom card is the jack of diamonds. Turning the deck back over, Dingo deals Maria a hand. No one sees him do it but when Maria turns her hand over it is obvious Dingo has dealt from the bottom of the deck. There is the jack of diamonds nestled in her hand.

"Can I borrow that deck, Dingo?" Maria asks. Dingo hands it to her. He notices she has large hands for a woman. Her fingers are just a blur as she shuffles the deck, all the while maintaining eye contact with Dingo. Then she hands the deck to Roger and says, "Please to cut." He does so and she takes the deck back and deals them each a card, face down, starting with Roger and ending with herself. "Take a peek, but don't show me," she commands. They do so.

"Ace of clubs," she says pointing at Roger. He flips his card over, it is indeed the ace of clubs. Turning she points at Dingo. "Ace of diamonds," she says. He flips his card over, revealing the ace of diamonds. "Ace of hearts," she says flipping her own card over. "And the big fellah, has the ace of spades," she says flipping his card over. "He wins," she says.

"Where on this earth did you learn to do that? More important, how did you do that?" Roger demands.

"Maria is a professional magician," Dingo says.

"My mother started me working with cards when I was two. Then I worked with a great magician, an American, in Egypt. Here in North America you call this kind of stuff 'up close magic.' I do it standing on a street corner and people give me money, and it's lots of fun. I can't tell you how I did it unless you are a Maslet, related to me by blood, or marriage."

"It's a professional secret, then," Dingo says.

"Very secret, yes," Maria says. "If you learned the secret, since you are not a Maslet, I'd have to kill you."

"Roger, while you and I are doing the Baccarat, Maria and Willie are going to play at Casino Edmonton on the south side. Maria is going to play, and Willie is going to do his wallflower thing. I know it's hard to believe but he can blend into the woodwork."

"I flirt and gossip and play and he listens," Maria says. "Maybe, he spots this Mr. Average Bob."

CHAPTER · 9

"Tell me straight," Willie asks as he and Maria drive to Casino Edmonton, "what do you really know about poker?" Willie is driving and drinking coffee, hot coffee. Eventually he'll learn not to drink hot fluids when Maria is talking.

"I was good enough to make a buck or two as a local," Maria says as she wriggles in the seat, trying to straighten her miniskirt. "I even played some second string in Yorkshire. I won some tournaments in Leeds and Plymouth. I love poker, but I'm a much better cheat than I am a player."

"You admit you cheat?" he splutters, spitting coffee all over the dashboard.

"Yes. Sometimes when I play poker for fun and competition, I don't cheat. Other times I play for money. For money I cheat as much as I think I can get away with. I'm super good at making cards doing things they aren't supposed to and not getting caught. So I cheat a lot."

At Casino Edmonton, Maria heads into the poker lounge. There are ten tables scattered around the room. Each one has at least a few players at them. Each table has eight chairs, at none of them are all the chairs full.

"How does this work?" Willie asks.

"It isn't the same everywhere, all the time. Here, this casino, tonight, the dealer works for the casino. They aren't playing, they are just there to deal all fair and square and collect the rake," Maria says.

"The rake?" Willie asks.

"The rake is the casino's percentage. Can be anywhere from one percent, very nice, to fifteen percent, robbery. Keep it too high, too long, no more poker players. There are a lot of players here tonight. That's because the house take is only three percent. For that you get a dealer and a place to play."

"But doesn't a dealer make it very hard for you to cheat?" Willie asks.

"Don't say cheat in here, don't even think it. Anybody could be listening. But the answer is no, it makes it a lot easier because everyone assumes you can't be cheating."

At first Maria just watches. She moves from table to table, staying far enough back she can't be accused of looking at anyone's cards. Some tables she only glances at the players for a few seconds before moving on. Three of the tables she waits through a number of hands.

"What are you looking for?" Willie asks her.

"I want a mixed table, a granny on a bus tour, a high roller, maybe a couple of locals, and, if there is one here tonight, a wing tester. Not a table of locals."

"Wing testers, locals?" Willie inquires.

"Poker players come in all kinds of skill levels. The great ones, every one just calls them players, but the way they say it you know what they mean; play high stakes poker and big time tournaments. The best of the best, like Amarillo Slim, play in the World Championship of Poker."

"Do all the best have nicknames?" Willie asks.

"I've never heard of any that were called Nick," Maria says.

"A nickname is a made-up name."

"All different kinds of poker players have these nicknames," Maria says.

"So simply because Average Bob goes by the handle Bobby Nevada doesn't mean he's a great poker player?" Willie asks.

"No. More likely he's a local."

"You said you didn't want a table of them. I guess you don't mean people who live around here when you said locals."

"But I do. In a way. Players travel, often a lot. But locals stick close to home. They might be good enough to play big time poker but for some reason they don't. Lack of capital, family troubles, jobs they can't get away from. They play a lot and most make money, they do it with careful, small bets, and good strategy. A table full of them is a hard place to make any money, good competition, small pots."

"What's a wing tester?" Willie asks.

"Someone who wants to be a serious poker player. It would be really excellent if they were good enough to take that step up. I like playing with good players, especially ones that lose a lot."

Suddenly Maria gets quite excited.

"Go and blend in," she orders. "Watch me. Look for Mr. Average Bob. I want that table over there," Maria says and then oozes her way into the game she's pointed out. The men standing around the small table, watching, part to let her through. Maria sits and plunks down a pile of chips in front of her. They haven't stop to buy chips yet and Willie wonders where she got them from, who she's stolen from this time.

At the table Maria has chosen there is the dealer and five players. One is clearly a tourist, all small bets and laughter, even when she loses. For a fact she's old enough to be a grandmother. One exudes confidence, he clearly expects to win, and win often. Watching him play for a while, Willie realizes this guy is the wing tester Maria was looking for and he is good, he wins a lot. Two nondescript men—they both look like Mr. Average Bob to Willie, they bet small, fold often, seldom lose much, and after a dozen hands are ahead of the game—sit on either side of Maria. These must be locals, Willie decides. The last player is a woman with brassy hair, a great gust of a laugh, zaftig and rich. She throws money into every pot, wins some big pots, and loses a lot of small ones and some big ones as well.

The big loser though is Maria. She loses conspicuously and consistently. She also radiates joy. Win or lose, she's clearly having a blast.

A man comes and joins the table. Willie has spent his entire adult life with people staring at him. Which is why he instantly sympathizes with the new player. A beach ball of a head rests on a barrel of a trunk. That whole, huge, upper body is supported by two of the thinnest, longest legs Willie has ever seen. He's not made less conspicuous by the lime-green suit with the yellow and orange fleck.

"Yankowich," the man says holding his hand out to Maria. He ignores the rest of the players in the game.

From the moment Yankowich sits down, Maria's luck changes. She starts to win. Not every hand, but way more than her share.

Willie can't believe how she reacts to her great luck. She throws a hissy fit, demanding a new dealer. Eventually the dealer gives in, a new dealer is sent for.

During the change-over Maria heads to the bathroom. On the way she signals frantically to Willie to follow her. First she tries tilting her head in little sideways nods. When Willie is oblivious to that she tries curt, regal waves delivered with her right hand, using her face to block Yankowich's line of sight. She puts both hands at her waist and makes scooping motions, trying to shepherd him along. That also fails. She raises her eyebrows at him. They get into an eyebrow raising contest. Finally she comes and grabs him by the arm and drags Willie off toward the women's washroom.

"Yankowich is security," she hisses at Willie.

"What do you care?" he asks. "The guy is your personal good luck charm."

"I'm doing it," she says, so softly Willie isn't sure what she's said.

"Doing what?" He asks.

"The c thing?"

"What's that?" He asks.

"Not playing fair," she whispers.

"You're cheating," Willie says, loudly. "Right in front of the security guy. Boy, you are good. Why didn't you cheat before he entered the game, no challenge?"

"I was cheating like mad before he joined the game," she says.

"Then you really aren't very good at it, are you? You were losing money hand over fist," Willie says.

"They are so bad the only way I can't win is if I cheat. Make them better than they are. Give them good hands. Heat of the infidel's desert, I nearly have to tell them how to bet." As she gets angry, her voice rises rapidly in volume.

"Okay. So now you're winning because you aren't cheating. Haven't been cheating since the security guy entered the game."

"No! No! I'm winning because as hard as I cheat to help the other players Yankowich cheats even more to help me. Then I have to cheat more. We're having a cheating war," Maria says. "The guy is good but I'm better. I'll end up losing."

"Why would he be helping you win?" Willie asks.

"Security guys do strange stuff. Who knows why?"

"Cash in and let's get out of here," Willie orders.

"I can't leave until I prove I can cheat better than Yankowich," Maria says.

It takes several hours but Maria finally finishes down about three thousand dollars. Maria bows formally to the other players at the table and picks up her chips. While she is doing that Willie winks broadly at Yankowich. Yankowich gives him a big grin.

"I've never had to cheat so hard," Maria says while she's cashing in her remaining chips.

"How much did you lose?" Willie asks.

"Lose? I made almost a thousand dollars."

Sure enough, she gets nine hundred and ninety dollars from the teller.

"My original stake, that was spillage. People are very silly, they come to a casino and they drink and they forget all about their chips. I know you think I'm telling you a big goosey fable, but it's truly true that every night at every casino in all the world someone leaves chips behind. The casino scoops them up as soon as the player is out the door. I just didn't wait quite that long."

"Did you even wait until they forgot their chips?"

"Don't be silly. I waited until they weren't paying any attention and I was sure they were going to forget. Then I took them. And no one kicked up a fuss so I must have picked a forgetter, mustn't I."

"You must have," Willie says. "And even after you lost three thousand dollars you still had some of those original chips left over. Good Lord! Why waste timing playing poker, why not just pick up the spillage?"

Maria squeezes Willie's arm. "I love you. You let me play poker and you ask all those questions about it. I've missed it so much. Draj swore if he ever caught me in a casino he'd pound both my hands with a tire iron until I could never pick up a card again," Maria says.

"Why on earth would he have threatened that? Surely you could have made a fortune for him."

"Not a fortune, Willie. I'm not that good. But a living, sure I could have earned him a living, him and his lazy family. He's a gypsy man, he makes all the decisions for his woman and there is no way he can do that while I'm playing poker. Every decision I make his hoolah shrinks."

They walk out into the parking lot. The evening is warm and moist. Maria shivers despite the heat, so Willie puts his arm around her.

"What I don't get is why you didn't leave your husband long ago."

"I tried once. We were still in England. I tried to go back to the Lees *kumpania*. Shaggy threw me out. I crawled away I was so ashamed. I ended up curled up underneath a tree, maybe a hundred meters from Shaggy's caravan. After dark he came out to see me. Said he had to wait for his wife to be asleep. He explained to me that Michla, his new Turkish wife, just an obnoxious kid really, wouldn't let him have anything to do with me. Insisted on my being thrown out in the first place.

"Shaggy thought of me as a daughter and I thought of him as sort of a grandfather and Michla though of us as possible lovers. Couldn't believe that we hadn't been doing it behind Agnes's poor back all these years. There wasn't much Shaggy could do for me, she had him by his humping apparatus.

"I managed to have a pretty good life for two months travelling all on my own, on foot. Then I was on a street corner in Plymouth when Draj caught up with me. I ran but Marko cut me off. The three brothers dragged me kicking and screaming off the streets and no one lifted a hand to help."

Willie frowns and tightens his grip on Maria's shoulders.

"Once we were back in their trailer Nana held my head and Marko my arms and Draj burnt me. He heated an iron until it was as hot as he could get it. Then he pressed it in to my feet. I'll never forget the smell of burning flesh.

"It was weeks before I could walk again. Draj told me the next time I ran away he'd cut off my feet. I believed him. I knew the next time I ran away I'd need a plan, a place to go, and someone to watch over me."

Maria looks up at the giant Samoan. "Then one day I see a man who has magic in his body standing over me. That's you. I also see his future and see I'm a part of it. In the hospital I saw how scared they are of you and I know as long as I'm with you I'm safe."

CHAPTER · 10

That night, once Willie is safely asleep, Maria slips out of the trailer. She tiptoes up to the main entrance of the trailer park. Across the road is a convenience store. In the parking lot two men sit in a Ford Explorer waiting for her.

When they see her coming, the man in the front passenger seat gets out and holds the door open for her. She gets in the front. He carefully closes the door for her, then gets in the back passenger seat.

"Did they buy it?"

"Dingo bought it hook, line, and sinker. Willie, I don't know. I can't figure him out," Maria says.

"If this is going to work he has to believe, both him and Dingo," Roger says.

"I know. Remember me? I'm the one who thought this scam up," Maria says.

"*We* thought this scam up, Maria," Average Bob points out. "You and I first, and then Roger adding all kinds of little flourishes. Without him we'd have no credibility with any collectors, and no marks to play. So show some respect, dear. Try to forget that Romni arrogance for a few minutes," the driver says.

"Yes, massah," she says. "I'm sorry, Roger. It's just you were so over the top with Dingo, almost slobbering on him."

"Still can't get the big Willie to screw your sorry little ass?" Roger says, venomously. "At least I'm sharing Dingo's bed tonight."

"I'm working on it. He'll fall. I know he wants me," Maria says.

"We'll just stretch the con out," Bob says. "Give you some more time. Willie's a pretty key player in convincing the marks everything is legitimate."

"Pretty key? Shit, he and Dingo are minor gods to some of these big time collectors of Americana, bailed them out of some sort of mining scam, helped them make a fortune. The two of them buy this and the rest of the dominoes fall into place."

"So reel Willie in. No excuses."

"You never told me he was Samoan," Maria says with a pout.

"What difference does that make?"

Maria just shrugs.

Roger checks his watch. "I'd better get back to Dingo. He was passed out when I came out, but with an alcoholic you never know. Bob, I'll catch up with you sometime tomorrow." With a flick of his hand, almost a salute, Roger slips into the night.

"This is probably the last time we'll see each other until the big night," Bob says.

Maria knows what he's asking. But she ignores his meaning and again just nods.

"Way things are going for you, I'm your last chance for sex for a month, like one of those gas stations in the middle of nowhere."

"He'd smell you on me. He's a primitive savage. How do you think he'd like that, another guy's smell on me?"

Even while she's speaking, she's climbing down from the SUV, giving Bob no time to think of a counter argument.

In the wee small hours of the morning, after a long walk through farmers' fields and industrial parks, Maria arrives back at the trailer, strips, and climbs into bed with Willie. Maria rapidly discovers you can't sleep in a waterbed with a man who outweighs you by two hundred pounds. Plus he smells weird, icky. She heads back to her own bed.

The next morning when Maria wakes up Willie is gone. He's left a cryptic note: Gone to listen to a rock! Maria has just had her usual breakfast, orange juice and coffee, when he returns.

"What's the story on this bowl?" Maria asks as Willie sits down beside her. "Why does it," she sniffs, "and you, smell so bad?" She is holding a large teak bowl.

"That was a gift from my Uncle Duncan. It's a bowl made especially to be used in various religious rites. Greeting guests. Negotiating truces. I used it last night to drink some Samoan beer. That's what you smell."

"Yuck. How could you drink something that stinky?"

"You hold your nose. Now let's go train."

They slip into sweats, and go for a run on the back roads between Edmonton and Sherwood Park. Next it is time to weight train. Willie has a fortune in weight-lifting equipment in what was originally a third bedroom. Willie figures that while Maria thinks she wants to be Samoan, what she really wants is to be able to stand up for herself.

Part of making sure you can stand up for yourself is getting fit. The fitter person wins almost every fight and that means running and lifting weights. At first Maria has trouble running any distance, so she and Willie run a little way and then they walk for a while. With the weights, right from the first Maria excels. She starts out bench pressing a hundred pounds, which can't be much less than her own body weight, and within a week is doing a hundred and fifty. By the end of two weeks she is up to two hundred pounds. Her squat is up to over three hundred, and she can snatch a hundred and twenty-five.

All of which means, by Willie's calculation, that she is in the top one percent of women in body strength. Not that she's changed her mind about becoming Samoan, in fact her desire grows each day. What Willie really likes is that she attacks the weights, the only woman he's ever met who lifts like he does. He also likes having a training partner, especially one who thinks weight training should be clothing optional.

Each day Willie measures the dark brown splotch on Maria's back. Each day it grows, slowly pigmenting her entire back. Maria gleefully turns to Willie and says: "See, I told you, I'm a Samoan woman."

"Not yet," he responds. But she is putting on weight at an unbelievable speed. Two weeks into their Samoan training regime she weighs a hundred and forty pounds, and most of it is clearly muscle. That's when it occurs to Willie to start measuring Maria's height as well. The first day she is 5'5" tall. Maria claims that she used to be 5' 3½ inches tall. Willie is dubious.

After the weights comes the shower. At first Willie thinks they will take separate showers but that isn't Maria's plan. As fast as he evicts her from the shower she slips back in. She claims it is her job to keep him clean.

Willie is driving her nuts in that he shows no interest in having sex with her. Well, not no interest. After all, lack of interest is a hard thing for a man to fake. But the fact that he isn't doing anything with his obvious desire is getting to her. From time to time, just out of curiosity, as she soaps her large brown man, she wonders what the Raklos are doing, and takes a moment to wish them the worst sort of luck.

CHAPTER · 11

If she knew what the Raklos are doing, Maria would be mightily worried. With Maria gone, Nana Raklo tells Draj to lie in the road. They only try that once. A guy comes down the Queen Elizabeth Hill in a nice new Crown Victoria, and Draj times his leap perfectly. The stunned motorist slams on his breaks, stopping just a hair from Draj's head. The motorist just sits in the car for the longest time. Draj remains motionless. Then the guy slams it in reverse, backs up about two hundred feet, shifts into drive and comes tearing right at Draj. At the last moment Draj manages to roll out of the way. The driver swerves to try to hit Draj as he rolls towards the ditch. Once he's dusted himself off and had a shot of vodka Draj announces, "This lying in the road, it's too dangerous."

Instead of extorting motorists each morning, the Raklo brothers get up and go check out new personal injury lawyers. They have heard at the Purple Onion that injury lawyers are always looking for "victims" for insurance scams. Late of a Friday night, after the band has packed it in, after last call, the Rom and the grifters and pimps and prostitutes sit around in tight little groups trading tricks of the trade, and providing the kind of support group that every professional needs. The rules, sort of, are you don't try to con a con man and you always try to give the other guy a fair break, unless you think you can make a buck off him. A lot of booze and some serious recreational drugs may have been consumed before the network meets, and you have to discount some of what you hear.

The Raklo boys meet Max Ferguson in the Onion the evening of Draj's near miss. Max is a true stand-up crook. He works the insurance circuit doing bump and runs. He stages fake car accidents — the accidents are real but they aren't accidents. And the claims are preposterous. Max has broken his neck eleven times in one month. He wears a neck brace as a permanent part of his wardrobe. In part, that is to make sure that no insurance investigator who is watching has any cause to suspect his claims are bogus but it is also a safety device so that when a car he's driving gets hit he doesn't actually hurt his neck. In the past the Raklos have picked up some work with Max, serving as passengers in his 'accidents'. But it isn't steady because Max has a large extended family, all out of work, all bone lazy as he puts it and they have to be kept employed in the family business.

Max gives the Raklos the idea of finding an unscrupulous lawyer to handle their accident claims. He won't let them get anywhere near his. It is nothing personal but a lawyer you can trust is worth his or her weight in gold and Max isn't going to risk losing a key part of his business empire. Especially not to Romanian pond scum like the Raklos.

The problem is, all the injury lawyers in the city, even real bottom feeders, take one look at the Raklos and think slimy criminals. Not that they have anything against slimy criminals, quite the opposite. It's just there isn't any work in the insurance business for people who look guilty. And the Raklos are a neon sign, flashing guilty, lighting up the night.

It's Yannis, the baby of the family, who finds a new career for them. He's in the main library downtown, reading about crooks, scams, and cons. One of the books he keeps passing over is about something called crossroading. Having pretty much used up all the other books on crime, even the serial killer bios, he finally takes it down from the stacks and goes to his favourite table. It's hidden away between the stairs and the vending machines. He's not doing anything wrong, but he still hates the idea of anyone catching him doing it.

"Draj," he says that night, after supper. He's the only Raklo who misses Maria's cooking, he prefers raw vegetables and simple salads. Meat in cream sauce, potatoes in cream sauce, and peas in cream sauce aren't his idea of a balanced diet. "I think I have a way we can make money."

Draj idly bats him on the head. "You are too young to have ideas. That's my job."

"What is it, boy?" Nana asks. She knows Yannis is the only one of her boys to get a brain. But he's so naive. If it's a good idea Nana knows that she can convince Draj and Marko it was her very own inspiration and if the idea sucks she'll let them beat on Yannis for a bit.

"We've all been to the casinos since we moved here, right?"

They all agree.

"Lost all my money," Marko says.

"How would you like to get it all back and a lot more?" Yannis asks.

"Out with it," Draj demands. His attention span is already limited by thoughts of the sexual adventures he has planned for the night. Draj has discovered he possesses talents that make young girls throw themselves at him. He can sing, dance, and play guitar, flamenco guitar and Romanian folk music. There are a few places where university students gather, not the sort who are into headbanger music, but the intellectuals, and the owners will let him play and sing. Hell, they even encourage him. Dressed in his finest clothes, clothes Nana has kept for him ever since they left Romania, he is an irresistible gypsy prince. He has no time for bright little brothers.

"There are crooks who specialize in stealing from casinos, conning casinos. They are called crossroaders."

"So what. How would we learn to be good cross-streeters?" Draj asks sarcastically.

"This book tells us how," Yannis holds it up, knowing he's the only one who reads, at least English. "Plus there are several sites on the Internet that explain how, and in FTP." Yannis can already see the plan unfolding. He's actually going to get to be in charge. As long as he doesn't ever tell his brothers, or mother all the details, he can call his own shots. Be the big man. If only he can appeal to their greed. "Come with me to the casino tonight," he says. "At least give me a chance to prove to you how much money we can make."

He finally wears Marko and Nana down. Draj is determined to go work on his professional gypsy routine. Yannis starts out at a blackjack table at Palace Casino. He's down nearly a thousand dollars in an hour. After yanking him around, Marko and Nana head off to the bar. Yannis comes home with six thousand dollars. Suddenly crossroading is everyone's idea. Everyone but Yannis.

That night Draj and Nana stay up late talking excitedly about what they are going to do with Yannis's money. With all the money he'll make for them in the future. They also talk about finding the witch, making sure she can't run away again. Later, drunk, angry, Draj decides to find Maria and kill her. Promises this to Nana, to himself. The next morning, sober, he's forgotten all about his vow.

CHAPTER · 12

Occasionally Willie and Maria vary their regime slightly, or rather Willie varies it. In the morning after breakfast they head out to the farm. Though only Willie ever thinks of it that way. It's a spruce bog with a couple of hills protruding from it and some aspen parkland surrounding it. The back of the property abuts on Elk Island National Park's east side. Willie often sees bison wandering on the other side of the fence that separates the two properties.

In the only real clearing on the one hundred acre property, Willie has levelled a piece of hummocky grassland to make a site for the trailer. He's installed a septic tank and dug a well. He's had the power and telephone extended from Wye Road into the site. He's also mowed some of the grassy clearing until it is almost a putting green. At one end there is a cement circle, with white chalk lines radiating out from it. This is where Willie comes to throw. If he goes too long without throwing he starts to ache all over. He doesn't think it's possible but sometimes he wonders if he's as addicted to throwing as Dingo is to alcohol.

Maria doesn't share Willie's passion for throwing but humours him by making a few tosses of the discus and running around the field picking them up and returning them to Willie. Cardiovascularly she's getting a much better workout than Willie. Her strength training comes later when she helps Willie with his latest farm project.

In the middle of the property the bog becomes a true lake. On the far shore from the trailer site, the lake actually has a stony beach. From there you can look back to the clearing, across the lake. On the beach Willie is building....well he isn't sure what he's building. He picked rocks from all over the farm, stuck them in his rickety wheelbarrow and wheeled them to the beach. Now Maria helps him. Some of the rocks are small as baby potatoes, others are as big as turnips, a few are the size of watermelons.

After every throwing practice, Willie cranks up his portable CD player — usually some chanteuse, Sarah, Holly, or Diana — and he gets the compass out of the leather bag he carries around his neck. Holding the compass in one hand they pick a rock from the wheelbarrow. If it's too heavy they use both hands and rest the compass on top of the rock. They walk whatever direction the compass points. There must be loadstone, or some sort of charged rock beneath the surface of the beach because the compass never points the same way twice. In fact the needle changes directions every few minutes, swinging wildly. When that happens, Willie and Maria drop the rock they are carrying. They repeat the process until all the rocks are distributed on the beach, then get another wheelbarrow load full of rocks.

Willie has been working away on this project for months and the result is a mound shaped like a giant cross. The main trunk of the cross is twenty feet long and eight feet across. The cross piece is fifteen feet long and three feet across. The whole thing rises up nearly two feet above the surrounding rocks of the beach.

Each time they come to the farm, after they've finished a session of working on the cross, they sit on the edge of the lake dangling their tired and hot feet in the cool water. That's when Willie says: "That thing is almost enough to make you believe in Christianity."

Maria isn't being as helpful to Willie's thesis quest as she would like. She can't figure out what the problem is. She's narrowed his search down to one short passage and that should have made everything much easier. It hasn't. Willie sits for hours every day reading the passage from *Dangerous Waters* over and over again. He writes down every idea he has about what the passage may mean. He's filled a ring binder with over one hundred and fifty pages of his jottings in two weeks.

Maria hates that binder. When Willie is working on "The Passage" as he calls it, he pays no attention to her.

They have come back from a hard morning working at the farm and Willie is drinking coffee in the kitchen when Maria says: "Today we are going hunting for chert."

"What's chert?" Willie asks.

"It's a magic rock," Maria answers.

"Is all chert magical?"

"No. All chert makes magic," Maria says.

"What kind of magic does chert make?"

"Say you're trying to tell someone's fortune and you aren't having any luck, you just can't see anything. You take a chert and you hang it from an old g-string," she says as Willie inhales and then blows coffee out his nose.

"From a banjo," Maria goes on, calmly ignoring Willie's coughing fit. "You hold the end of the string in your hand and the chert hangs down. You take something like a book or a newspaper and hold the chert over that and it points at various letters. The chert answers your questions. You don't need any binder or even to think, not with chert."

"Where are we going to get this chert, then, oh magic gypsy princess?"

"In a river, big, brown, stupid man."

"What's it look like?"

"It's not what it looks like, it's what it feels like."

"What does it feel like?" Willie asks.

"It feels soft, softer than a rock should. But if you rub it, it starts feeling hard," Maria answers, ignoring Willie's Groucho impression. Then she spins around and around until she is so dizzy she almost falls down. "We will drive that way," she says, pointing west, "until we find chert."

"How will you know when you have found a river with chert in it?" Willie asks.

"I'll get out of Truck every time we cross a river and smell the water. Eventually I'll smell chert. It has an odd odour, burnt pasta. It'll be fun."

"It has to beat reading The Passage again. I'll go on one condition. I get to take my fishing rod and I can fish while you look for chert," Willie says.

"Deal," Maria says.

Willie makes peanut butter and banana sandwiches, fills his two old canteens with water, and they head off to find chert. First they cross the Blackmud, which fails the chert test. Then the Whitemud, which is even less promising, chert-wise. Their route crosses and re-crosses the North Saskatchewan River which doesn't smell like chert. Neither does the Wolf. The Brazeau smells like chert.

Willie finds an old logging road that leads right down to the river. They park Truck in the shade of a huge pine tree and sit on the tailgate eating their sandwiches. As they eat Maria tries to explain to Willie how to listen to a river. How to tell if it's magic or not. The Brazeau is. Willie thinks it sounds just like all the other brooks he's fished in over the years.

After lunch Willie breaks out his fly rod and walks a little ways up river from where Maria is hunting for chert. He spends a wonderful summer afternoon casting for rainbow trout and brook trout. Standing knee deep in the crystal clear water he can see the fish swimming by his legs but none rise to his fly. Occasionally he glances over to where Maria is searching.

First she searches the river bank near the truck. Then she raises her skirt up above her knees and wades across to the other side of the river and searches the bank there. The next time Willie looks she has taken off her skirt and blouse. Wearing nothing more than panties two sizes too large for her — she plans to grow into them — she is searching the river bed a handful of rock at a time.

It is past suppertime and Willie's stomach is growling loud enough to scare off all the fish when Maria comes running up to him along the riverbank. She jumps into the river beside him, grabs his hand, peels his fingers back and slaps a shiny, round and smooth black rock into the palm of his hand.

"Chert," she says.

Willie turns it over in his hand.

"Rub," Maria orders.

Willie rubs the rock. At first it feels soft to the touch. The longer he rubs the harder it feels.

"Chert," Maria says. She is so excited she is bouncing up and down. Willie reaches out and gently presses down on her shoulders, briefly pinning her to earth. Then he bends down and kisses her. It is a chaste kiss but a kiss nonetheless. Maria wants to say "gotchya" but doesn't.

In Drayton Valley they find a restaurant, Dimitrio's, that serves Lebanese and Greek food. They have *cous-cous* and *dolmades*. After supper they drive home with the setting sun behind them. Maria curls up against Willie's massive chest and sleeps.

That night, after she is sure Willie is sound asleep Maria charges the chert. This is a step she hasn't told Willie about. It's a secret, the very first Grandma Nose ever taught her.

"The power is in us," she'd told Maria, "and all those like us who have the gift. We can see the future clear as a bell, sometimes. But other times with all the noise in our head we can't see so clear. So we take a piece of rock and we give it some of our power and then we let the rock do the work for us. But only rocks that feel soft when you first pick them up can take that power, and only those that go hard when they are rubbed are useful."

Grandma Nose had charged her cherts by sucking on them. She'd put them in her mouth and go around all day sucking like the chert was some sort of hard candy. When Maria tried to charge up a chert that way it didn't work. She could keep it in her mouth for days and it still didn't work, the chert wouldn't tell her anything useful.

"You must find your own way to give the rock your power. My way doesn't work for you. Remember you are a Maslet, not a Romni. I think my Da told me that only the Rom suck on the rocks, other peoples have other ways. I wish I could tell you how to charge chert but I don't remember the old stories too well anymore, not all of them anyways. My mother could have told you all about when the Rom and the Maslet lived together in India. She would have known how a Maslet girl charges up a teller stone."

Eventually Maria found a way of charging chert. She used the magic her mother had taught her when she was a girl. Maria can remember her mother sitting her down the day after Maria first menstruated and beginning to teach her the "woman's magic." It embarrassed Salma and fascinated Maria.

"Long time ago," Salma began, the two of them sitting on a little hill on the west edge of town, "the Maslets didn't live here in Shadipur. We lived way up there," she pointed off to the northwest, "in the big mountains. And we practiced real magic. The women did, the men farmed, hunted and fished. We knew how to make the moon stop and the rain fall and all manner of useful and amazing things. But the most amazing thing of all was that we knew how to use our bodies to make magic happen. Men and women they do these things together, things that bring pleasure and make babies and being nosy little you I bet you know all about these things."

"Yes mother, I do," Maria says.

"Well, you don't really, but enough for me to tell you the story of the Maslet people. The women would use the men, their excitement, their urges to cast spells. The more excited they got the men the better the spells worked and the more powerful the women became. The women kept this magic to themselves, a secret that no man must ever learn. This made the men very jealous and they ordered the women to stop doing this kind of magic. Being good, obedient women they did what their husbands asked and stopped doing their body magic.

"The rain didn't fall when it was needed and it fell when it wasn't and the crops failed. But the men could still hunt and fish and they wouldn't let their women practice the forbidden magic. Then the snows came early and were too heavy and the big deer and the little rabbits all died and the men couldn't hunt. But the men could still fish and they wouldn't let their women practice the magic. Then all that rain and all that snow made the rivers silt up and the fish couldn't be caught anymore. The men came to the women and demanded the women teach them the magic.

"The women thought about this for a long time and then they disobeyed their husbands for the first time. They taught them magic all right. Magic like Father does. But not the body magic. That they kept a secret.

"The men brought their women and children down from the mountains in order to find people to amaze with their simple tricks. This is how we ended up in Shadipur. It's why women can't perform in public, and eventually you'll have to stop. But the women, they kept their secret and still do. I know how to do that kind of magic and I'm going to teach you and you must never teach a man but you must teach your daughters and they, their daughters.

"Mummy, do you do this magic?" Maria asked.

"No! The men say we mustn't so we don't."

"No matter how bad our lives get?"

"No matter how bad it gets little one. We struggle and we survive or we die but we don't practise the magic of sex."

"Why should I learn it?"

"Because Maslet women know that some day the men will say, 'please use your special magic.'"

"Mommy, does this magic have a name?"

"We call it Tantra, my little one."

Now laying naked on top of her bed Maria begins working the chert by rubbing it over her belly in gentle circles. From her belly she expands the circles until the rock is rubbing over everywhere she can reach, her face, her breasts, her stomach, her groin, and down her thighs. She imagines it's a man trying to seduce her, the cold stone. Gradually she begins to concentrate on her groin, rubbing the rock over her mound of Venus and the inside of her thighs. She flicks it over her clitoris giving herself a little shock, and then begins to caress her pudendum ever so lightly, teasing herself. Despite herself, despite the revulsion she feels every time she charges a teller stone, she becomes aroused.

When she is hot and wet she spreads her legs. Slowly she inserts the rock up inside her. Once it is firmly in place she begins to rub her clitoris with two fingers, one on each side. Up and down, faster and slower, and then fast she rubs and as she rubs she contracts her vagina squeezing the rock. Finally her whole body contracts and in that moment she can feel her power being transferred to the teller stone.

Slowly and carefully Maria removes the chert and puts it in a special case. It is just a shoe box filled with bubble wrap and tinsel. But Maria imagines it is a magnificent jewel encrusted case. Lying there, holding the box to her chest, Maria hopes Willie appreciates everything she is doing for him.

CHAPTER · 13

Draj's first response to being displaced as head of the family by his baby brother, not to mention being abandoned by his wife, is disastrous.

He's been watching Biography on A&E. He always watches Gangster week with rapt attention, and Bad Boys, Mobsters, and any other criminal success story. The night after Yannis usurps his role he sees a bio of Willy Sutton.

One thing sticks with him. Keeps him awake for several nights. When asked why he robbed banks, Sutton said, "Because that's where the money is."

Draj thinks he has what it takes to be a successful bank robber but Yannis has taught him the importance of research. That's why he goes to see Max Ferguson at the Purple Onion. Draj knows Max spends every waking moment trying to plan the perfect crime. Max is fond of saying, when he's had a little too much single malt, "I'm an encyclopedia of thuggery, skulduggery, scams, and capers."

"What do you know about bank robbery?" Draj asks over saketinis. Designer cocktails, an Onion speciality, are for business, whiskey is for the blarney, according to Max. Draj has to fight not to puke whenever he's forced to try one of Max's "favourite drinks."

"Low return, low risk. Though they nearly all get caught sooner or later. Bank robbers."

"What's this low return? Those banks, they've got lots of money."

"Yeah Draj, but not that you can get at. Not unless you want to tunnel underground or use enough explosive to take out a city block. Over the years there have been more than a few yobs like you and me thought we could make a good living knocking off banks. Now they keep the serious money in a vault. It's on a timer. Nobody who works at the bank can get into it. No combination for them to know, just a clock deep inside it. Or a central computer somewhere miles away calling the shots. All the tellers have is a few thousand for regular transactions."

"What happens if they need more than that in the drawer?" Draj asks.

"Somewhere behind the counter, back out of reach, is their own ATM. It's got a lot of money in it and whoever designed them gave it some thought. Those little pigs are damn near impregnable."

Max sips his crèmedementhetini. "So that leaves you with those few bucks in the teller's till. But the banks, they're run by anal accountants. That means the teller has a silent alarm she can push and an alarm in the till she can set off just by removing the last large denomination bill. Plus she can always throw in an ink packet when she's stuffing your Christmas stocking full of the bank's money."

"Ink packet," Draj says.

"Blows up, turns your money all pink."

"Sounds tough," Draj says.

"Actually all that security, that's the good news. Most banks don't feel they need armed guards anymore. Plus you even look at a teller funny and she's been taught to give you the money in her till and it takes a few minutes for the police to respond to that silent alarm. That's why you keep hearing about bank robberies on the news, pull just one and chances are you won't get caught."

"Great," Draj says, thinking it's just the thing to impress Yannis.

"Hey Draj," Max says as Draj is leaving, "don't forget to wear a disguise."

The next morning Draj tries his first bank robbery. Nobody would ever recognize him. He's a bag man. He's wrapped himself up in a filthy duffel coat he dug out of the garbage. He has on a toque and scarf.

Draj is right that people on the street won't remember a homeless man, won't even look at him. On the negative side, he can barely move in the coat, which is two sizes too small. He also hasn't allowed for the smell of the hideous thing. It assaults his nostrils, nearly gagging him. The smell and discomfort grow worse as Draj begins to perspire profusely. It's t-shirt and shorts weather.

Before he enters the TD bank at 106 Street, Draj ducks into an alley and strips. He leaves his own clothes in a dumpster, puts his wallet, keys and money into the pockets of the coat. Naked under the coat, Draj feels much cooler and can move easier. He stuffs Kleenex up his nose to block the smell.

Joe Ashton manages the branch Draj has chosen to do business with. That's too bad for everyone concerned. At twenty-two Joe is the youngest manager in the whole system, maybe the country. A lofty position he's achieved in the fourteen months since he graduated with a B.Com. from McGill. His meteoric rise is the result of his compulsive attention to details, particularly to rules. Everything must be by the book. Joe's constantly testing his staff and finding them wanting. They just don't understand the rules.

This day he has a very special test planned for them. A fake bank robbery. He's hired an actor to play the part. Joe knows his staff will fail miserably, unable to follow the simplest rule.

What Joe doesn't know is that his staff have had enough.

Draj can't believe his rotten luck. There are six people in line in front of him. By the time he gets to the front of the line, reaches a teller, his brain is starting to melt and his nose is over-stuffed with Kleenex. He has a hard time remembering why he's there.

"Don't give me any pink money, you runt," he says as he steps up to the teller. A six-foot-tall woman looks down at the smelly little man and says, "I don't think runt is the word you meant to use, sir. As for pink money I think the closest we come are fifties. If you don't want any fifty dollar bills then I'll be only to happy to give you tens and twenties instead."

"No! You souped ditch, this is a bubbery," Draj screams.

"Nancy, I think the gentleman is trying to tell you this is a robbery," the next teller, a grey-haired spark plug says, trying to be helpful.

"Thanks, Trish." Nancy says. "That would make so much more sense. Please don't take this the wrong way sir, but you look a little under the weather, would a glass of water help?"

Draj nods as vigorously as he can and Nancy walks over to a water cooler. She takes a mug from a shelf under the cooler and pours water into it. Draj chugalugs it and instantly begins to feel better. But he still can't make Nancy understand him. A third woman, a suit, emerges from the back of the bank and asks Nancy: "Is there some sort of problem?"

"Yes," Trish volunteers, "this young man seems to be having difficulty communicating."

"We think he's trying to rob the bank but we just can't be sure. He isn't making too much sense," Nancy adds.

"Maybe he should try taking all that Kleenex out of his nose," Beth says.

"Then I'd skell myself," Draj says.

"Well the rest of us have to, why should you be any exception," Beth points out.

Free of Kleenex, Draj's confidence begins to return.

"This is a robbery," he says.

"Yes dear. We have that figured out," Trish says. "The question is how can we help?"

"You can give me money," Draj yells.

"That's probably the place to start all right," Nancy agrees.

"I'm not convinced," Beth offers. "I'm a personal banker and financial advisor," she explains to Draj.

"So why can't I have money?" Draj asks.

"I think we have to look seriously at your ROI here," Beth says.

"What's an ROI?" Draj asks.

"Return on investment. I'd have to crunch the numbers but I'd think that you'd be better off robbing a grocery store."

"Or a bar," Trish says.

"A casino. That's where the money is," Nancy says. Which sends Draj over the edge.

"Just give me my damn money, now! And no paint bombs. I swear on my mother's grave, any tricks and I'll come back and kill you all."

"He's probably right," Beth says. "He's the professional."

"This is our first robbery," Trish confides to Draj.

"It's so nice to know we are in the hands of a professional," Nancy says. None of them make any attempt to get Draj his money.

The truth begins to dawn on him. These women aren't ever going to give him any money and there is no way he can force them to. He sinks lower than he has ever been. He slumps out of the bank, completely defeated.

Inside the bank Joe remains blithely unaware of what's happened. His office is surrounded in glass, but soundproof. He makes a habit of sitting, menacingly, with his back to his staff.

Tromping down 106th Street, dejected, Draj bumps into an old friend and gets a second chance to make a first impression.

"Draj. You stink."

"Trinh. Have you got a gun on you?" Draj asks.

"Come on Draj, you know better than to ask that."

"I'll give you five hundred dollars for it," Draj says.

"Cash?" Trinh asks.

"Cash. Right now."

They step into a nearby alcove to do the deal.

"Be careful with that weapon," Trinh tells Draj, passing him a lethal-looking pistol. "It's loaded and it has a hair trigger."

"Now they'll have to respect me," Draj says.

Back in the bank, Draj gets in line again and waits patiently to reach the tellers.

"This is a stick-up," he yells at Nancy, pulling the gun out of his coat pocket. Or trying to. It's hung up in the lining of the coat. He tugs on it, and comes within an inch of blowing his testicles off. The bullet hits the floor between his feet. But he gets the gun free. That's when he sees that Trish is also being robbed.

"Hey, who are you? This is my gig," the florid redheaded robber at the next wicket yells at him.

"This gentleman was here first," Nancy points out.

"I think we have to let him rob us before we can serve you," Trish says.

"Too right," the other robber says.

"There's a proper way to do these things. An etiquette," Nancy says.

Meanwhile a horrified Joe Ashton is looking on. He's standing in his office waving frantically, trying to get his staff to understand that there is a real bank robber in the building. He succeeds in attracting Draj's attention. In a rage of frustration Draj points the gun at him and pulls the trigger. The gun explodes in his hand, bucking. The window shatters, the manager goes down. The window absorbs the force of the bullet. But Mr. Ashton faints.

Draj bolts. He's shot a man. The police are undoubtedly on their way. All Draj can think about is that they'll be looking for a man in a duffle coat. At the dumpster he tosses off the coat. Goes to put on his own clothes. They are gone. He can't wear the coat. Has no clothes. He's seven blocks from home.

He puts the coat, toque and scarf into the dumpster then runs into a nearby funky clothing store. Grabs the first clothes he sees. A tartan kilt several sizes too big, a denim shirt, a woman's straw hat that barely fits on his head. He's so fast all the staff can remember later is that he was naked.

Later, safe at his own door, Draj discovers he's left his wallet and keys in the coat. He has to hide in a utility closet with the janitorial supplies until Marko gets home. The entire three hours he waits he keeps repeating to himself, "I will not ask Yannis how to rob a bank, I will not ask Yannis how to rob a bank."

CHAPTER · 14

The morning after she has charged the chert, Maria and Willie head off in search of a used banjo. It doesn't take Willie long to discover that what Maria considers a banjo isn't what most of us picture. Every time he points out a banjo in a music store or a pawnshop she says very definitely, "Not banjo!" The Rom, Willie learns, have their own form of banjo, a six-stringed instrument, the neck of which is longer than a conventional banjo and which has a smaller, more oblong drum than the round base of the modern banjo.

"In England I met all kinds of wonderful people as we moved from camp to camp and some followed the same routes we did. My favourite people were the Rastafarians from Jamaica. They had these awesome dreadlocks and dealt weed. The *gaujo* hated them even more than they hated us.

"My Rasta friends in England they tell me that the slaves brought the banjo to Jamaica with them from Africa. Didn't actually bring it, hadn't time to grab nothing, but first thing they get to Jamaica they sit down and make themselves musical instruments. Those old time Rasta called the instruments they made banja. They played their banja like a fiddle.

"Somewhere out on the road, many years before my time with them, the Rom took to calling their own stringed instrument a banjo. When I showed Shaggy Lees' banjo to the Rastamen they tried playing it like they would their own instrument, it worked just fine, the sound was maybe even richer and stranger coming from it. I guess at some point they were the same instrument but I've tried using a string from a banjo like they play here with my chert and it just doesn't work. So I need a Rom Banjo."

It takes them nearly four hours going from pawn shop to pawn shop before Maria finds the right sort of banjo. In the junk at the back of the Cash and Go Maria finds an odd looking instrument. Willie thinks it looks like a cross between a ukulele and a sitar.

"That is a banjo," she tells Willie.

Maria haggles endlessly with the owner of the Cash and Go. He wants sixty dollars for this weird and dusty instrument. Maria is prepared to pay him five dollars. Eventually they meet at twenty and Willie thinks, "Great. Now we can get out of here." The place is setting off his dust allergies. Willie is ready to pay when Maria reaches into her pocket and takes out a diamond ring.

"Trade you this instead of the twenty," she says to the shop owner.

The pawnbroker takes the ring from her and examines it closely through a jeweller's loop. His eyes light up. The greed fuse has clearly been lit. Willie starts to say something to Maria about is she sure she wants to do this. She kicks him.

"Even up?" the owner asks.

Maria looks at Willie for an explanation.

"He means you give him the ring, he gives you the banjo," Willie says.

"Deal," Maria says and spits on her right palm before holding it out to the pawnbroker. He nervously shakes Maria's hand. Immediately afterwards he wipes his hands against his pant legs. Maria hands him the ring and he gives her the banjo.

Once they are outside Willie looks at Maria, who is cradling the banjo in her arms like it is a baby, and asks: "Did you just trade a thousand dollar diamond ring for a twenty dollar banjo?"

"No, Mr. Willie. I just traded a $550 diamond ring for a thousand dollar banjo."

"How do you know it was a $550 ring?" Willie asks.

"That's what he had it on sale for," Maria answers.

"Who had it on sale for?"

"That guy back there in the Cash and Go, the guy I traded it to for a thousand dollar banjo."

"What are you talking about?" Willie asks.

"That store we were just in, the Cash and Go, had all this really cheap costume jewellery on sale for three to four times what it was worth. I took one of those rings, probably cubic zirconium, the sign on it said $550. I gave that fake ring to the pawn guy for this beautiful banjo."

"I never took my eye off you, there is no way you could have palmed that ring," Willie states. "Plus why wouldn't he have known it was fake just as well as you did."

"Oh, Mr. Willie. I know you never take your eyes off me. Well, when you work on The Passage, maybe. Then I could dance the dance of the seven veils and I think you wouldn't notice. But since I was little I've had to help earn money for my family by pocketing things. That ring was nowhere near as hard to pick up as a mango."

"Maria, you can't just go around stealing things," Willie says.

"I didn't steal the ring. I gave it back to him, didn't I?"

"I guess technically you didn't steal but you did defraud that guy of a $20 banjo that you think is worth a thousand dollars."

"There was no fraud. I out-traded him. He thought the banjo wasn't worth anything and tried to sell me his worthless banjo for twenty dollars. I got it at the price he thought was fair, nothing. I out-trade him. I think, maybe you don't last too long as a gypsy."

"I give up. What's next?" Willie asks, shaking his head and shrugging his massive shoulders.

"Take me to a real music store, please. One where they sell guitars, violins, stuff like that," she says.

On the way to Lillo's on Whyte Avenue Maria removes a string from the instrument. Willie is prepared to take her word for it that this is the G-string she needs. At Lillo's she gets a new string to replace the one she removed.

That is a two-minute errand. But Maria stays in the store for nearly an hour. She spends much of the time flirting with the staff, none of whom seem to be able to take their eyes off her breasts. Maria calls them her vacuum cleaner breasts, when they are turned on they suck men's eyeballs towards them, there is nothing the men can do. Willie wants to drag her out of the store kicking and screaming. However, he thinks maybe he should begin to trust that Maria has some method to her madness.

Maria also gives an impromptu concert. She plays the big ugly banjo like she is in a Dixieland band. The customers and staff keep time, some even dance a little jig. Maria finally says goodbye to her admiring fans and she and Willie leave the store.

"So what did you steal from them?" Willie asks.

"What do you think I am? They are good people, those people in that store. True gypsies they never steal from good people. Maybe they try to trick them but they don't steal from them. Those nice people told me where I can find someone who will want to buy my banjo.

"The Raklos they never hung out much with other Rom. Nana and Draj thought that all the other gypsies were beneath them. I don't know where in Edmonton to find some Rom who might want to buy this. But the thing about gypsies is we love our music, our stringed instruments: our guitars, our violins, our banjos. The place to find gypsies is to go to a music store that sells such beautiful music makers. The people who work there will tell you all about the local gypsies that come in to look, to play, and sometimes even to buy these wondrous things. If you'll take me to Millwoods I'll sell this banjo."

When they get to the address she has in Millwoods, it doesn't look too promising. It's a complex of business condos, mainly doctors, dentists, and lawyers. Maria's address is the office of a Dr. Morgan, who is apparently a psychiatrist.

"So who are you looking for?" Willie asks. "The receptionist?"

"This Dr. Morgan is who I want," she says.

"Dr. Morgan is a gypsy?" Willie asks.

"That's what the people at Lillo's said. It's quite cool these days to be a gypsy and I've met a couple here in Canada who tell everyone they meet whether they are asked or not. That's what this Dr. Morgan did at Lillo's. Besides, Dr. Morgan is a good name for a gypsy."

"Okay, I'll bite. Why is Dr. Morgan a good name for a gypsy?" Willie asks.

"Many Rom names are hard to say in English. Grandma Nose, her maiden name was Ooskloosk. In Yorkshire they just couldn't say that so she called herself Smith because that was what her dad did. He was a blacksmith. The Rom they'll use whatever comes to mind when they need to give themselves an English name. In England we still ride around in the traditional horse-drawn caravans, at least some of us do, and a lot of those caravans are pulled by these mighty little horses, which are called Morgans. I think you'd better let me talk with this doctor on my own. He's a psychiatrist and he might want to shrink your head."

Forty minutes later Maria emerges from Dr. Morgan's office without the banjo. She has a big grin on her face.

"How much did you get?" Willie asks.

"Six hundred and fifty dollars," Maria says and shows him the money.

"I thought you said that it was worth a thousand."

"That's the price before you negotiate."

"In other words this guy out-negotiated you," Willie says.

"I sold him a twenty dollar banjo for six hundred and fifty dollars and you think he out-negotiated me."

"How did you convince him to pay that much, oh shrewd negotiating gypsy princess?"

"That's better, roly-poly brown klutz. Worship my brilliance. There are very few gypsy banjos available in the Edmonton area. That one we had, once it's cleaned up, will be beautiful. It has all this wonderful hand painting on the wood and a good song inside it. I dusted it off while I was waiting for the doctor to see me and then I played him that same little tune that I played in the music store. In Canada you say 'value added' a lot. I added value to that banjo.

"Dr. Morgan told me that sort of banjo is called a *solmo*. I never heard it called that but that's what he said. I mostly just let him talk. He says that it's a type of sitar from India and is proof that India is where all gypsies come from. I let him sell himself the banjo. The negotiating was easy. It was all the cash he, his partner, and his staff had in the office."

To celebrate her newfound wealth Maria takes Willie out for supper at the Asian Hut. She asks if she can order. Willie says sure. Even though he knows she's said that she grew up in India it's still a surprise to him when she starts talking with the waiter in what Willie assumes is Hindi.

"Did you speak Hindi when you were little?" Willie asks.

"Well I learned to speak it when I was little. The audiences that my dad and I had in Delhi were always Hindus or spoke Hindi as a second or third language. But in Shadipur where we lived we spoke mostly Maslet."

"Where is Shadipur?"

"It's on the edge of Delhi. It's where all the magic people live."

"Magic people?" Willie asks.

"Nasreeb, my father, did street magic. He did all the classic routines, swallowing swords, decapitating little girls, lighting himself on fire, and so on. Other people who live in Shadipur they do other tricks, stick swords through their bodies, walk on coals, lie on a bed of nails. It's all magic. That's what the Maslet do, they make magic.

"Only the men are supposed to perform but Nasreeb and Salma only had one small girl, me. So I'd dress like a little boy and perform with my father and to do that I learned Hindi. At night after we were through my mother would teach me all the secrets of Maslet magic, not just the ones Nasreeb knew. That was so that someday I could teach them to my sons and daughters."

"How on earth did you get from being a Maslet in Shadipur to being a gypsy in Canada?"

"That's a long story, Mr. Willie. I think that The Higher Power must have been guiding my feet every step of the way. Though of course I didn't think so at the time."

CHAPTER · 15

Maria tells Willie the amazing story of her life. As she got older, and her breasts developed, it became necessary for her father and her to travel farther and farther away from town. Unfortunately, the farther away they got, the less the crowd was familiar with street magic. In Allahabad, the decapitation of Maria caused a riot and left the girl stranded, hiding in an abandoned house, away from the screaming, irate crowd. A Canadian couple found her and, being good Canadians, took her to the police to take her home.

"I know they had good hearts but still I wonder if they rescued me because they wanted to know how the decapitation trick is done. That's the first thing they asked me and the last thing they said to me.

"I couldn't speak much English back then, "Hello, Mister! One, two, three! Goodbye, Mister! Hello! How are you today? Where is you from? Good morning and good night! I don't speak English very well, thank you. I love you!" that was my English. But I understood a lot.

"The Peacocks did the logical thing, they took me to the police. Everyone in Shadipur hates the police, always with their hands out. It doesn't matter whether you have permits or not, if you want to perform in a public place half your take, or more, goes to bribing the policeman whose 'corner' it is."

The appetizers appear just then. It is a platter heaped up with pakora, samosa, and deep fried paneer. Both Willie and Maria give it their full attention for a while.

"In England I used to slip away from the caravan and go to the Tandoori Takeaway. It was to remind myself that I was Maslet, but somehow I ended up Romni anyway. That's why I think I can become Samoan. It's no bigger change than Maslet to Romni," Maria says when they've finished devouring the appetizers, racing to see who can eat the most.

She continues her story. Turns out the police hated the Maslet as much as they hated the police and refused to take the girl home. The couple tried to rescue her but the police then arrested them and put them in a cell "to rescue them from the girl." Maria was tossed out and snuck into the jail while the guards were sleeping and let the couple out.

"Allahabad is not more than three hundred miles from Delhi, but the Peacocks couldn't find Shadipur on their map. For some reason they decided the best thing to do is to take me to the Canadian Embassy in Delhi. That's fine with me, once in Delhi I can find my own way home, and, Allah willing, Father will be there.

"We caught the first train in the morning. It was crowded and I used my magic to make room for them. Without warning the Peacocks, I removed a long knitting needle from the secret folds of my sari and rammed it through my nose from side to side, about an inch up from the nostrils. Blood flew everywhere and the crowd parted. I slowly drew the needle out, and uttering my magic chant: shuckee, shuckee, tantru, restored my nose to its pre-needle condition. The crowd gave us a wide birth the rest of the way.

"In the mash of people getting off the train, with Mrs. Peacock holding one hand, I picked several pockets. Waiting for a taxi to take them to the embassy I bought the Peacocks tea and cakes. I was having too much fun to recognize the danger.

"The Peacocks took to me to the Canadian Consulate and left me with a very stupid man. They told him that I came from Shadipur and that he was to make sure I got back there. He asks everyone in his office if they've heard of Shadipur and no one has. He takes a book out of his desk. It has maps of all the world in there. He searches India looking for Shadipur and then he moves on to other countries.

"Finally he decided Shadipur is in Turkey. I tried to tell him, 'No! No! Delhi. Shadipur, Delhi!' Like I said, he was very stupid. And he puts me on a plane for Ankara."

The main course interrupts Maria at that point. It consists of three dishes, each of which Maria inspects in detail, looking for the slightest imperfection.

"With Dum Alu the secret is popped mustard seed. First step in Dum Alu, before the onions and potatoes is to fry mustard seed. When you put the mustard seed in the hot oil, it pops, and the popped seed flavours everything. Here smell, smell that, it's mustard seed. Isn't it glorious?" Willie can't actually smell much of anything, or rather he smells everything, the restaurant is overwhelming him with odours. But he nods anyway, and grins.

"With Binji Baji it's what you do to the okra, see how this okra looks like it's been coated in curry and deep fired."

"Fried," Willie says.

"Fried, and they've done it just right. Chana Masala is just chickpeas in sauce and you'd think it would be hard to mess up. But they've gone and done it. It's way too runny, the sauce."

"Well I guess we'll just have to send it back," Willie says.

"Oh, Willie, it's not that bad. I can manage it, I think. We don't want to make a scene," Maria says.

Maria and Willie mix the dishes together along with some fragrant saffron rice. They spoon the mixture onto chapatti, rounds of flat bread, and rolled up the chapatti. These they eat with their fingers, the excess food spilling out of the bottom. It is a messy business, which makes carrying on a conversation impossible.

Once they finish eating, Maria announces she's too full to continue her story. Though that doesn't stop her ordering dessert.

While they are waiting, Maria slips out of her shoes. She isn't wearing socks.

"Want me to show you a sex trick?"

"We're in a restaurant," Willie says.

"That's good because this is a food tantra." Maria begins gathering up all the little bits and pieces of food their exuberant gorging has left lying around. She clumps it into a ball. Then she starts to shape the ball. "Think that looks like my breast, Willie?" she asks.

"Yes."

"No, it doesn't. My breasts are much bigger than that," Maria says indignantly.

"Oh certainly, But you got the shape right. Sort of conical."

"You think my breasts are comical," Maria's voice is icicle cold.

"No, conical," Willie giggles.

"Conical, what's that?"

Willie picks up his napkin and forms it into a cone.

"Like an ice cream cone," Maria says. "You think my breasts look like ice cream cones."

"No. Not like ice cream cones. Just conical, as is an ice cream cone," Willie says.

"I guess there are worse things you could be thinking about than ice cream cones when you look at my tits. What do you do with an ice cream cone, Willie?"

Willie answers, "You eat it."

"But how do you eat it?" Maria asks.

"I lick mine," Willie says.

"Like I said, there are worse things you could be thinking about. Now use that napkin, make me a model of my breast."

"Which one?" Willie asks.

"What difference does that make?" Maria asks. "Aren't they the same?"

"Not even close. The left one is about an inch longer and almost that much thicker. But the right one has a much larger nipple, especially when it's excited."

"So you do notice?" Maria asks.

"The left has the more perfectly symmetric aureole though," Willie says.

"Oreo?" Maria asks.

"Aureole," Willie gently corrects her. "It's the ring around your nipple." He reaches across the table and with the tip of his right index finger traces the outline of her left aureole.

"Such strange names the *gaujo* have for things," Maria says.

"You don't know the half of it in this case. Aureole are what religious people call the halos around the heads of saints, Christ, and other deities."

"And that's what you call the dark ring around a woman's nipple?" Maria asks.

"Want to know why?"

"Yes." Maria puts her head in her hands with her elbows resting on the table and stares at Willie intently.

"Because it's the ring that makes a breast taste so wonderful. It secretes chemicals that babies seek out to start suckling. And which can make a grown man weak in the knees. The ancient Greeks thought such a wonderful thing must be the mark of the gods on a woman's body."

"Okay, my large philosopher, take that napkin and make a proper model of my breast. The right one."

Willie does his best.

"Now just hold on to that for a second," Maria says. She gets up and goes from table to table looking for anyone who might have a safety pin, or a hairpin. She has no luck and returns to their table frustrated. Willie reaches into his pocket with the hand that isn't holding the napkin together and digs out a couple of safety pins.

"Why didn't you tell me you had pins?" Maria demands.

"You didn't ask me," Willie says. "And I kind of enjoyed seeing you embarrass yourself."

Maria takes the pins and uses them with some skill, pinning the napkin into something stable.

"How close do you think you got?" Maria asks.

"Pretty close," Willie says.

"I think you made it too big," Maria says. She lifts her sweatshirt. Under which she is wearing nothing. She slips the napkin cone over her right breast. It is in fact a little too big. She tries it on her left breast, where it fits snugly. "Not bad," she says. By now everyone in the restaurant is either staring at her breasts or staring very intently at their food.

Maria removes the napkin from her breast and lowers her sweatshirt. Then she begins to stuff the napkin with the ball of food. There is nowhere near enough to fill it. Once again Maria goes table to table, this time gathering food scraps.

Back at the table she finishes modeling her breast. Then she removes the napkin mold. Gently, Maria lifts her breast on to one of her discarded plates.

"Boy the service here is slow," she says putting the plate in front of Willie. "Eat that," she says.

"Are you out of your mind?" Willie asks politely.

"Do you want to learn Tantra or don't you? Right, then eat."

Willie manages to force the first mouthful down. It actually doesn't taste too bad. It's mostly saffron rice, curry sauce, and pakoras.

"Okay, Indian witch woman, I'm done. Now what?" Willie asks when he's finished.

"Now you're my sex slave forever," Maria announces, loudly enough for everyone in the restaurant to hear. "When you eat a woman's breast you give her complete power over you."

"You think so, do you?" Willie asks.

"Well that's what my mother taught me," Maria says. "I think we'll have to wait and see."

"Why did you take off your shoes before you started all this?"

"Everyone knows you can only do Tantra in your bare feet," Maria says with a sniff.

Then, finally, dessert arrives.

CHAPTER · 16

Dessert is shaved red beans on ice and coconut shakes. Once they are finished eating and paying, Maria asks Willie if they can drop by his office at the university.

"If I am going to use the teller stone tonight I need you to pick a book."

"How does a teller stone work, exactly?" Willie asks.

"Nothing in fortune-telling works exactly, Mr. Willie. What we will do is pick a book, an article, a newspaper, or something. It's got to be something written about what you want to know. You want to know about Mark Twain so you have to pick something written about him or by him. Then I read your numbers."

"Read my numbers?"

"All over your body you've got numbers, everybody has numbers. You can't see them but I can. They're on your hands and your feet and in your eyes. We are all just numbers. When I first started travelling with the Rom, Grandma Nose taught me how to read those numbers. She was Shaggy Lees' grandmother, he was the leader of the group of Rom, the *kumpania*, that I was adopted by. I lived with them for nearly fourteen years.

"Grandma Nose could take one quick look at you and see all your numbers. She'd 'do her sums' as she called it and then pick up the Bible and tell your fortune. The numbers told her where to look in the Bible to find your personal fortune. Honestly, me, I don't always see the numbers. On you I see them all very clearly. Your numbers sort of glow."

"I'm wandering around covered in glowing numbers," Willie says, secretly pleased with the idea.

"Yes," Maria says.

"How did you end up living with this company of Rom?" Willie asks.

"That's *kumpania*," Maria says spelling it out. "Once we've picked out a book I'll tell you that story. I promise."

At the office Maria takes a scarf she's carrying in her fanny pack and ties it around Willie's head, blindfolding him. Then she spins him around and around until he is completely disoriented. Once he is barely able to stand up she gives him a little push. He stumbles into the bookcase. Willie reaches out to stabilize himself and his hand touches a book. It is the *Complete Short Stories of Mark Twain*, the Bantam Classic edition. It's a hardbound book no larger than the palm of Willie's hand. He holds it and feels a tingle run through his body. What is Maria doing to me, he wonders, not for the first time.

On the way home Maria rests her head against Willie's shoulder and starts to talk.

"In Ankara I ended up falling in with a bad crowd, though I loved them like family. They were Kurdish street kids. Pickpockets, purse snatchers, and smash and grab artists. We mainly went after tourists. There were a whole pack of us. But the three I was closest to were Alvin, the leader, Betty, his girl-friend, and Fallio, who was a how you say, cross-dresser. A boy girl."

"Here they say transvestite. In Samoa we called them *fa-afafine*."

"Did they beat up on them in Samoa? In Turkey Fallio was always getting punched, kicked, once he even got badly beaten. And here, I'm not sure things are a lot better."

"In Samoa when I was a kid, being a *fa-afafine* was not only not looked down on, sometimes it was encouraged."

"Encouraged, Mr. Willie?" Maria asked, puzzled.

"Samoans have big families. And if there weren't enough girls to get all the work done to look after the family then some of the boys would end up acting like girls. People thought, good for them, they're helping out.

"Maam raised me to be one. There was just her, but she looked after all eight of her younger brothers until they left the house to have families of their own. She always claimed she needed my help. It was only as an adult I realized she did it to keep my uncles from 'corrupting' me."

"What was it like, did you wear a dress?"

"Only until Maam's back was turned. Every morning she'd apply makeup to me, and get me dressed all pretty. Then I'd help her cook, wash, clean, shop, and cook some more. It was fun when I was little. But later, boys, and not just other *fa-afafines*, but supposedly straight boys, would make passes at me. I didn't like that. I knew I wasn't interested, and was just leading them on. It led to all manner of bad feelings. But I'm interrupting your story," Willie says.

Maria smiles and shrugs. "The problem with being a criminal in a Muslim country is you never know when they are going to crack down on criminals. The Turks decided to start chopping off the hands of pickpockets. Particularly Kurdish pickpockets. Alvin, Betty, Fallio, and I fled late one night, tipped off to a police raid. Stowed away on a cargo plane that ended up taking us to Cairo. We thought we'd discovered paradise, tourists everywhere, all laden with gold, ours for the taking. Unfortunately, we weren't very good pickpockets. The first day, working one of the bazaars frequented by tourists we made over a thousand dollars. U.S."

"I thought you said you weren't any good at it. That sounds like you were doing just fine," Willie says.

"After we'd finished up for the day we split the money up and started for the old hotel we were staying in. Betty got about two blocks before someone picked her pocket. Alvin must have got nearly halfway back when he lost his, we were never really sure. I figured that there wasn't much point in hanging on to mine so I bought anything I saw along the rest of the way. Fallio lost some of his money but hung on to a hundred dollars that he'd stuck in a little pouch that hung down below his balls. Cairo is full of pickpockets and many of them are very good indeed."

The gang switched to robbing suitcases from fancy hotels when the valets weren't looking. They were making a good living but one day Maria got caught.

"I come tearing around a corner carrying a suitcase I've stolen from the Hilton. I'm using back alleys to get home. Around this corner a big stick of a man is standing waiting for me. 'My name is Ed," he says. He takes the suitcase from me and he carries it and drags me back to the Hilton. I think he's going to turn me in. Instead he sticks that suitcase back right where I picked it up. Then he drags me into the hotel and into an elevator. No one does anything to stop him. Next thing I know I'm in his room.

Willie isn't sure he wants to hear this story. "How old were you?"

Maria squeezes Willie's arm. "I think I know what he wants. But I'm wrong. Ed sits me down at the table in his room and he starts showing me card tricks. For four hours he shows me card tricks and teaches me how to do them. We can't speak to each other but he's good at letting me figure the tricks out by watching him do them really slow. At the end of the day he gives me twenty dollars and then very politely escorts me back to the street.

"I'm so curious that next day I go back. Ed answers the door, bows real pretty and asks me in with a sweep of his long arms. Five hours later my hands are numb from doing card tricks. And he pays me thirty bucks.

"For a month every day Ed and I worked together. At night I'd go to the lounge in the Hilton and watch him perform. The cards did impossible things for him, but he wasn't much of an entertainer. Father could have taught him so much. When Ed finally had to leave Cairo to go on to his next job he gave me a bunch of decks of cards. Managed to make me understand that if I always had the cards with me and always practiced I'd never have to steal suitcases again. I didn't know what he thought I could do with the cards to earn money but since then being able to do card tricks has come in handy in many ways."

"Is that where you learned to do the trick with the four aces?" Willie asks.

"No, the stuff Ed taught me was far more complicated than that. The four aces I learned from a book. Shaggy Lees used to take me to book stores and libraries, part of his campaign to teach me to read, and once I learned, to get me keep improving. Somewhere I stumbled on a book of card tricks. I read it. Memorized it. Then, eventually I'd find another. In one of them, I saw that trick. Taught myself to do it."

"What happened to Alvin and the rest?"

"They got themselves arrested. Tried to rip off some rich American businessman. In his hotel room, no less."

The American turned them in and they begged for mercy, saying they'd been hoodwinked by a brilliant criminal. It wasn't 'til she was nearly caught in the streets of Cairo that Maria realized the brilliant criminal was her.

"And were you?"

"Really, Mr. Willie."

"In other words you were."

"I take the fifth."

"That's only in America, Maria," Willie says.

"What's only in America?" Maria asks.

"That people take the fifth. The Fifth Amendment of the American Constitution gives its citizens the right not to incriminate themselves when under oath. Doesn't apply here in Canada."

"So what do people here do?" Maria asks.

"We lie. But what did you do? The police are after you."

"I grabbed my share of the money, and ran. Used a part of it to bribe a tour bus operator and get a ticket to Israel and on to Greece. I have no passport, no way to get one. But I'm safe, I'm alive, and if I end up in an Israeli jail at least I'm better off. I'm stunned when the Israeli border patrol just waves us through. We are in Israel for six days. I spend my time trying to acquire a forged passport and looking over my shoulder."

"When I'm not doing that I hang around with this older couple, the Leeses, and see the sites of Israel. Shaggy Lees is fiftyish and built like a teakettle, Agnes isn't quite as round but her skin's pink and she's very jolly, everything is funny to her. She calls herself a matron in an apron, and always over her knit skirts, polyester blouses, and wool dresses, she wears an apron. Together we see the Wailing Wall and the Temple of the Mount. They don't speak any of my languages, only later do I learn they are speaking English, which I think I know a little of, just not their English, The King's English."

"No one else on the tour will talk with the Leeses. I can't figure it out. It's like I was back in India and they belonged to some lower caste but to me they look just like all the other people. They seem well off, dress like everyone else."

"One day I hear Agnes say to Shaggy 'I just hope we are right and she's the one Grandma told us to watch for.'"

"They got me a passport and took me to England with them. That's how I met the Leeses and started travelling with the Rom," Maria ends.

"You've told me that you *became* Rom," Willie objects. "You mean just because they adopted you that made you Rom?"

"No. Grandma Nose tested me and initiated me and trained me and I lived with her and the Leeses and that's how I became a Rom." Maria crosses her arms across her chest. "I said all I have to say about that. Now we need to solve your problem."

They are now sitting in the living room of the trailer. Maria is kneeling on one side of the strange coffee table that Willie's built for his dining room, mainly so he can rest his massive feet on it. He's found a solid oak door somewhere and it's resting on four huge metal jugs that Willie has told Maria are milk cans. Willie is sitting opposite her. Maria has placed the book, the sacred text, *The Complete Short Stories of Mark Twain* between them on the old oak door. The box with the teller stone is beside her right knee on the floor.

Studying Willie intently, Maria opens the book and starts flipping through the pages. She is over half through when she starts flipping back. There are only a few pages left when she stops. Maria lays the book down on the table. It is open to pages six and seven. The title of the work is "The Story of the Bad Little Boy."

Maria reaches down and lifts the shoebox onto the table. Very gently she removes the lid and, after taking several deep calming breaths, reaches in with her left hand and lifts the teller stone out. Maria ties the G-string to the rock using an intricate knot unlike anything Willie has ever seen. She holds her right arm rock steady out in front of her, the elbow bent, and her fingers spread so that her thumb points at her heart. With her left hand she drapes the banjo string over her ring finger. The teller stone is pointing down at page six. Nothing happens.

"Aren't you supposed to mutter some sort of mystic mumbo-jumbo at this point?" Willie asks nervously.

"Mr. Willie, the mystic mumbo-jumbo has already been done," Maria answers.

Maria holds the teller stone over page seven. It points down at the centre of the page, dangling from its G-string. Then the teller stone begins to swing.

At first it is just a slight fluttering, but the arc grows larger and soon the rock is making circles covering most of the page. It's like it is looking for something.

Each circle is of a different diameter. If Maria is guiding it, Willie can't explain how. When the teller stone finally stops, the G-string appears to be defying every law of physics.

The string hangs straight down from Maria's ring finger, the stone painting at the centre of the page. After a moment, the teller stone zips to the top of the page, pulling the string behind it. It gives Willie goosebumps.

The teller stone is clearly pointing at the word "go." Nothing more happens on page seven. Maria picks up the book and leafs ahead to pages 308 and 309. She begins again.

Maria begins with page 309. Soon the teller stone is swinging wildly again. It points out the words "to" and "the" and Willie thinks they hardly needed to come to page 309 to find those words. Then the teller stone climbs up to the top of the page to the title. It moves up and down the words, "Is He Living or is He Dead?" before it finally stops on "dead."

That turns out to be the entire message. Go to the dead.

"Frankly, my dear, that isn't much of an improvement over The Passage in scrutability," Willie says.

Maria is deeply angry. She knows that Willie understands the message perfectly. She was watching his eyes while the teller stone worked. She saw it. They are about to have a major fight when someone begins pounding on the door.

CHAPTER · 17

Roger and Dingo are at the door. They are very excited and a little drunk. Tonight Dingo has been playing against Average Bob himself. Once Bob left, Dingo and Roger followed him home. Home turned out to be in Pleasantview, a very middle-class neighbourhood built after the Second World War to provide housing for veterans.

"But this wasn't any middle-class house," Dingo says.

Roger nods. "It had its own private driveway, almost like a back alley between all these neighbouring houses. Back in there was a wood lot, a whole bunch of trees and in amongst them was a very large house."

"We couldn't get a real good look, but it sure seemed to be large," Dingo confirms. "I made four thousand dollars off Average Bob but I got the feeling his heart wasn't in it. That he was just waltzing through the steps, ignoring that we were jiving."

"Coming home we were trying to decide what we do now," Roger says. "We saw your lights on and thought we'd stop and ask the two of you what you think."

"There are a lot of things you could do," Willie says.

"That's the oily rub of the gristly little bugger," Dingo says.

"Give me some ideas," Roger requests.

"You could find out what newspapers Bob subscribes to and then you could place classified ads in those papers."

"What would these advertisements say, Willie? Eccentric collector seeks the truly gruesome. If you happen to have a spare brain, call," Roger says.

"How about, 'Desperately seeking pickled President.'" Maria asks.

"I'm serious!" Willie says.

"How could you be sure he got it?" Roger asks.

"If, after a few days you haven't heard anything you mail him the ad, you circle it in red and fold the paper open to that page," Dingo says. "Willie and I've done it before when we didn't want to go rushing through the bush and get bitten by some snake. I don't know in this case. He sounds like he might be a bit brighter than our usual perpetrators. I think the next time we are playing poker I should just casually work the brain into conversation."

"Oh, and how do you propose to work Kennedy's brain into the conversation?" Roger asks. "Speaking of Gretzky coming out of retirement to help the Oilers, whatever happened to Kennedy's brain? I don't think so. I think I should just walk up to him and say, 'Hi. I hear you've got Kennedy's brain. If the price is right I'd like to buy it off you? If he's as bright as we think then he already knows what it's worth."

"I wonder why he hasn't sold it already?" Maria asks.

"Maybe he has," Willie says.

"If he had I'd know," Roger says. "Someone in the business would have said something, you could never hope to keep that quiet. But I've got to admit I'm also curious as to why he hasn't. Maybe he's a collector of Kennedy memorabilia. Maybe he's just been too busy."

"I think you are all turned around backwards," Maria says. "First we should find out everything about him that we can. Not just wild stories but real things: his name, how old he is, what he eats for breakfast, who he loves, who he sleeps with, is he really a good poker player, what kind of car he drives, does he own this house, how much money does he have in his bank accounts or under his mattress, what are his hobbies, does he have any diseases, any addictions, how he dresses. Maybe also we should find out if he has the brain, where he stores it, if it is really Kennedy's brain, is it weird keepsake or an investment."

"I think Maria has chased our ideas right back down the rabbit hole," Dingo says, a trace of pride in his voice.

"Indubitably," Roger says stuttering over every syllable.

"What does that mean?" Maria asks.

"That we all think you're a lot smarter than we are," Willie says.

After Roger and Dingo leave, having kicked the plan for learning all about Average Bob around for more than an hour, Maria asks Willie: "Why do men do that?"

"Do what?" Willie asks.

"Beat a simple idea with a stick, beat it until it's black and blue, and then poke it just to make sure it's dead," Maria says. "The Raklo boys did that, they'd go over a plan a hundred times until Nana would tell them, 'enough, enough. Just go do it, put the meat on the table.' Then it never went the way they planned it anyway. It was just a waste of time all that planning. You think once, you act, you're lucky or you're not."

Willie frowns. "It's evolutionary, I think. For thousands of years men went on hunting trips, many miles from home, as far as they could walk. When you are facing a trip like that, on foot, no protection from the weather, using spears, trying to kill large animals before they or some other animal kills you, you plan. Maybe you realize you've tried that hunting place before and the water was no good. Someone may have heard that another tribe, another clan is already hunting there and why pick a fight. And as they planned our ancestors tried to get themselves excited, excited enough to dare a world they knew very little about. Not to mention that if the men were really lucky, they spent so long planning that the women went out and found enough food that the men didn't have to go anywhere."

"You made that up," Maria says indignantly.

"It's not made up, Maria. What I'm doing is speculating. I'm guessing what might have happened."

"Now you speckyoulate on what 'go to the dead' means, you big brown speck."

"I don't have to speculate, little gypsy mystic, I know," Willie says.

"I knew you know," Maria says.

"What did you know I know?" Willie asks.

"I knew you know what 'go to the dead' means," Maria says.

"In Samoa, my family, everyone, believes that we don't ever have original ideas, nor do we create original paintings, songs, or stories. In Samoa everyone knows that an author doesn't write a book and a composer doesn't write a song. Life doesn't work like that," Willie says, settling in at the kitchen table.

"How does it work in Samoa?" Maria asks, sitting beside him.

"An ancestor, usually a long dead ancestor, one you never even met, writes your book, composes your music. The ancestor gets inside your head, just for a little while, and tells you what to put down on paper. What's the last movie you saw?" Willie asks.

"*Go*. It was great. It tells the same story four times, from four different points of view, for four different characters. These people, in that film, were almost as stupid as the Raklos," Maria answers.

"All right. In Canada, the film critics, just like you did, say what a great film. The director is a genius, the writer is amazingly profound, the producer has courage and recognizes talent. We think all these creative people are wonderful.

"In Samoa, we would also say what a great film. The director's ancestors are very clever, the writer's ancestors sure know how to tell a story, the producer's ancestors sure know how to recognize a good project when they see one. We worship our ancestors."

"So why don't you ask your ancestors for help, Mr. Willie?" Maria asks. "I bet they must be pretty awesome ancestors."

"I'm sure they were, especially if half the stories my mother tells are true. However, it's not that simple. When I was a child my uncles, my mother's brothers, started training me to be a shaman, a medicine man. Part of that training had to do with telling stories. These stories are supposed to heal the sick, save marriages, make the infertile woman pregnant, and help the lame rise up and walk."

Willie goes to the fridge for some cold water. He pours two glasses. "In pre-medicine I took some courses in anthropology. They told us that in the South Pacific many indigenous peoples have flexible beliefs. What they meant was that we tell whopping great lies and if something happens that doesn't quite fit with the story we've made up we just incorporate that new fact into our story and keep right on going as if nothing has happened. My uncles, for example, told stories about how man came to be created. These stories were supposed to help the barren woman have children.

"I'd follow them around on their calls and listen to them tell these stories. They never told the same creation story twice. They personalized them a great deal. If the woman was a Catholic the Pope figured prominently in the story.

They tell the woman that one morning the Pope's head started to itch. Now with that strange hat on there the Pope can't scratch, and he's not supposed to have his head uncovered in public. He either wears the big high hat or the little cap that just covers his bald spot, but he doesn't go with a bare head. All day the Poor pope's head itches, it's driving him crazy but he has a busy schedule of public appearances and he just can't get a moment to himself in order to scratch. 'God,' the Pope says. 'You are sorely tempting me to commit a sin. I will be good, and not be tempted, but Lord you'd better make it worth my while.' At the end of the day the Pope finally is able to take off his hat, and it must have been that high pointy one because underneath there are all these people, all these beautiful, friendly, brown people, all these Samoans."

Maria holds out her glass for more water. "Then what?"

"The next woman they saw would have been to the United States and been very impressed with planes and cars and skyscrapers. 'Honey,' they ask this woman, 'has anyone ever told you how the President made the Samoan peoples?' That story went on and on about how Washington or Roosevelt or some other dead President had discovered Samoa, and he thought it was the most beautiful place he'd ever seen, all that was missing were the girls. It needed girls that were as pretty as the islands. Well the President reached into his valise and he pulled out a bunch of dolls, the dolls went everywhere with him just in case he wanted to play with them. Well as soon as he took them out of the suitcase they started to burn. To keep them from burning up he started blowing on them. And that brought all the dolls to life. Now there were all these beautiful women on the islands and they were perfect so he left. Not that long after he left, all those doll women had perfect little brown babies and there have been Samoans on the islands ever since."

Willie shakes his head. "My Uncle Dunk had an incredible number of these stories. But each one ended exactly the same way. 'This story comes straight to you from my ancestors. They want you to have it.'

"'But uncle,' I said. 'You told me that only the ancestors can make up stories, and you don't talk with the ancestors before you tell these stories, so where do they come from?'

"'Little giant, the ancestors live in our heads. That is why we are medicine men. Why we can tell stories. We are not like other people, we don't have to go to a clearing and drink kava or chew betel to talk with our ancestors. All we have to do is listen to their voices in our heads. When you are older your ancestors will come to live in your head because you are one of us.'

"Ever since then I've been terrified of my ancestors getting inside my head. My uncles are wonderful men, caring and kind. They are also crazy, and chronic liars. If they heal anyone, and I think that they do, it's with the herbs they hand out, not the wild stories that they tell. But they believe the magic is in the words, not the plants and they've got everyone else in Samoa convinced as well. They get calls from the sick and lovelorn all over the islands, wanting them to come and tell one of their stories.

"Everyone except my Maam. When she became a Mormon she decided my uncles were bad, evil men. I had to promise my Maam, on my father's soul, that I'd never let myself get sucked into my uncles' madness. My Maam she went even further, she raised me so I'd be unacceptable as a medicine man. She raised me as a *fa-afafine* which, like I told you, left me all confused. I wasn't supposed to like girls, but I did. I was supposed to like boys, but I didn't. I went to church with her, first to the Catholic church, then to the Baptists, and finally the Church of Jesus Christ of the Latter Day Saints. But none of it helped. At fourteen I started hearing voices in my head.

"When she found out what was happening to me Maam moved us to Los Angeles. Which was a disaster. There were these boys, they belonged to a very tough street gang, the Sons of Samoa. And they didn't like me. My Maam told me that Los Angeles would be just like Samoa. The part of LA we lived in, it was."

"How was it like Samoa?" Maria asks.

"Everywhere I went all I saw was Samoans. There are more Samoans in LA than there are in all of Samoa. All of whom thought I was weird. The *fa-afafine* thing didn't go over in LA, I knew that after the first week, but by then the damage was done. I was a fag, a homo, and fair game to beat the crap out of, a walking target."

"You got beaten up a lot?" Maria asks.

"No, most of my tormentors I could out-think. The rest I could out-run."

"Out-run, you aren't exactly fast."

"Hey, I had a weight advantage. The Sons of Samoa all weighed well over three hundred pounds. Woo-woo Fat, their leader, he was somewhere around four hundred and still growing."

"Woo-woo Fat?" Maria asks puzzled.

"He told me, the first day I met him and his gang, that they called him that because he liked to sit on his victims, squeeze the life right out of them. The only sound these poor souls could make was woo-woo. Those voices I told you about, they said things to me, things that came out of my mouth unedited.

"I told him that he must be very fast or a fool. Since he had to catch a victim before he could sit on him. And he sure didn't look fast. He took offence, once he finally realized I'd called him a fool, dissed him right in front of all his home boys."

"So what happened?"

"I ran as fast as my chubby legs would carry me with a screaming gang of massive Samoan boys right behind me. I didn't know my way around very well then. I ran right out of Samoan territory."

"Samoan territory?" Maria asks.

"Every street gang in LA has a part of the city they think of as their territory and that they defend like rapid dogs. I ran into the Cripps territory. My pack of pursuers followed me. Pinned me in a dead end alley. They were going to make short work of me when this tiny black boy with a machine gun shows up.

"I couldn't understand a word he was saying but it sure got the attention of the other boys. I thought they'd been pretty fast chasing me. But their hearts must not have been in it. Because they vanished like smoke as the black kid waved his gun around. Didn't even stop to assure me they'd get around to killing me.

"I was going to follow them. But the black kid says, "Where do you think you're going." Up close he wasn't a child at all but a mature man. "Want to know why I saved you?" he asked. "For a big man you can really run. I coach track and field and I'm always on the look out for new talent."

"Coach Evans taught me how to throw, and the more I threw, the more I practised, the less I heard voices. At practice I met whites, blacks, Asians, and various mixtures. I began to realize I wasn't Samoan at all. That half of me is WASP."

"WASP, what's that?" Maria asks.

"Well it could refer to a vicious stinging insect. But in this case it means white, Anglo-Saxon, Protestant. Like my dad. And I like that half of myself much better. Once I got to know it. As long as it's in control I'm all peaceful. My brain works great. I make good decisions, and I don't hear voices. Every time the Samoan part of me comes out I get in trouble, bad trouble. Being like my uncles, even for a few minutes, isn't a good idea. They go *musu* so easily."

"*Musu?*" Maria frowns.

"Going *musu* is likely going postal or going berserk except worse. A Samoan man in a state of *musu* is not only violent, they are also capable of awesome feats of strength. The island I grew up on is called Falemusu, island of bad moods. The men there are notorious for incredible *musu* fits, they tear up trees, knock down buildings, nothing and nobody is safe. My Uncle Duncan crushed a car once."

"I don't believe you," Maria says. "You're jerking my leash."

"I saw it. My uncle stepped in front of a moving car. An old Buick. It had almost run over some school kids trying to cross the street.

"It bounced off him. At about thirty miles an hour. Then he lifted it by the front bumper and flipped it over on its roof. The driver just got out in time. Then my uncle, the sweetest man I've ever met, systematically destroyed that car. Tore off the doors, smashed the windows, rolled it over and over until the roof collapsed, and finally, using just his hands he crushed the frame. Then he took me out for ice cream like nothing had happened."

"I don't think I'd like to see that."

"No, I don't want to be like my uncles. I've gone *musu* just once, and I ended up in jail. I swore never again." Willie smiles at Maria. "Now you use your Romni magic, or maybe your Indian magic and tell me to go to the dead, to ask them for answers. I knew exactly what you meant but I can't just go and do it. I don't even know how."

"Your uncles would know how, wouldn't they?"

"Yes."

"You could ask them."

"No I couldn't," Willie says and heads off to hide in his bedroom.

CHAPTER · 18

Later, sitting alone in the living room, Maria thinks about crazy people and people who tell stories. She thinks about Grandma Nose and all her stories. She had a story for every problem, every event. Riding in the caravan with her, Maria listened with two big rabbit ears to every word. Grandma Nose was Mommy and Father combined. Maria loved the woman and found her love returned manyfold. But it hadn't started out that way.

Maria wasn't ever supposed to be found. The Lees *kumpania* was on a run of very bad luck. They traded away their best stallion for a racehorse that showed no interest in running. There hadn't been any babies born to the *kumpania* in over a year. The Yorkshire government had decided to crack down on gypos as they were called throughout the dales, and was hounding them with a new law. It said they could only camp anywhere for one day at a time, so they had to keep moving, constantly. It was all getting to be too much, and it was all Grandma Nose's fault, as the resident fortune-teller and medicine woman.

Grandma Nose deflected the criticism by fabricating a little foreign girl who'd be found in Israel (she spun the globe and blindly stuck a finger out to pick the country). She'd speak a language that sounded like Romni but wasn't. She'd be on the run, and need help. And when they found her, then everything would start going right. If she couldn't be found that wasn't Grandma Nose's fault, she was too old to go looking herself.

Then damned if Shaggy and Agnes hadn't returned with the girl. The *kumpania* rejoiced. Grandma Nose announced she'd have to test the girl, make sure she was the one.

The *kumpania* was working their way back from the pilgrimage to Ste. Marie de La Mer in the honour of Saint Sarah, the servant girl that gypsies believe is their patron saint. They were camped on the outskirts of Paris trading horses with other Rom that had completed the pilgrimage, all equally convinced that the effort of the pilgrim would now be rewarded with great good fortune in horse trading. They were also there for the Arc de Triomphe, the horse race of the year.

As long as there have been horses and there have been gypsies the Rom have shared a special relationship with the horse. They love their horses. Horses get fed before humans. Campsites are chosen for the horses, not the humans.

Not all horses pull wagons of course, many race. And on those the Rom bet. Every man, woman, and child of the Rom believes they have a special affinity with fast horses, an affinity that allows them to pick sure winners. They don't, but they believe that they do and they lose often and in large amounts. Which is why the Rom revere those few individuals who can reliably pick winners, the handicappers par excellence.

Grandma Nose claims that "Nose" is her nickname because she can so reliably smell a winner. She always could, according to her, smell speed. Her nose just grew into the job as she got older. If Maria is the one, then she must have the horse sense, like Grandma Nose. So this year the little girl will pick who the Rom should bet on. If she's the one, they will all get rich. If not, they'll send her back where she came from.

Maria learns all this later. Her first meeting with Grandma Nose is unpleasant. The old woman looks at her with eyes like a hawk, as if calculating how much soup stock her bones might make. They are the oldest, coldest eyes Maria has ever seen.

"She doesn't look like much, Agnes. Not much at all. Tomorrow, Shaggy, you take her to the track, let her pick us a winner."

That night is Maria's first night in a wagon. The wind rustles the canvas and sings Maria a song. The bed is firm and soft all at the same time. It's goose down stuffed inside layers of intricately patterned quilting. The pillow is also down. Maria sleeps in luxury, in a strange country, with the strangest of people.

Early the next morning Shaggy Lees takes Maria to the track. He drives an odd little truck with only one front wheel and a round front end. It's painted blue and yellow, hand-painted. Maria thinks it's the most beautiful truck she has ever seen. It's race day. Maria can sense the excitement in the people wandering around the track, smell it on the horses. Somehow Shaggy gets into the stables. Morning workouts are over and the horses are all back in their stalls. Some are being brushed down. Others are quietly chewing. All glisten with good health. Shaggy leads Maria through a complex of stalls and corrals. "These horses are racing against each other today. Which will win?"

Alone, she walks up to the first of the stalls. Maria remembers it as the loneliest day of her life. She so wanted to fit in, to belong to these people. But she'd never seen horses before and they terrified her. As she approaches, the first horse, all grey and white blotches, whinnies. Maria jumps back. She can hear Shaggy laughing.

Slowly, Maria moves forward again. She stops just out of reach of the horse, who is straining his neck, trying to reach Maria. Tentatively she puts out her hand. He makes no attempt to bite it and she pats him, strokes his neck, rubs his ears. She can't believe how muscular his neck is.

Moving down the line of stalls Maria learns each horse has its own personality. The second horse is a big black monster. Maria knows his sort, she's met plenty of men like him. He's full of himself and mean to boot. Several of the other horses are like the black, but less so. If these horses race, the big black will win.

There are horses that she can tell live to run. Maria has met men like that too, in Shadipur, in Ankara, in Cairo. Good-time Charlies, Betty called them. They just wanted to have a good time and the sooner the better. None of these horses would be able to beat the big black either. Running isn't the same thing as racing.

There are several horses that don't belong in any kind of race. They don't like to run, and they hate to race. Eventually Maria learns that in any horse race some horses are entered simply to flatter the ego of the owner, not because they have the slightest chance of winning. The bigger the race the more likely some of the horses will be outmatched. In amongst the certain losers is a little roan, almost a pony. Maria likes that little horse, every time she gets close to him he tries to kiss her. When she dodges out of his way the horse makes a nasal snorting sound that simply has to be a laugh.

By the time Maria reaches the end of the stalls she is certain the big black brute is going to win any race amongst these horses. She is just about to tell Shaggy this when she looks back at the little roan one last time. He smiles at her and blows her a kiss and somehow she knows he'll find a way to win. That's what she tells Shaggy.

"We'll see girl, we'll see. He's an awful small horse after all," Shaggy says.

Shaggy and Maria spend the day at the races. It's amazing, all the beautifully dressed women, the little jockeys in their bright colours, some of the men in jeans, others in suits, some in tuxedos. Everywhere Maria looks people are drinking champagne in tall fluted glasses. The race between the big black brute and the little roan pony is the last race of the day. Maria sits in the stands near the finish line watching horses run their hearts out. It makes her cry and laugh all at the same time. During the day the bleacher seats fill with Rom; word has spread beyond the Lees *kumpania* that the little magic girl from the east has picked a sure winner and they are there to bet their life savings, such as they are.

When the last race comes to the post, Shaggy takes Maria by the hand. She knows her test is about to begin. Out of the gate the little roan is dead last. The big black is in the middle of the pack. As they round the first turn the little roan falls further and further behind.

"Don't worry girl, it's a long race," Shaggy says to Maria but his grip tightens.

Around the second corner the big black bullies his way to near the front of the field. The crowd is screaming his name in several languages. "Thunder," they cry, "come on Thunder!" "Allez Tonnere!" It's hard for Maria to tear her eyes away from the big black as he bursts out in front and begins to pull away from the field.

As they round the third corner she looks to the back of the pack for her little roan. He isn't there. Her first thought is he must have dropped out. Then as her eyes cross over the pack, headed back to the front to watch Thunder run home, she realizes the roan is in the pack, hidden by the bigger horses. And as the pack turns that last corner the roan rockets out from amongst them and is suddenly in second place. Only Thunder remains ahead but he is a very long way ahead.

The big black is eight or more lengths ahead and running well. But the little roan is actually making up ground with each stride. Maria stares hard but can't see the roan's hooves touching the turf. It's like he is flying. Even the jockey is clearly holding on for his life. Two strides from the finish the roan is a full body length behind, an impossible distance. But at the tape, somehow a little roan nose crosses the line first.

The crowd is silent at first. Then the grumbling begins, the talk of doping. Shaggy Lees is jumping up and down and hugging Maria. He is saying, "We knew you had the gift, we knew you had the gift."

That day Morning Sunrise won the last race of the first day of the meeting at a thousand to one odds. The only heavy betting on Morning Sunrise was done by the Rom. There were a number of investigations. Dirty, stinking, cheating gypsies the papers said, fixing a grand old race, ruining it. The Rom, accustomed to eons of persecution, found the French hysteria hilarious. For the rest of race week the English gypsies drank and danced. They also gambled away all their winnings and thumbed their noses at the French. It was grand, they'd say years later, just grand.

Grandma Nose was a realist. She knew she was now stuck with Maria. Oh well, she thought, maybe I can make a silk purse out of this little sow's ear.

Meanwhile, as Maria is sitting in Willie's trailer remembering her first great fortune-telling success, the Raklos are learning to cheat the casinos.

CHAPTER · 19

Yannis is a patient young man. He needs all of that patience to deal with his pig-headed brothers and interfering mother. It's not that they don't have the skills to be great crossroaders. It's that they fight him on everything. For example, he wants to play craps. They don't.

There are a number of reasons for his decision. It's the form of cheating that the most has been written about. Alberta has just started allowing craps to be played in casinos so it's likely that none of the staff have ever seen anyone cheating at it. The potential profit is enormous. All good reasons. But the best one is that after rehearsing them all, it's the one the brothers are best at.

Finally Yannis wins the craps battle. He fixes up the kitchen like a real craps table at a real casino. That's where the Raklos practise their crossroading technique. Draj is a master at getting the rigged dice in and out of play. Marko is a wonderful roller. He pretends to be drunk and fumbles with the dice and generally acts like a klutz while rolling winner after winner, appearing amazed each time he wins. When he loses he sulks for a few seconds and then grins and starts killing time waiting for the dice to come back to him. Yannis suspects Marko is never entirely sober but it doesn't matter, his betting is small potatoes, sometimes in his drunken stupor he forgets to bet altogether. What counts is that Yannis is stone sober and calculating odds and maximizing his betting. He never touches the dice, if they come to him, he just waves them on. He's the one killing the house, apparently able to predict when Marko's hot streaks will begin and end. But that is the source of all the fights. Yannis is the one making the money. Baby brother. It should be Draj.

Draj goes whining to Nana. Nana demands Draj be the one doing the betting. Yannis thinks to himself, during one of his mother's harangues, "I must have been switched at birth." Nana orders a change in playing order. They try it her and Draj's way in the kitchen casino.

Draj can't master the basics of betting. With him handling the bankroll, the house has a very unfair advantage. He claims it would be different if they were playing for real money.

Yannis has Nana take his place. He becomes the casino. His own money is on the line. Wanting desperately to make his baby brother look bad doesn't improve Draj's betting. It makes it worse. After two hours of playing for real money Draj has lost five hundred dollars and is out of money. According to Draj the table is unfair. He forces Yannis to trade positions with him. Nana bankrolls Draj. Yannis ends up with a thousand dollars of her money in twenty minutes.

Yannis knows one of these days he's going to pay for his success.

With Yannis back in charge, practice resumes. Eventually even Yannis thinks there is nothing more for them to learn in the kitchen. It's time to try a real casino. The first trip to a casino they aren't there to try to take the house, just to learn what a casino is, a massive machine for taking your money.

Yannis takes three hundred dollars of his own money, makes his brothers promise to leave all of theirs at home. He even searches them before they leave the house. Yannis doesn't believe in leaving anything to chance.

Outside the casino he gives each of his brothers one hundred dollars. Draj loses his in minutes playing twenty-one and then grouses around, learning nothing. Marko, with great luck, wins consistently. But he drinks the profits faster than they come in. In an hour he's broke. Yannis holds even for almost two hours at the craps table before a streak of bad luck wipes him out. Yannis is pretty sure that with a big enough bankroll he could legitimately beat the house at craps. He's read about it happening, someone with a great ability to work out the odds on every bet, betting mostly with the house, surviving the bad times by drawing on a thick bankroll and walking away from the table ahead.

They meet outside, once Yannis has lost. Out into the fresh night air away from prying ears.

"Okay. What did you see?" Yannis asks.

"Those waitresses all have goodly chests. They are a pleasure to bump into," Draj says.

"Why do you think all those women are so pretty and wrapped up so nice, Draj?"

"I don't know, but I surely like looking at them."

"That's why they are dressed that way. It's meant to distract you a little bit, put you in a good mood. Men tend to lose more money gambling and much quicker than women. Casinos are filled with eye candy, pretty women, flashing lights, mirrors, anything to distract men from how much they are losing. You've got to learn how to ignore all that stuff."

"They water down their drinks," Marko says.

"Not exactly," Yannis says. "Not most of them, anyway. They practice flow management. That's what they call it. The drinks keep coming to you if you're betting enough, free of charge, and each drink has the right amount of booze in it. But it has more water or more mix than it should, or the drink is just bigger. They've got two reasons for doing that. First you feel like the drink doesn't have the usual kick, which encourages you to drink more, to make up for the fact the drinks are so watery. Second it makes you need to urinate. A man with a full bladder makes dumb gambling decisions. A drunk man with his bladder about to burst makes terrible gambling decisions and sometimes goes broke just so he can go take a pee."

"A man was staring at me. A little *gaujo* in a cheap suit. He was giving me the eye. I think maybe he was a hoho at first. But as I make more money he looks harder."

Yannis says: "That was the pit boss. I wasn't winning much, mostly just not losing and he's on me. He's only got about two weeks worth of experience. Imagine what it's going to be like when we start winning thousands, maybe tens of thousands of dollars, and the staff have learned what to watch for.

"And it won't just be the pit boss. He'll call security and they'll have a camera trained on us from up above the table, watching every move we make. If we keep winning, the head of security will come to the table and enter the game. Many of those guys are first class magicians and card mechanics. If we're cheating, and not doing it well, they'll catch us.

"That's not a problem for me, I'm not doing anything wrong. If they think I'm up to no good they'll play back the tape they make of every game. It will show I never touched the dice, so how can I possibly be cheating? In fact I'll probably have been here playing for hours before you guys arrive and may play for hours after you leave. But that tape might show Draj taking the dice in and out of the game and that could send us all to jail. Which is why, Draj, the first thing you must do each time you go to play is figure where the cameras are and make sure you can't be taped placing or removing the dice. And, Draj, it can't be obvious, you can't appear to be avoiding the camera. It's all got to look natural."

Draj scowls and kicks a clump of dirt.

"So what else could trip us up?" Yannis asks. His brothers look at him with blank stares. Yannis sighs, quietly. They still haven't learned the most important thing of all.

"Even in a little casino like this one the head of security is a talented cheat. They'll be in the game just waiting to get their hands on the dice so they can check them out, and it'll only take them a millisecond to determine the dice are funny. Draj, you've got to learn to spot those people and get the dice out of play before they grab them. Marko, you have to keep watching Draj, without anyone realizing you are doing it. If he gives you the signal you have to help him get those dice out of play.

"Remember, security doesn't want to make a scene but they will if they have to, so once again, whatever you do to get those dice out of play you have to do with style. Making it look like an accident is probably the best. We all have to remember the other reason why security might want to touch those dice without your knowing they've done it. With luck they can switch clean dice into the game and before we realize the dice aren't friendly anymore the casino will have won back a bunch of its money.

"And what do we say if they catch us?" Yannis asks.

"Nuttin, we tell them rotting pumpkins full of gabble," Draj answers belligerently, thinking "It's not like we are amateurs."

"Exactly, Draj. You tell them nothing. If we've done our jobs right they have no evidence. All you've got to do is stay deaf and dumb and next thing you know you'll be free to go.

"But the problem is that once they've caught us cheating, even if they can't prove it, we'll be on the list. Most casinos work closely together circulating dirty pictures. That's what they call them, the pictures the video cameras have gotten of us. If a casino thinks we've been cheating they will isolate our picture from the video and circulate it to all the other casinos on their distribution list and the next time we walk into a casino, security will be on us before we can sit down at a table. That's why, every time we go into a casino to cheat, we wear a disguise.

"I know that guys like you, tough guys, you aren't too worried about getting arrested. That's why I want you to remember that even in Canada there are people in the casino business who don't like cheats. I heard a story at the Palace Casino yesterday, from a girl, she's in security, I've been yapping her up."

"Ah, our little brother has found out about girls," Marko drunkenly giggles.

Yannis blushes. "Listen, this important. She told me about an Indian band that has a casino. That's where she broke into the security business. She caught a crossroader and turned him over to her boss. A few days later she learned that a couple of thugs had taken this poor guy out into the prairies and pounded his hands into a bloody pulp with a sledgehammer. She worked for three years in Vegas and she'd hear stories about the great cheats, even met some of them. Everyone knew they were jerking off on the casinos but nobody could figure out how. Then one day they simply weren't around and never were again. Later she'd hear stories of them being buried in the desert or buried in the forest or equipped with cement overshoes and dumped in a handy lake or burnt to cinders in a blast furnace. Sometimes she'd hear that they were still alive at the time. So let's not get caught, right."

The boys nod their heads slowly.

"How do you make sure you don't get caught?" Yannis asks.

"We do it good," Marko says.

"That's part of it for sure," Yannis says. "We'll practice until our fingers bleed, until we are flawless. The three of us are already a good team. But there are only three of us, and there should be at least four, maybe even five if we want to keep the casinos guessing. The team in these books all used seven."

"They'd totally control the table. That let them stay playing for a long time without the casino being sure they were cheating. The person putting the die into play would be right before the roller they'd be betting on. They only put one die into the game and once they'd done that they were out of there, out of the casino, quick as they could make it without drawing attention to themselves. They used dice that only had ones and sixes on them. That drove the odds of winning up significantly. They couldn't be sure they'd win on any one roller so two or three of them in a row would use those dice and all the while another bettor further around the table would be doing the heavy betting. When the third roller in the line finally lost they'd take the funny dice out of the game and they'd all gradually drift out of the casino. Maybe stop and play a little keno, or the slots.

"With just the three of us we've got to wait for the dice to get to Draj so he can switch in the loaded ones. And we have no choice but to use loaded dice since we can't be seen next to each other or it'll be really apparent that we are cheating. They can't be too loaded or the people who handle the dice before Marko will realize they aren't right and then the fun really begins.

"Before we can really score big you have to wait for the loaded dice to reach Marko. Because the dice we are using are weighted you know whoever is rolling them is more likely to come up with a seven than average and you can bet accordingly. And you must be betting since otherwise you'll be asked to leave the table. Now when the dice get to Marko he knows how to roll them in order to greatly increase the benefit of their weighting. We've seen how good he is."

That he's good is the first thing Marko has got out of Yannis's lecture. Draj has been spending his time thinking about ways he could stop an armoured truck. Maybe stick up some security guards with a lot of money. And women, Draj is thinking about women. He's thinking about Maria, about how sorry he's going to make her.

"If Marko gets on a roll..." Yannis continues. He knows his brothers aren't listening, but he knows they have to pretend to be, and that's enough for him. This way when they get it hopelessly wrong, and they will, he can say, I told you so, "...and is winning every time he rolls the dice the money will be flowing off the table into our pockets and you'll forget the most important thing of all. That's to not overstay our welcome. Three or four wins and then Marko rolls wrong, makes sure he loses, passes the dice on to the next person. When they come back to Draj he takes them out of play, puts the right one back. If we all think Marko's first run hasn't attracted attention and I'm handling the betting well, so the house isn't sure how much I'm up, we can let the dice go on around and repeat the process. But no more than three circuits, Marko doesn't win more than fifteen times maximum and maybe he has some loses in there just to confuse them.

"Done right, in an evening we'll win ten or fifteen thousand dollars. We get greedy, we get caught. That's a promise."

His brothers are nodding and grinning. But Yannis knows they aren't ready. They are Rom and he's the youngest, and thus the dumbest. They are almost certainly going to ignore the little he's managed to teach them as soon as play gets underway.

Later, Yannis goes on the Internet, talks with everyone he's come to know in the casino business. He wants to make a dry run. One where they can make some money if they're lucky and not get into too much trouble, if as he suspects, they twist up. His contacts suggest he try Medicine Hat. Yannis rents a Transport minivan and they take off. Having Yannis control the transportation makes his older siblings nuts. But he's the only one with a valid driver's licence. He's the only one who drives.

For the entire six-hour drive Draj demands he be put back in charge of the operation. After all, Yannis must have taught them everything he knows by now. It's Draj's job to make the decisions.

There is a casino that's held in the basement of the Medicine Hat Lodge. It's well laid out and lighted but Vegas it isn't. The Raklos take one look and Draj says, "Shrub league," and Marko says, "Minnie Mouse."

Yannis asks: "Would you like to know what their handle is? Well, on a really busy night two hundred thousand flows through here. Let's see how much we can make stick to our fingers."

After the constant harangue of the trip, Yannis has had enough of his brothers and leaves them to go get ready in the room he's rented for the three of them under an assumed name. He goes to play the slots. He's a system player and in the next thirty minutes his system pays off handsomely. He's up two hundred dollars when his brothers return in disguise.

Yannis has to admit they haven't chosen badly. Draj is wearing a baseball cap and overalls and has a nice stubble. He looks like a lot of the other players. Marko has a fake mustache of real human hair. It's so exuberant that it's all you see when you look at him, and he's made his cheeks all puffy with wadding. Otherwise he's dressed in blue jeans and a golf shirt and looks good. As long as no one pulls on the mustache he'll be fine.

Yannis came prepared in a good quality suit, which makes him stand out, and his hair is slicked back. He looks like a moderately successful real estate agent or mutual fund salesman and he's busy networking, looking for that next sale, which makes everyone avoid eye contact with him.

Even with the great disguises, it takes the Raklos less than an hour to get caught. Caught in the shrub leagues by Minnie Mouse. Marko's caught holding the loaded dice. They've made Draj as his partner. They look so much alike, act so much like undisciplined pigs. Yannis is home free, all he has to do is walk away, up three thousand dollars and let his brothers rot. But they are his brothers.

He catches the next elevator upstairs and gets his supplies from the van. His new disguise is remarkably simple and effective. It's a pair of overalls and some grease which he applies to his face and hands. He's got to move quickly if he's going to free Draj and Marko before the RCMP get around to responding to the complaint from the casino. He carries a tool chest with him.

He knows that as long as the casino hopes to extract some of the Raklos's winnings from them they won't make that call. It's one of the reasons he's told them to keep their mouths shut if they are caught. It encourages negotiation.

In the men's washroom in the basement he disables the security camera. He cuts its cable. From his tool chest he extracts some grease and gasoline soaked rags that's he's carefully stored there. He puts the rags in the paper towel receptacle. Next Yannis uses an awl and a hammer to punch a few holes in the metal of the receptacle. Then he takes a lighter out of his pocket and lights one last remaining rag on fire and drops it into the receptacle. In seconds the bathroom is filling with bilious black smoke. Yannis walks out into the hall and does his duty. He pulls the fire alarm.

In the resulting confusion, Yannis is able to recover the security video tapes of the Raklos in action. He thinks they might make valuable teaching aids. He hopes his brothers are smart enough to escape on their own given the opportunity. But he wouldn't want to bet on it.

CHAPTER · 20

On a steaming hot afternoon, the staff of International Investigations meet to let Roger know what they have learned about Mr. Average Bob.

"His real name is Robert Montgomery Peterson." Dingo begins. "Willie found that out by doing a title search on the property in Pleasantview, which turned out to be owned by a numbered company. But Willie has contacts in Corporate Registry and for a donation of a few hundred dollars he got the name of the owners of the numbered company. There were only three of them, a lawyer and an accountant who hold one percent each, and Robert Montgomery Peterson.

"From there I took over. I made several guesses, that he was born in Alberta and that he is between thirty and forty. Then I started searching various databases, I got a half dozen likely hits from Alberta Genealogical Research. I cross-referenced those names with holders of a valid Alberta driver's licence, that's a database we have access to because of all the insurance investigations we do. With that additional information it was pretty easy to track our man back to his birthplace. Robert Montgomery Peterson was born in Vulcan, Alberta. That's just a little southeast of Calgary. He's thirty-nine.

"We've talked to a number of people who knew him while he was growing up, and none of them remembered anything unusual about his childhood. He was a good solid B student according to his teachers. He belonged to the volleyball and basketball teams but was a bench-warmer. His most significant accomplishment seems to have been winning a contest where he picked a group of stocks on the Toronto Stock Exchange and invested five thousand hypothetical dollars. In six weeks he turned it into twenty thousand. He beat high school and university students from all over Canada."

"How did you get all these people to talk to you?" Roger asks.

"Mostly we told them that he was being screened for a high level security clearance, we let them assume that we were some sort of government agency," Dingo answers.

"Aren't you worried someone will tell Bob you've been asking about him?" Roger asks.

"Well it's always a risk. But in this case it seems unlikely that anyone will pass it along. Bob hasn't been back to Vulcan since his parents were killed in a car accident about twenty years ago. He had just turned nineteen and was a student at the University of Alberta, pre-med. The funeral was on a Saturday and Monday he was back in class," Dingo answers. "Maria did all the work on Bob's university career."

"I found out that he was a pretty average student until his parents died," Maria says, batting her eyelashes at Roger. "They use a nine-point marking system at the University of Alberta, and the first year and a half he was there Bob average a little less than 7.0. The next year and a half he averaged 8.8. I make friends with the boy who works the information desk in the Academic Building, that's were they keep the records, and he tells me all this, just by looking on the computer. And that's not all he was able to tell me. Bob, his marks aren't quite good enough to get into medical school so he goes ahead and finishes his bachelor's degree in science. I have to ask Philipe, who works the desk, and tells me this, why you have to be single to get a degree in science.

"He takes me out to lunch, and explains all about the different kinds of degrees and the history of universities and he brings along Robert Montgomery Peterson, of Vulcan, Alberta's transcript. Bob's transcript gets really weird once he doesn't get into medicine. He keeps taking biology courses but now he gets threes and fours and gets put on academic probation. Then in his fifth year of school he begins taking statistics courses and math courses and his marks jump back up and he's on the dean's honours list.

"Philipe has a friend upstairs in Registration and he's able to get the full file. Bob was at risk of getting expelled, had to undergo counselling, which doesn't seem to have done much good. There is no record of what turned it around for him but suddenly he's a brilliant student again."

"I want to know what you paid Philipe to get all this information out of him?" Roger asks.

"I didn't pay him anything, Roger. I never pay nobody unless I have to and Philipe just wanted to help me. He'd never met a female private dick before, he'd never met any private dick before. And to thank him I went with him to a dance at Dinwoodie Lounge and he showed me off to all his friends, and after he'd had a little to drink he felt up my back end and got all bothered and then I slipped away while he was getting us both drinks. If I ever have to use him again he'll be like silly glue in my hands."

"I don't doubt that for a moment," Willie says, feeling both jealous and a little excited by Maria's account.

"So what else did you learn about Bob?" Roger asks.

"I tracked down some of his professors from that last year," Maria says. "They said he was a good general mathematician, good enough they remembered him years later. Almost a prodigy. But that he really came to life in probability classes. Could calculate the odds of almost anything in his head.

"He went on to Yale to do graduate studies in statistics and probability. Bob got his Ph.D. in just two years and was working as a junior professor when he started drinking."

"We know this how?" Roger asked.

"I talked with the guy who shared Bob's office at Yale when they were both Ph.D. students," Maria says.

"She talks real low and slow and the men she's talking to bleat just like sheep as they are fleeced," Willie adds proudly.

"He's a professor now at Boston College, this guy who shared the office," Maria says, ignoring Willie's interruption. "Before he hit bottom Bob ended up as a dealer in a casino in Atlantic City. That's where we lose him for the first time," Maria concludes.

"I called up an investigator I know in New Jersey and asked him to see if after all this time he could find out what Bob did next," Dingo says. "It took some digging but it seems that Bob went from Atlantic City to Los Angeles. He supported himself waiting tables and handicapping horse races. In the meantime he worked with a local magician, who, despite having been born with no fingers on one hand and only three on the other, could do amazing card tricks. That's where Bob learned to cheat at cards. Once he thought he was good enough he moved to Las Vegas.

"It wasn't hard to pick up Bob's trail in Vegas. I've spent enough time there gambling and losing money at it to have some very good friends in the industry," Dingo continues. "He couldn't have been in Las Vegas more than a week when he got a job as a security guard at the Freemont Street Casino. He progressed quickly from there to being a pit boss at the Gold Dust and finally became the eye in the sky at Circus Circus. Sitting at his console in a room way up in the rafters he could view every corner of the casino through one of the closed circuit TV cameras. With his background, he could spot a card cheat in an instant and he learned how to recognize all the other kinds of crossroaders quite quickly."

"I thought you said he was a gambler," Roger objects.

"When he wasn't working he was gambling. He was a regular loser at games like craps and roulette, but every time he got anywhere near cards he started to win. None of the casinos seem to have worried too much about his winning streaks because he simply turned right around and lost it playing other games of chance or betting on sporting events or horse racing. Then he started playing poker exclusively.

"The casinos don't care who wins or loses at poker, they take their rake, their fee for providing the space, the drinks, the snacks, and dealing the cards. As long as a lot of money is bet they're happy. Bob started off playing on the low stakes tables. My source said he was probably winning two or three hundred dollars a night using very conservative betting strategies and picking his tables carefully."

Dingo pauses. "At this point I have a picture of a very conservative guy, hard-working, relying on the power of his ability to calculate odds to make a decent buck playing cards, a romantic, a bit of a loser. Then in 1990 he tried to pull off a major scam in Reno, playing blackjack. It was a one-man show and it was audacious. He wore a pair of very retro eyeglasses into which a tiny fibre optic camera had been built, that was transmitting to a very small but powerful computer in his shoe. The shoe computer would then send a signal to a hearing aid he was wearing pressed deep in his ear, where it was hard to see.

"And the thing to keep in mind is that he spent years building up to this. Right from the time he started working as a security guard he complained his hearing was failing, went to a doctor, convinced them he needed this hearing aid. When he started working at Circus Circus he complained his eyesight was failing and got these prescription glasses, these massive, retro glasses. Wore them for two years before Reno. Bob played just enough blackjack for every casino in Las Vegas to identify him as a regular with wildly unpredictable betting habits, just shy of being a high roller.

"He took a month's vacation from Circus Circus and played poker in Reno, higher stakes poker than was his habit, and after a night at the tables he'd unwind, losing most of his winnings playing wildly eccentric blackjack. At least twice he got up thirty or forty thousand dollars playing blackjack before he came back to earth and lost it all."

Roger grins. "This guy is the opposite of dumb."

"So when he walked into the Silver Glitter security already knew who he was and that they wanted him playing blackjack there. Bob's sting began with him winning over sixty thousand dollars playing poker, it looks like several of the other players conspired with him, letting him win money from them that he shouldn't have. It seems he provided them with that money in the first place. But it made him look like he was on a roll. So when he went to play 21, blackjack, whatever it's called at the Silver Glitter the casino security boss was not surprised that he was betting more than was his regular habit. Nor did he panic when Bob's winning climbed above forty thousand, he knew Bob's luck would run out eventually, there was nothing about his play that suggested he was counting cards or cheating. But Bob kept playing and kept winning.

"They changed dealers on him, started playing with four deck shoes, mechanically shuffled, they even changed the order they dealt. The pit boss tried to pressure him into packing it in, calling it a day. They tried to get him drunk. They even tried to remove him from the table by force but by then there was a very large crowd. Bob ran his winnings up to $1,800,000 then cashed out."

Dingo looks around the table, but nobody says anything. He carries on. "Bob thought the casino would sick some goons on him. Had a plan for that. Instead they called the police. He nearly bluffed his way out of it. No one could figure out how he'd cheated. But they had him sweating pretty good. He took his glasses off to wipe his brow and they slipped out of his hands.

"A young detective, trying to be helpful, beat him to them, realized they weren't right. It turns out that using electronic aids in a gambling house is a fairly major no-no. Bob got seven years at a minimum security institution. But Willie will tell you the rest."

Willie glances down at a file. "Bob ended up doing his time outside of Calistoga, in the Napa Valley. Ever since I started working as a private detective I've often been struck by the strange world of coincidence that we all live in. I did time at Calistoga State Correctional Facility. I was a model prisoner. Went on and made something of my life. In other words I'm something of a poster boy for the state's correctional programs.

"Calistoga isn't exactly a social club like some white-collar prisons, with their tennis courts and swimming pools. The residents work hard in the vineyards as day labourers and over half of them are serious career criminals, counterfeiters, check kiters and con men. The rest are amateurs, right now some of them are hackers, others are entrepreneurs who got in over their heads and created bizarre scams to keep their companies afloat. They have a certain *joie de vivre*, these guys, it's hard to keep them down. Bob seems to have fit that pattern, he pumped iron, taught the other inmates how to cheat casinos, and listened carefully to any advice he was given," Willie says.

"What were you in jail for, Mr. Willie?" Maria asks.

"Assault and reckless endangerment."

"Who did you assault and endanger?"

"Long story," Willie says. "Let's move on. From the time he was released from prison we lose all track of Bob until about 1995. That's when he had a real shot at winning the World Championship of Poker. It was televised and a Robert Montgomery made it to the semifinals. In 1997 he was arrested but not charged in a plan to offer offshore gambling over the Internet. The Internet Casino itself was a little troubling to government regulators but it was the listing of the company on Nasdaq and its subsequent promotion that made the money and tap-danced on the edge of legality. In any case Bob got out just before the roof caved in and, as I said, escaped prosecution. That's when he bought the house in Pleasantview."

Dingo nods. "Mostly, as far as we can tell, he plays poker for a living and runs the odd con for fun. He also seems to have some legitimate business investments in the gaming industry. We checked his credit rating with Equifax and Creditel and he has no black marks and a credit line of over five hundred grand through the same numbered company that owns the house.

He owns several antique cars that he bought as wrecks and has restored to mint condition. He gives heavily to United Way, Catholic Social Services, Habitat for Humanity, the Bissell Centre and the YMCA. Bob subscribes to *Science and Spirit, The Journal of Applied Mathematics, Penthouse, Nude and Natural, Yellow Silk, Travel Abroad,* and *The Smithsonian.* He has three Basset hounds, and a purebred Burmese cat. He has his suits handmade."

"Come on Dingo, how can you possibly know all that?" Roger asks.

"We traded some information with a couple of the larger consumer marketing research firms."

"You mean they knew all that?" Roger asks.

"And more, much more. He buys six boxes of shredded wheat every six weeks. He prefers Kleenex brands but will use Purex if he has to, feeds his dogs Eukenuba dog food, and so on," Dingo says.

"What do you think all this means? Does he have the brain or doesn't he? Is he trying to con me, do you think?" Roger asks.

"I've tried to figure out the answers to those questions and the best that I can say for sure is, yes, I think he has the brain. I doubt he's trying to con you, I doubt he knows you exist. If he is conning you or someone else he sure has a funny way of going about it."

"So, what do we do now?" Roger demands.

"Well, Maria, Willie and I have discussed that at great length and concluded that we are going to have to break into his house and have a look see."

"You're going to steal the brain?"

"No, Roger. We aren't going to steal anything. We are going to try to slip in and out without Bob ever knowing we've been there and see if he has got the brain and what else we can learn about him. We want you to come along but only if you promise to do exactly as we say, since none of us want to go to jail," Dingo says.

"When are we going to do this?"

"Bob is flying to Vancouver tomorrow afternoon and returning the next morning. It seems like a good time for us to peek inside his inner sanctum. We'll bring some treats to keep the Basset hounds happy. Maria will serve as our watch dog and you and I and Willie will reconnoitre."

CHAPTER 21

That evening Willie takes Maria out with him on his recycling run. They start at the dump. Maria can barely breathe for the smell.

"You'll get used to it," Willie promises her. "I did."

"This from the man who drinks putrid beer in the middle of the night."

"It helps me sleep."

"Are you doing it every night?"

"Not every night."

Maria glances around the dump. "What are we looking for, Mr. Willie?"

"Anything we can sell or use. But mostly I'm looking for some extra parts for Truck. I'd like a heavy duty winch, a crane, super shock absorbers, maybe springs."

They don't find any of those things.

What they do find is a wooden crate full of wine bottles. Maria is the one who spots it. The crate is partly buried under old newspapers and rotting, mouldy towels. Maria has a very hard time convincing Willie he should dig it up.

"Why don't you do it yourself?"

"You're the one with the gloves," she says.

"I could lend you mine," he says.

"They'd be way too big."

Finally she annoys him into action. He uses his garbage-poking stick to move the most repulsive of the towels. Then Willie bends down and pulls the crate out where they can get a good look.

Maria bends over and extracts one of the bottles. It's empty and dusty. She carefully brushes dust off the label. Then she begins to laugh.

"I'm good at this," she announces.

"I guess we could recycle the bottles," Willie says, not wanting to burst her bubble.

"We could sell the bottles Willie, for a lot of money. I know someone who would buy them."

"Why would anyone pay large amounts of money for old wine bottles?" Willie asks Maria.

"You don't read much do you? Except for some dust, these bottles are in mint condition with immaculate labels," Maria says.

"So?" Willie responds.

"They are Chateau Latour 1982. Collectors pay big money for that."

"But that's only if they are filled with wine," Willie points out.

"This guy I know, Pete. He'll fill them with wine. Might even taste like Bordeaux. Then he'll sell them," Maria says.

"You are a devious girl," Willie says and smiles.

"There is just one problem," Maria adds at the last moment.

"Which is?" Willie asks.

"He's a business associate of my husband. Maybe even a friend. I'll have to stay out of sight, which means you'll have to negotiate with him."

"No problem," Willie says.

"He'll beat you into the ground. By the time he's through with you, you'll be lucky to not end up paying him."

"No problem," Willie says. "You just tell me how much you'd get and that's what he'll give me."

"Yeah, sure."

"Nobody tries to negotiate with me," Willie says and frowns. "It makes me angry." Now he gives Maria his most belligerent look. Willie's look terrifies Maria. She figures with Willie smelling the way he does and his size, the look will probably get the job done.

"Where are we going?" Willie asks as he loads the wine bottles into Truck.

"Place in High Street. Premium Spirits and Fine Wines."

"Your guy owns a wine store."

"No. Pete just works there. It's how he meets prospective clients for his service," Maria says.

"Victims, you mean."

"Not at all. Most of the people Pete sells to want to impress their friends without breaking the bank. He fakes a wine, puts it in the right bottle, and sells it for a fraction of the price of the original."

Pete isn't too happy to see a smelly monster walk into the store and ask for him by name. Not until he sees the bottles. Willie names his price and Pete gladly pays it.

Outside he hands the money to Maria.

"Keep it," she says, surprising herself. "For Truck."

On the way to the Pick a Part, Maria asks Willie if used his "look" on Pete. Willie says, "You know, he just smelled me. I think he would have paid me to leave the shop."

They have to go to three places but eventually they find everything Willie wants for Truck.

Before they head home Willie takes Maria to Capilano Park.

He hoists her up on top of the middle boulder. The one he's being trying to move.

"Listen," he commands.

After a few minutes he can't contain himself anymore.

"Hear anything?"

"Is this the rock you came to listen to the other morning?"

"Yes."

"I'm sorry, Willie. I don't hear anything. But I wouldn't, would I, not if it's your special rock."

Willie is disappointed but not surprised.

He spends the rest of the evening and well into night putting the various parts on to Truck. He's not sure what he's doing it for. Or why he's in such a hurry.

Maria watches Willie for a while from the trailer window. Her frustration with him isn't just sexual. To her alarm, she finds herself angry when he ignores her, or talks about some other woman at the gym. Her job is simply to string him along, as Average Bob says. But who is stringing whom?

Around 2:00 A.M. Maria gets up to check and Willie is still hard at work. She brings him a Pepsi. Willie is under Truck putting in the new shocks. She has to kick his feet to get his attention.

"This rock is that important to you?"

"What do you mean?"

"Aren't you fixing up Truck so you can steal that rock? The one you think is singing to you."

Willie thinks about her question for several moments. "You know what, I am. I can't believe it but I am."

"What's so special about that rock? I mean besides that it sings."

"Isn't that enough?" Willie asks.

"I really want to know," Maria says.

"That boulder. Those three boulders. They come from Frank."

"Frank? Who's he?"

"It's a little town in southern Alberta. It was a prosperous place a hundred years ago. A mining town. Then one day the mountain that overlooked the town split apart and a massive slab of it fell on the town."

"Kind of like what happened to your Dad."

"Yeah."

"Come on, Willie. Tell me the rest."

"Meeting you. Living with you. It's got me all shook up. I'm acting Samoan. Remember what I told you? The Samoan part of me gets me in trouble. Well, it's running rampant these days."

"And?"

"And nothing," Willie says.

"Don't kid a kidder," Maria says.

Willie shrugs. "I've got myself convinced my Dad's spirit is trapped inside that rock, listening to alternative radio and going slowly crazy."

CHAPTER 22

The next morning, yawning and stretching in bed, Willie has an inspiration. A dream just past awakening. A gift from the rock.

First he'll have to get rid of Maria. She's sticking to him like superglue. He's rehearsing possible excuses when she comes running into the bedroom and jumps on the bed wearing a tight new red dress.

"What do you think of this dress?" Maria asks, spinning around.

Willie grunts appreciatively.

"Do you think my ass looks fat in this?"

Willie nods happily, noting that in fact she is looking fatter all over.

Maria smiles back at Willie. "We'll have to skip training this morning," she says. He notices that she's not only dressed nicely, but dolled up.

"Why do we have to skip?" he asks.

"Bob Struter invited me out for breakfast, at the High Level Diner," Maria says.

"I kind of have other plans," Willie says.

"You're not invited," Maria says.

"What are you two going to talk about?"

"You, of course."

"I shouldn't have asked," Willie says. "When are you meeting him?"

"In an hour," Maria says.

"Could you drop me on the way?"

"Where? Who are you meeting?"

"Dingo and I have been trying to recruit this guy, Eugene Mitchell, to join up with us. You know his mother. Mrs. Mitchell, she was at your party."

"The woman who had to fly off to look after her daughter in Arizona."

"That's her. Eugene's sister had sextuplets," Willie says.

"Sextuplets?" Maria asks.

"That's what happens when you have too much sex. Six kids. All at once," Willie says. "Imagine that."

"You'd never have sex again," Maria says.

"Not if you're smart. Dingo and I have been working on Eugene for months. Whenever one of us has the chance we go by, take him out for a bite, shoot the breeze. It's just at the end of the freeway, across from the McDonald's there. I'm going to take him out for breakfast."

"Want me to pick you up on the way home?"

"No. I'll walk, it's only a couple of miles as the crow flies. The exercise will make up for missing training this morning."

Eugene's shop is very discreet, masquerading as an appliance repair business. He sells spy equipment. His clients find him. He also publishes and prints *The Complete Spy Handbook*, a yearly compendium of the latest gear, markets, and trade craft. He calls himself The Genie. Willie humours him but thinks of Eugene as The Badger, the animal Eugene most closely resembles.

"Genie," Willie says, exchanging a high five over the counter.

"Willster," Eugene replies, bumping fists. "Want to see my latest business card?"

Eugene is on a quest for the perfect card, one that will sum up the inner Gene. He hands Willie a beautiful creamy white card stock with embossed gold foil print. Eugene Mitchell, Ph.D., P. Eng. Techno-creep. Eugene has a fortune in printing equipment in the back of his shop.

"Let's *dim sum*," Willie says.

"It's Sunday already?" Eugene asks.

"Yup."

A half a block away is the Red Diamond. It has great *dim sum*. Willie and Eugene are well-known and liked at the restaurant. They get seated almost immediately.

As carts of steaming dumplings and pastries go by the two men just point at random. Neither of them has ever figured out what filling is in what dumpling or bun. They agree that knowing would ruin at least half the fun of *dim sum.*

"I've got a problem, Genie."

"If you're looking for me to fill in for my Mom and give you advice on your love life forget it, I have enough problems with my own."

"You don't have a love life, Genie."

"That's the problem Willster." They both laugh. It's an old gag.

"I need to know about conspiracy nuts. I thought you'd be the guy to ask."

"Being a nut myself."

"No, Genie. But consider your clientele. Where do you advertise? *Soldier of Fortune, The Alien Invasion, Spy Book.* Surely you know some serious conspiracy fanatics."

"We prefer the term realists."

"So, I have come to the right guy?" Willie asks.

"What do you need to know?"

"Let's say I had an item I thought might appeal to you realists, that I wanted to sell, how would I go about it?"

"I'd have to know what Willie. Say it's a bit of UFO, I'd advertise in *Fortean Times.* Marilyn Monroe's diary, I'd place an ad in *True Confessions.*"

"How about Kennedy's brain?" Willie asks.

"Jesus! That would cross boundaries. *Soldier of Fortune, True Confessions,* you name it."

"You have any of these magazines?" Willie asks Eugene.

"Promise you won't tell my Mom."

"Promise."

"I subscribe to them all. But I can't tell you if anyone has advertised Kennedy's brain. Business is booming, I've been run off my feet. Come back by the shop and I'll let you have a look through them."

"But your guys might be advertising on the Internet, anywhere from eBay and Amazon to Fetish Land and Dark and Dangerous."

"Aren't those last two porn sites?" Willie asks.

"Lifestyle sites, Willie."

"Can you give me a list of the ones you think are most likely targets for ads?" Willie asks.

"Sure, but you're paying for *dim sum*."

"*Dim sum* and I'll buy a couple of bugs off you. The slap and sticks."

"And not ask for the trade discount," Eugene says.

"Genie, you drive a hard bargain."

"I'm going to give you something else," Eugene says.

"What?" Willie asks.

"I have a list, don't ask how I got it. It's a short list."

"What sort of list?" Willie asks.

"*Dim sum*, four bugs, and I get to meet this girlfriend of yours."

"Okay," Willie agrees after a pause. Eugene believes he's irresistible to women. Maria thinks she's irresistible to men. Willie can't wait.

"It's a list of people who bid at the Kennedy auction at Sotheby's."

Back at the shop Willie digs through the magazines while Eugene gets the list and writes down some Web Sites.

Willie's already found what he's looking for by the time Eugene returns from the back room photocopier. He's carrying several phone books.

"What are those?" Willie asks.

"The bidders."

"Genie, it will take me years to wade through those. Looking for who knows what."

"That is why you come to the Genie. I've organized it for you. Not everyone was successful. That's successful bidders there on the top. Starting with the ones who paid the most money."

Halfway down the page Willie knows what the Genie has been trying to tell him. He pulls his cell phone out of his pocket and starts to make a call.

"Stone Age, man," Eugene says. "Here, use a secure phone." Eugene tosses him a brand new phone, still in the wrapping. "Digital," Eugene says.

"Dingo," Willie says when he finally gets an answer. "I have to see you. Dig a hole."

Twenty minutes later Dingo arrives.

"Anyone follow you?" Willie asks.

"Please," Dingo says.

"As if," Eugene says. He worships Dingo.

"Let's start with the ads," Willie says. "This is the latest one from *Soldier of Fortune.*"

One of a kind item. Recently rediscovered. Conspiracy Americana at its finest. Verifiable. Unique auction. Call now.

"When did the first one run?" Dingo asks.

"Couple of months ago."

"You try calling the 1-800?" Dingo asks.

"Yes," Willie says. "It's a canned voice mail saying, 'If you are interested in our ads and want to know more, leave your name and number and we'll get back to you.' That's it."

"No way of telling where it's being answered?" Dingo asks.

"I already cracked it, boss," Eugene says. "It's right here in Edmonton, somewhere in the 432 region."

"That takes in Pleasantview?" Dingo asks.

"There are some 432 numbers in Pleasantview," Willie says.

"Our instincts were good then, it's a scam," Dingo says.

"Yes, though I'm still not quite sure how it's supposed to work," Willie says.

"Me neither," Dingo says.

"But that isn't why I dragged you down here," Willie says. "I think we're being used. Eugene got his hands on a list of people who are big time collectors of Kennedy memorabilia. Near the top of the list is Dudley Scott. Mike Riley is on the first page as well."

"Riley and Scott are the two guys you saved from going to prison in that mining scam, aren't they?" Eugene asks Dingo.

"Yeah. But come on guys, you can't expect me to believe anyone could be that devious. In all my years in the business I've never met anybody that clever. Where is the payoff for all that work?"

"When we learn how the scam works we'll know that," Willie says.

Willie knows that nothing he can say will change Dingo's mind. It's just past noon and already Willie can smell the booze on Dingo's breath. He isn't thinking clearly. Booze and sex, a potent combination. Willie's seen it fool other people into thinking they're in love.

When Willie gets back to the trailer he finds Maria sound asleep in his bed. He slips out of his clothes and climbs ever so carefully in beside her. She's learned to ride the waves of his presence. He cuddles up against her, wishing things were different. Soon he too is sound asleep.

They wake up in time to wolf down some supper before heading off to begin surveillance of Bob's house. Dingo and Roger will tail Average Bob from the house to the airport, make sure he gets on a plane. Willie and Maria's job is to stay behind, try to figure out if it's a setup, a trap. Make sure nobody else is in the house, or shows up later.

They have brought some of Eugene's toys for the purpose. The two of them sit on 70th Avenue in a white utility van. Ron's Contracting. The ladders and pipes on the roof hide a variety of antennas. The van fits in almost anywhere. In any neighbourhood, at any time, someone is having something fixed.

The star piece of equipment is a parabolic mike. It amplifies sound many thousandfold. Unfortunately, once Bob finally leaves for the airport, the only sound coming from the house is an odd "skritch, skritch."

Listening to nothing gets very boring after a while so Willie tries to get Maria to tell him what Bob Struter said. She won't. He threatens to use an old Samoan torture on her. She still refuses. He grabs her right foot, strips off her sock and shoe. She tries to fight him off but is helpless.

Willie starts by rubbing the foot gently between his palms.

"What are you doing?" Maria asks.

"Warming it up, the torture works better that way," he says. Then he lifts her foot up to his mouth. Begins to lick it. She's reduced to giggles. "Tell me everything," he says.

"Never," Maria responds. Willie begins to suck on her big toe. At first it's like he's sucking a lollipop. Soon he's sucking her toe fully into his mouth, right up to the sole of her foot, and then forcing it back out with his tongue. It's intensely sexual. She feels herself rushing towards orgasm, but every time she gets close he stops sucking.

She's about to spill all the beans when Roger and Dingo's car pulls up. Willie puts Maria's foot down.

"Can all Samoan men do that?" Maria asks breathlessly. "Can they all do that?"

"I don't know," Willie says. "On *falemusu* it was something we learned after we learned to kiss and before we started going down on each other. It's a perfect size, the toe. Midway between a penis and a clitoris. Now help me with my gear."

Willie has a vest to carry all the tools he may need. It's worn like a corset and tied very tightly so that no loose material catches, leaving telltale clues. Maria has to put her foot in Willie's back and lean back like she was sailing to pull the cinches tight.

Next comes the headgear. It's a series of straps that holds a small camera on Willie's head. Maria will sit in the van and watch a monitor. She will see and hear everything Willie does. In Willie's thick, dark hair, the straps almost disappear.

Finally Willie steps into his climbing shoes. They are very quiet, but their real benefit is that, if he has to, he can go almost straight up a wall. After checking every piece of equipment one final time, Willie steps out of the van and walks toward Roger and Dingo.

"Hey," Maria calls after him.

"Yeah," Willie says, stopping.

"He thinks you are a repressed homosexual."

"Who does?" Willie asks.

"Dr. Struter. That's why you have writer's block."

"What did you tell him?"

"That you're a repressed heterosexual."

CHAPTER · 23

Breaking into the house isn't easy. The toughest part of most break-ins is looking nonchalant so the neighbours will think you belong. Carrying a clipboard helps and so does wearing coveralls, but even with all kinds of costumes and props there is still a period where the neighbours might be watching you and wondering what you are doing. That is a big part of the jazz of being a burglar. But in this case, the neighbours can't see the house. It's walled off by trees and hedges and the garage.

By the time Willie joins Dingo and Roger they've already found the alarm box and it's a lulu. Often, stupidly, the alarm box is just up under the eaves, or hidden in the garage and all the various wires are labelled telling you what door or window is represented by what wire. That makes the job of the burglar a lot easier.

In this case the alarm box is on the side of the house midway between the second floor and the roof. The three men make a return trip to the van for an aluminum extension ladder, cutting through one of Bob's neighbours' yards. In this case they know that the neighbours in question work nights.

One of the reasons that Willie would like Dingo to sober up and stay that way is because Dingo is much better at gaining illegal entry to all manner of places than Willie will ever be. At least he is when he's sober and his hands aren't shaking with the DTs. Willie hates heights, and the idea of climbing a flimsy ladder in the dark gives him the heebee-jeebies.

When Willie gets up to the alarm he discovers it has its own alarm. That's when he realizes just how difficult this job may be. Willie takes out his toolbox and, balancing on the shaky ladder, wires his way around the alarm box alarm. He uses alligator clamps to connect up the circuit and then carefully removes the alarm wires from their terminal. He takes the alarm box off its bracket mounts and lifts it free of the wall, at least as far as the wires that remain attached will let him. Experience has taught Willie that it is best never to work with an alarm in its brackets. It's too easy to exert more force than you mean to when you are attaching and detaching clamped wires. Holding his flashlight in his mouth, he gently pries the box open with a screwdriver. He is careful not to leave a scratch.

Inside the box none of the wires are labelled. The wires cross and recross and Willie is pretty sure that this was meant to confuse any thief, to make them wonder if each alarm has its own alarm. He's fairly certain that it's all just smoke and mirrors. If it was really wired in that complicated a way, false alarms would then be a common occurrence and no one would respond to a real break-in. So he goes eenie, meanie, minie, moe and picks a blue one. He thinks it's probably a ground floor window alarm he's messing with. Willie places the clip from one end of his jumper wire to the terminal of an incoming wire that he isn't planning to play with, and connects the other end to a outgoing terminal. Once again he gently removes a wire from its terminal. The alarm should think it's still getting a signal from an intact window.

Once he's finished with rearranging the wiring of the box he reattaches it to the wall bracket mount. That's in case someone wanders by while they are in the house. Nothing like a alarm dangling in the night to let every Tom, Dick, and Harry know there is a burglary in progress.

Then he walks around the house using his magnetometer to search for an electric field, or the absence of one. The first three windows he tries are all hot, the fourth, a bay window, is not. He gives Roger and Dingo, who've been watching the entire process in silence, the thumbs up sign. The part of the window that opens to allow for ventilation, in this case a juicy side panel that even Willie could fit through, is locked on the inside. The first thing Willie tries is giving the window a little push with a crowbar, gently, gently, just in case the window isn't really locked. An amazing number of people pay a fortune for state-of-the-art locks and then don't use them properly, or at all. Unfortunately, in this case the window is well secured.

Willie thinks about the problem for a time, squatting beside the window. None of his tools will fit through the gap between window and frame and reach the lock. He tries anyway. Even if they did reach, the lock is a screw-down. Somehow Willie would have to reach in and wrap something around the screw and loosen it.

Willie heads back to the alarm box. He thinks he may now understand how the wiring is set up. Ten minutes later he's reconnected the bay window and successfully disconnected the rear door from its alarm, but there is a new complication, a cctv. The damn little camera will record anyone approaching the door. If Willie cuts off its power supply, he may trigger another alarm. Willie's solution is simple, he connects the leads from a powerful battery to it and fries its internal circuits. With luck Bob will think it's a lightning strike or an internal malfunction that is responsible, which would actually be the smart money bet. Willie is pretty sure that the camera is still broadcasting a signal, but one that looks much like TV static.

It is half an hour of nerve-racking work to pick the three locks on the back door. Willie holds the pick in one hand and the tumbler depressor in the other and fiddles, cursing and muttering under his breath. Willie is pretty sure the entire set-up is far tougher than average, that even a pro would be having problems. With each new barrier, Roger gets more and more excited. He's sure there must be great riches inside. Willie isn't convinced.

He would have long since been inside the house if he hadn't been trying so hard to leave no evidence that he had been there. If all he'd wanted to do was pillage and plunder he'd have been in and gone by now, with his arms full of loot, if there was any loot to be had.

When Willie finally gets the door open Dingo and Roger are all ready to rush inside. Willie grabs each of them with one massive hand, holding them back. With the two of them literally pushing up against his back Willie slips on a pair of night vision goggles he picked up at an army surplus store in Missoula, Montana. The entryway is crisscrossed with infrared sensors. It looks possible, if they lie on the floor and crawl, that they can slip under the beam of the lowest sensor.

Willie goes first. He lies on his back and wiggles along the floor. He watches through his goggles to see if at any point he interrupts the beam. His theory is that if a man his size can slip underneath the sensor it should be no problem for the svelte figures of Roger and Dingo. Willie is staring intently at the beam as his chest goes underneath it when he feels something wet on his face.

Suddenly he is under seige by Bassett hounds. It seems to Willie there are more than three of them. They are licking his face and jumping up and down on his chest, repeatedly breaking the beam. The three dogs are also howling joyously, a sound at least as loud and annoying as any car alarm. Dingo and Roger are reduced to giggles by Willie's predicament.

Thinking about it, Willie realizes the infrared has to be a joke, a way of amusing the dogs. It's the number of beams, the intricate pattern. He thinks about sharing this with Roger and Dingo but doesn't. Why spare them the fun of getting a facial massage? Past the sensors he climbs to his feet and Roger begins crawling under the sensors. Willie waits for the dogs to descend on Roger. They don't, instead they remain at Willie's feet, woofing, and jumping up and down, paying no attention to Roger. Once Roger and Dingo are both through, they set out to explore the house. Willie is still accompanied by his three new pals.

The house is beautifully decorated, but it has sort of a show-home feeling, as if no one really lives there. None of the furnishings tell a story. Usually when you break into a house, the furniture and possessions tell you a great deal about the person who lives there. Not with this house, not with Average Bob, who maybe wasn't so average after all.

Even Willie is impressed by how clean everything is, especially with the dogs and cat. The bed in the master bedroom looks like it was made by a Marine master sergeant. The flowers have been freshly watered. Willie can't find any sign of any of the magazines that Bob supposedly subscribes to and that troubles him.

Before Willie has much chance to work out what all this cleanness means, Dingo finds a floor safe, cunningly hidden under the cat's litter box. He comes over to Willie who is searching the kitchen cabinets. Dingo tugs on his sleeve. Points at the safe. Willie gives him the thumbs up sign and then holds up two fingers.

Before Willie can do anything about the safe he has to do something about the dogs. They are beginning to drive him crazy. His solution is to try feeding them. There are two bags of food in the pantry, President's Choice and Eukenuba. Willie fills a bowl with the Eukenuba and puts it down. The three hounds dive at it simultaneously. The bowl goes skittering across the floor with the dogs in hot pursuit.

"Can you open that?" Roger whispers. Willie considers mentioning the possibility of voice activated mikes. But knows the damage is already done.

"I can't," Dingo says. "Never could."

"How about you?" Roger asks Willie.

"I doubt it," Willie says. "I've got the tools and I understand the concept but safe-cracking isn't a skill I've spent much time on."

Maria is watching this all through the camera and finally she turns on the two-way radio. Static fills Willie's ears.

"Use the squelch knob," he tells Maria. After a brief pause the static increases dramatically.

"The other way. Turn the knob the other way."

Maria swears, then says: "Try 21 right, 32 left, 43 right."

"Yeah, sure," Willie says, humouring her.

"I'm serious, just try it. I'll tell you all the ways I know to please a man if you do."

For some reason, in a darkened house, over a two-way radio, this sounds very sexy. Willie kneels beside the safe and cautiously spins the combination dial to the right until the indicator arrow points to 21, then he goes left to 32, and back right to 43. Nothing seems to happen but when Willie pulls on the handle, the safe door opens. Inside there is one plain manila envelope. On the cover it says, "To Whom It May Concern."

"How did Maria do that?" Roger whispers. Willie briefly considers choking him. No names, they told him over and over again before they entered the house.

Willie, the only one with a two-way mike, relays the question to Maria.

"A trade secret. If I told you that I'd have to tie you down and have a buzzard eat your eyes. Actually it's his student ID number from the University of Alberta."

"What do you think?" Dingo asks Willie. "A will, real estate deed, what? If we open it, he's going to know we were here."

"Guys, I think we put it back, close the safe, and, if I can convince these dogs to let me go without a fight, we get out of here lickety split. The place is giving me the creeps. I think it's all some sort of elaborate practical joke." He pauses to tickle one of the hounds under the chin, and another behind the ear.

"Steam it open," Maria's disembodied voice says.

"Does that actually work?" Willie asks.

"If you are very careful it does," Maria says. "I used to steam open all of the Raklos's mail. They never caught on."

After hunting around in the kitchen for a teakettle and putting water in it and bringing it to a boil, Dingo, Roger, and Willie are wound tighter than a golf ball. The letter shakes in Willie's hand as he tries to hold it just right so steam soaks the glue strip without getting the rest of the letter wet. Finally he lays the letter down on the kitchen table and begins to gently probe the flap with the thinnest blade of his Swiss Army knife. Minutes pass as the blade works its way carefully from one side of the envelope to the other. Finally Willie lifts the flap. Rather than reach into the envelope, he dumps the contents on the table.

The contents of the envelope are clear and unambiguous. First there is a photograph. The star of the shot is a brain floating in a jar filled with clear liquid. The jar is lovingly held by Average Bob. The only other thing in the envelope is a standard business card. Just a plain white business card. But there is no printing on it, just a hand-written note. "If you want to talk about Kennedy's brain, call (780) 555-7258."

It takes Willie, Dingo, and Roger almost half an hour to backtrack out of the house, removing all evidence of their presence, though Willie isn't certain why they are still bothering. They all pile into the back of the van for a conference.

"It looks like we've been hornswoggled," Roger says.

"Bamboozled," Dingo says.

"Hoodwinked," Willie says.

"The question is, how did he know we were coming?" Willie says.

"The question is, was it us he intended that message for?" Roger says.

"The question is, why go to all the trouble of setting up such an elaborate front?" Dingo says.

"The question is, what are you going to do now?" Maria says.

"I say we call him up right now and I make an offer for the brain," Roger says.

"I don't think it's that simple," Dingo says. "If he didn't intend that message for us then there is another player in the game and there might be a bidding war. If he did intend it for us then who does he think we are, a local PI firm, or a very serious collector? And in either case why doesn't he just come to us? That would seem the simplest way."

"Maybe he's afraid that we are part of the conspiracy to kill John Kennedy or to cover it up," Roger says. "I mean, if he's a conspiracy buff."

Willie shrugs. "But we don't know if he is or was ever interested in the Kennedy assassination. He's got us playing guessing games. I think we've got to go back and check everything again. Try to figure out how much of his background Mr. Average Bob planted for us to find."

"Honestly, how much could that brain be worth, to go to all this trouble?" Maria asks.

"I know at least one collector I could sell that brain to for a million dollars or more. If I got an auction together I think it would probably end up going for two and a half or even three million dollars. I could get more if I could auction it off in public, let the entire world know I had it, but of course that'll never happen," Roger says.

"Why not?" Maria asks.

"Well first up there is the little issue of ownership. The law in the United States is pretty vague but usually the remains of an autopsy — the body, organs, blood, and tissue samples — belong to the family. If the family doesn't claim them, then they belong to the state.

"On top of which, in this case there will be some very heavy players wanting to control that brain."

"Like who?" Willie asks.

Rogers shrugs. "FBI, CIA, all the electronic and print media, the Smithsonian, the National Archives, the Senate, even the Supreme Court. Thinking about it, maybe the military as well. None of them, with the possible exception of the Smithsonian, are going to want to pay for the pleasure of ownership. The Smithsonian has quite a collection of Kennedy assassination memorabilia but they usually pay about a tenth what the same object would fetch at auction.

"I never intended to auction it, of course. My plan has always been to call a large press conference, announce my discovery and introduce a panel of experts that have been given a chance to examine the brain. I've got a hand-picked group lined up, all eminent pathologists and forensic scientists, and all sworn to secrecy. In order to ensure their silence, they've agreed, if I ever find the brain, to being locked up in a remote laboratory where there will be no outside communication possible. At this news conference they'll tell what they've learned and then I'll give the brain to the Smithsonian on behalf of the American people. But none of that is possible if I have to pay too much for the brain."

"What would too much be?" Willie asks.

"I might be able to go as high as a million, if I had a chance to get a good look at the brain."

"I want to know what Maria thinks we should do next," Willie says.

Maria frowns. "I think Dingo is right. Average Bob has us playing guessing games. I think maybe we should make him start playing some guessing games of his own. Mr. Willie, those dogs loved you, right?"

"Yes, they certainly seemed to be excessively enthusiastic in my presence."

"Well, I think you should give them a gift."

"A gift?" Willie asks.

"Tomorrow we get some fancy wrapping paper and a shoe box. We put those sneakers you are wearing in the box and we wrap the box all up in pretty paper and leave it on Average Bob's doorstep. He takes it inside. Long before he's opened it, the hounds will be all over it. He opens it up and it's this old pair of sneakers. His first thought is going to be, 'What type of weirdo sent me this? What does it mean? Won't those dogs ever stop barking? Did someone break in? Has my message been sent and received?' Now who is playing guessing games?"

"It's brilliant," Dingo says. "It would make me ask questions."

"It think it's crazy," Roger says. "Though I must admit it would make me speculate."

"It would sure make me stop and rethink who was in control of the process. It might even make me a little peevish," Willie says.

"I'd be downright grumpy. It's like we are saying he has to do better than that or we aren't interested in playing. And after he went to the trouble of setting up this elaborate charade, all designed to put the ball in our court. Then we toss it right back at him," Maria says.

Everybody nods in agreement. Willie starts the van and pulls away. Meanwhile, Maria is wondering to herself why Bob and Roger are stalling.

She assumes they are having trouble lining up marks, but as long as they are, she might as well have a little fun with it.

"Hey boys, maybe we should put advertisements in various nutbar magazines claiming to have the brain. That'll smoke him out, I bet."

Roger breaks out in a sudden sweat. Looks quite grey.

"What's the matter, Roger?" Dingo asks. "The excitement too much for you?"

CHAPTER · 24

The morning after the burglary Willie measures Maria, at her insistence. He's been trying to ignore the obvious. Maria is growing at an astonishing rate. He measures her three times, trying to figure out if she is cheating somehow. He even checks the tape measure to make sure it's accurate and that she hasn't tampered with it.

"Five foot nine and three-guarter inches," Willie says.

"Five foot, ten inches," Maria says.

In the bathroom, before they shower, Willie weighs Maria.

"One hundred and sixty-four and a half pounds," Willie says.

"One hundred and sixty-five pounds," Maria says, looking down at the scale.

The pigment blotch that started in the small of her back has spread all over Maria's body. The only patches of Maria's skin that are noticeably lighter than Willie's are her armpits, her elbows, her knees, the palms of her hands, and the soles of her feet.

"I think it's my womb genes," Maria says.

"Womb genes?" Willie asks.

"I find another article in the paper, *The Times of London*, that's a good paper isn't it?"

"One of the best," Willie says.

"Well this article says that in the womb all kinds of genes are working that don't work once you are born and gravity starts to take a hold."

"Do you have a copy of this article, Maria?"

"Just wait," she says and dashes out of the bathroom. In a couple of minutes she is back and hands Willie a short clipping. He sits on the toilet to read it.

Gene Changes Found In Weightless Space

Nigel Hawkes
Times of London

For years, enthusiasts from the United States space agency NASA have been saying that space stations will be a wonderland for manufacturing all kinds of exotic materials, from new drugs to perfect crystals.

Sceptics have seen this as a political claim designed to lever money out of Congress. Until now, few experiments in space had shown dramatic differences from the same experiments carried out at much lower cost on Earth. But a flight in April 1998 by the space shuttle Columbia produced far more interesting results. Experiments on board showed that the quantity of proteins produced by genes was altered by microgravity. "We found that there were dramatic effects, that many, many genes change, " Prof. Timothy Hammond, of Tulane University told The Scientist.

The experiments, briefly reported in Nature Medicine *earlier this year, involved human kidney cells. The cells were kept alive in a culture dish and their behaviour compared with similar cells from the same donor kept on the ground, both stationary and in a device, called a rotating wall vessel, that simulates some of the conditions of microgravity.*

At the end of the flight the cells that had been in the weightless conditions in space were compared with those that had stayed on the ground by using microarrays, small ceramic chips on to which many short sections of DNA have been attached. These chips are a way of measuring which genes have been active.

On Earth only five of the 10,000 stationary genes monitored had changed their expression during the six days of the experiment. In the microgravity machine on earth, 914 genes had changed, while in space, 1,632 had changed.

One theory why this should happen is that the cells are, in effect, returning to their behaviour in the womb, when a different repertoire of genes is used by the developing embryo.

The womb is a semi-weightless environment because the embryo floats in neutral buoyancy. It may be, says co-investigator Thomas Goodwin, of NASA's Johnson Space Centre in Houston, that the cells flown in Columbia were reprogrammed into an embryonic state by the flight and reverted to long forgotten patterns.

The idea is to try to understand why microgravity has the effects it does, and then try to replicate the effects in Earth-based laboratories.

"I think my genes have reverted to long-forgotten patterns," Maria says.

"I don't know, I'm pretty sceptical but I'm worried that there might be something seriously wrong with you. If you'll cooperate, I want to talk some of my friends into doing tests on you," Willie says.

"I'll let them do whatever tests they want, but there is nothing wrong with me. I feel scrumptious," Maria says.

They get in to see Freddie Egan, Edmonton's pre-eminent endocrinologist the next day. "It must be her hormones. They must be out of whack," he says. Then he has her go for blood tests and a urinalysis.

Once they are through with those tests, they go to see Wayne Mahovich, Edmonton's pre-eminent neurologist. "This isn't good. Maybe some kind of tumour," he says. Maria just laughs but Dr. Mahovich sends her for a NMR and CAT scan. That eats up the rest of the day. Willie looks worried but Maria is not. She thinks to herself, I'm turning Samoan.

From the hospital they drive over to resume surveillance on Mr. Average Bob. Once he leaves the house for the day, Willie delivers the evocatively wrapped dirty running shoes. Maria, in a fit of creativity, has used wrapping paper from a wicca supply store. It is covered in astrological signs and ogham script. She thinks that will discombobulate Mr. Average Bob even more than the shoes.

Dingo has struck a deal with one of Mr. Average Bob's neighbours, who thinks Bob may be a dangerous drug-dealing pervert. The neighbour's certainty is based on the fact that Mr. Average Bob likes to lie naked, in the privacy of his back yard, suntanning. In return for two hundred dollars, the neighbour has granted Maria and Willie access to the ancient motor home he has parked in his back yard. From the roof of the motor home they can watch Mr. Average Bob's front door, and his back yard.

Willie works on his thesis while they await Bob's return. Maria is practising her tarot-reading skills. She's using a *Sforza* deck and she's using the

Romanian technique, about the only useful thing she ever learned from the Rakloses. She is trying to figure out the key to igniting Willie's lust.

The Devil card keeps coming up in weird ways. He straddles a dry well to which a man and a woman have bound themselves. The cord that binds the man and the woman is long. It fits snugly around her neck and his wrists but fits loosely through a ring at the base of the fount. The man's hands are tied at one end, yet it appears that the cord is very loosely wrapped around his wrists. The rope is slip-knotted around the woman's neck, but her hands are free so that she can liberate herself or the man at any time. She is looking passionately at the man and he is looking passionately at the devil.

Maria tries to draw parallels with her relationship to Willie. She certainly looks at Willie with that sort of passion. She didn't set out to fall in love with him. She simply planned to use and then discard him, once she had her money and, even more importantly, once she became a Samoan woman. But each time he dodges one of her sexual gambits, her desire for him increases. Even weirder is the fact that with each pound she gains, she finds herself feeling increasingly guilty about her plans for Willie.

Maria looks at the card. The question is: what devil is Willie worshipping? Maybe if it weren't for Mark Twain, Willie would chase her around the trailer, trying to have her. Or perhaps it is the ancestor practices of his Samoan family calling to him, maybe that's the siren call of the devil. And what is the right thing to do? Should she push him at his devil? Should she keep trying to get Willie to talk with his ancestors, finish his damn thesis, or should she deliberately sabotage him?

The other card that keeps coming up in the power position is the Tower. It seems to Maria that the Tower is erupting like a volcano. It is spewing forth knowledge and a new beginning as it releases the Eclipsed Sun and the Star. A hanged man and a woman leap out joyously. Nana Raklo taught Maria that this new beginning comes from changes within, not from external forces.

If you put the two cards together it's like they are trying to tell Maria that she and Willie have enslaved themselves but it is within their power to set themselves free. The question is how? Maria lets herself fantasize about the possible sexual significance of the imagery. Lately at night she hasn't been sleeping very well and has been getting up and reading her way through Willie's home library. For a solid week, her reading has consisted of the

Collected Writings of Freud. She believes that Freud was probably right about the central importance of sex in shaping lives and wrong about nearly everything else.

Maria thinks that even in the Renaissance, when the *Sforza* deck was created, the artists understood the sexual tableau they were playing out in those cards. A woman dominated totally by a man, possibly sexually aroused by strangulation, certainly by the domination. The first man enthralled by the devil, an unambiguously virile male, with overtones of homo-eroticism.

Then in the Tower, the Eclipsed Sun, representing the Dark Lord, and the Star, representing the Mother Goddess, emerging together, blissful. They have sex of a cosmic sort and the power relationship has changed. The man has given up his homo-erotic fixations and now he's completely under the woman's power.

That, Maria concludes, is the secret to completing the transition to becoming a Samoan woman. She must succeed in seducing Willie, and the sex must be amazing. He must become her love-slave. That's what will finally set her free. And maybe him too.

Maria's ruminations are interrupted by the return of Mr. Average Bob. He approaches the package with great caution. He kneels beside it for some time, then edging carefully around it, he lets himself into the house. In a couple of minutes he emerges with the Basset hounds. They head straight for the package, all crowding in, trying to be the first to get a good sniff, pushing the package around with their noses. Then in unison they start to howl and hop up and down.

Mr. Average Bob bends down and takes the package away from the dogs. They go crazy trying to climb his leg and get at the wrapped box. With a fine attention to detail, he manages to remove the wrapping paper intact. He lifts the lid of the shoebox. For a moment he just stands there staring down at the box. Then he extracts Willie's old running shoes and tosses them, one at a time, out into the night. The hounds roar after them, snuffling and growling and howling as they fight over them. Mr. Average Bob stands on his front veranda and laughs; at first it's just a giggle but it evolves into a deep, belly-shaking guffaw. It isn't quite the reaction Maria had been hoping for. In fact, for a woman used to controlling men and events, nothing is really going according to plan.

The next day Maria and Willie revisit Drs. Egan and Mahovich. Dr. Egan looks over all the test results. "You're fine, endocrinologically speaking," he says. "All your hormone levels are completely normal, nothing to worry about in that department. Honestly, I'm a shade mystified. I'd like to run some more tests." Dr. Mahovich looks over the CAT scan and the NMR, "You're fine, no placques, no lesions, no tumours. Your brain is perfect. I'd say we have to look elsewhere for the answer to your problem. I'd like to run some more tests." Maria declines to allow either doctor to poke beyond the limits of their speciality.

They move on to Dr. Felicity Sebastian, Edmonton's pre-eminent dermatologist. "Very, very interesting," she says. "Some sort of fungus perhaps, or a weird drug interaction, maybe Lyme disease. Never seen anything to equal it. We'd definitely better run some tests, take some skin samples, both from the affected area and those small patches that haven't changed yet, do some blood tests. You aren't taking any drugs, are you?" Once Maria has reassured Dr. Sebastien that she is drug-free, she heads off to get more blood taken.

From Dr. Sebastian's office they head on see Dr. Freida Washington, Edmonton's pre-eminent obstetrician-gynaecologist. "You aren't by any chance pregnant, are you?" she asks. "Perish the thought," Maria answers.

For that you have to have sex, Maria thinks to herself. And she and Willie haven't had sex, haven't had sex, haven't had sex. That's really beginning to bother her. Not nearly as much as Dr. Washington's plan to do a pelvic exam and Pap smear. Willie gets to leave, lucky man. Maria entertains herself thinking about creating elaborate schemes for punishing Willie for putting her through this when there isn't a damn thing wrong with her except she's turning Samoan. After the pelvic it's off to have an ultra-sound. That's also tons of fun, trying to blow up your own bladder. All doctors are sadists, Maria thinks and adds more sins to Willie's growing list. He won't have sex with me but I have to have a pelvic and an ultra-sound.

The next morning Willie and Maria return to see Drs. Sebastien and Washington. Dr. Sebastien examines all of Maria's test results and says: "Normal, they are all normal, there is nothing the matter with your skin, nothing. I find that hard to believe, I mean you are visibly changing colour. If you were getting lighter, there are diseases that cause that, but not darker, not like you are. You would be developing raised patches with any of those diseases. I think we should run some more tests."

Maria politely declines.

Dr. Washington examines her test results. "There is nothing out of the ordinary here. You seem to be a remarkably healthy young woman."

"Don't you want to run more tests?" Maria asks.

"I don't think I'd learn anything, nothing I'd be likely to understand, anyway. You seem healthy and vital and that's all that counts. You should know that there are other cases like yours."

"People turning Samoan?" Maria asks.

"No. But similar things. A man who grew a foot and a half in a week. A woman who turned blue, she thought she was a space alien, and turned blue to prove it to the rest of the world. Even one well-documented case where a woman turned into a man, without drugs or surgery. The mind can play amazing tricks with the body.

"That said, I'd like to forward your file to a psychiatrist. Dr. Nigel Dempster. He's done some interesting work on bizarre cases."

"Freudian?"

"I believe so."

"Why not," Maria says, thinking she might finally have some fun.

CHAPTER · 25

The next morning Willie is sitting in the kitchen eating grapefruit and reading the *Edmonton Journal*. Willie is a newspaper fanatic. Before Maria entered his life Willie started each morning by reading Canada's two national newspapers; *The Globe and Mail* and the *National Post* as well as both of Edmonton's dailies, the *Journal* and the *Sun*. Watching Willie waste a perfectly good morning reading newspapers offends Maria. Willie is now lucky if he gets time by himself to read one paper.

While he reads, Willie is thinking about Maria. He's not sure how much longer he can ignore Maria's naked body parading around his trailer. His WASP side found her original self to be attractive, but he had been able to submerge his feelings. Now that she seems to be transforming herself, his Samoan half is becoming *very* attracted to the new Maria. But he still feels a need to keep his guard up. He isn't sure why, but he has learned to trust his instincts.

Maria comes into the kitchen in a huff. She is dressed like a Wall Street investment banker. Except she's gone a little overboard and looks like a male investment banker.

"Mr. Willie, get a move on."

"Why? What's up?"

"We're going to be late for our appointment," Maria says.

"What appointment?" Willie asks.

"With Dr. Dempster."

"That's this morning?"

"In about forty-five minutes. So cart ass."

The doctor's office is all cool pastels and oak trim. Very neutral, peaceful even. Dr. Dempster sits behind a giant oak desk. He is a thin gnome of a man. Willie expects him to object to Maria's insistence that Willie accompany her into the session.

"Pleased to meet you, Maria, Willie," Dr. Dempster says, standing up. He pauses in front of her, admiring the suit. Then he clicks his heels together, bows formally, lifts her right hand to his lips and kisses the back of it. Maria giggles. They all sit down.

Dr. Dempster jumps right in. "I want to hear all about how you are trying to turn Samoan. Let's start with why."

Maria takes a deep breath. "I always felt tiny. Tiny and helpless. Tiny and helpless with big breasts. Men would look at me and want me and think they could just take me because I was small and weak. When I came to Canada with my new husband and his family I didn't have the protection of my *kumpania*, of my extended family, anymore. My husband beats me and he and his family take advantage of me in all sorts of ways. Then one day in a magazine in a doctor's office I see this picture. It's of a Samoan princess, the daughter of a big chief and she's enormous, the ground must shake when she walks on it. I think that if I get to be huge and strong no man can ever hurt me again."

"Do you think being this huge Samoan woman is going to stop men from wanting you?" Dr. Dempster asks.

"Men, they all want Marilyn Monroe, not Oprah Winfrey when she used to be big."

Dr. Dempster nods. "Let's say that at least some men want those girlish sorts of women. Why do you think that is? Let's try Marilyn first. She wasn't exactly skinny. Why did men want her?"

"That's easy, they thought she was a willing slut and would be really good in bed."

"Why did they think she was sexually available?"

"The way she walked, the way she talked."

"What about the way she talked?"

"She sounded like Shaggy Lees. Once at the fair, he inhaled helium, and he sounded like Marilyn Monroe, kind of."

"Who else might sound like Marilyn?"

Maria frowned. "I don't know."

"Do some little girls sound like Marilyn? Did Marilyn sound like she was still a little girl?"

"Yes. She did, didn't she? Wait. Barbie-big boobs, little girl, models-big boobs, little girls, almost not women, Marilyn-big boobs-little girl. You're saying men want little girls with big boobs."

"If they do, why do they?"

"They want little girls because little girls they can control."

"Why do they want big boobs, do you think?"

"The big boobs mean the little girls are sexy people. They are big enough to have sexy feelings, those little girls, but small enough that men can overpower them."

The doctor looks at Willie who stares at the carpet.

"In conventional psychiatry they call what you're talking about the rape fantasy of the undeveloped ego and all men have the fantasy. Even gay men have their own versions. Having sex with someone you can completely dominate is one of the meta-themes of human sexuality."

"That's nonsense," Willie says.

"We'll deal with your issues later, Willie. But first, tell me Maria, were you ever raped?"

Dr. Dempster sits back in his chair. Almost nonchalantly.

"No."

"Never had sex when you didn't want to?"

"Yes. But that doesn't make it rape, does it?"

"Doesn't necessarily. Did you say no, let your partner know you didn't want to do it?"

"No."

"Should they have known you didn't want to have sex?"

"I don't know."

"Then you're in an area of vast debate. Many feminists believe that unless you make your interest completely clear, say something like, 'yes, do me, please do me, I want you, I beg you, do me' then you've been raped. And I don't mean to make fun of their position, it has considerable merit. Were any of these men in a position of power over you?"

"What do you mean?"

"Father, older brother, uncle, teacher, husband, boss, doctor, policeman, and on and on."

"Yes, they were in a position of power over me."

"Did they use that power to make you have sex?"

"I don't think so."

"But how can you know for sure? It can be so subtle. Maybe you want to please them that night because the next day you're going shopping and you hope they'll buy you something nice, or worse maybe the next day you have a big test they'll be marking, worse yet maybe you know that when you don't please them in bed they beat you. The truth is men are almost always in a position of power over any woman they sleep with, and it's easy for them, often inadvertently to use that power."

"Let me try turning all this on its head. Do you ever fantasize about raping a man?"

Maria glances at Willie and blushes.

"I guess that flushing means yes and its none of my business. But have you ever considered that you just want to get big in order to be able to rape men for real?"

"That's ridiculous," Maria says it for Willie this time.

"No, it's not. Men have been raping you your entire life and you're mad as hell and you aren't going to take it any more. You are going to get big and strong and then they are going to see how it feels."

Maria sticks out her tongue at the doctor.

"My wife does that too," he continues, unfazed. "Tell me more about how you think you brought about this sudden change."

"You'll just make fun of me."

"Whatever else I'll do, I won't make fun of you, Maria. Let me prove I'm not the ogre you think. I'll tell you how I think you did it."

"Okay, egotistical man, you go for it," Maria sniffs.

Dr. Dempster sits back in his huge chair. "You prayed. You probably believe in God in several forms. I'd guess you were raised in India, that's an easy one given your medical records say you are East Indian by birth, but I'll bet you were born in one of the lower castes. I'll go way out on a limb and narrow it down for you; you were born in one of the following classes: Kanjar, Kalander, Bajigar, Nat, Jadugar, Lohar, Banjara, or Maslet. I'd bet on the Lohar, the Kalander, or the Maslet."

Maria nods, wondering if Freud taught fortune-telling.

"So my guess is you prayed to Allah, you prayed to the Father, and you prayed to Shiva. Kind of covering all your bases. The more I think about it the more I'm sure you have to be Maslet. I think you cast tantric spells and chanted magic chants. How am I doing so far? Judging by the fact your mouth is hanging open I guess pretty well. Though that expression on Willie's face suggests he thinks I'm cheating, and to a certain extent he's right.

"In your medical records you are pretty clearly identified as a gypsy woman who was born in India. All I did is ask myself what sort of person, from what caste, could fit into Romni society and get along. There are only a few castes that would be able to make such a transition. Frankly, people born in most of those castes wouldn't be up to convincing themselves that they could turn Samoan. But the Maslets, particularly the Maslet women, they'd be capable, though the circumstances would have to be extraordinary. Then the question becomes what sort of process would a Maslet woman follow to try to become Samoan and how would years spent among the Rom affect that.

"Unfortunately, the accuracy of my guessing has made you begin to wonder if you really do just want to get fat so that you can rape men. In psychiatric jargon we call that position I argued you into the opov."

"The opov?" Maria asks.

"The opposing point of view. I've been up all night reading your medical files and some articles and books, then I kiss your hand and something deep in the back of my brain goes bitz, beep, honk, hey! over here stupid. Now I have a bizarre theory for why you are turning Samoan, but I want you to stumble upon it yourself, with me just providing a little help. The easiest way to force you towards the discovery I want you to make is to present you with a rational explanation that makes you uncomfortable and then you will, recoiling from that, begin to edge towards my truth. The opposing point of view needs to excite you enough that you may momentarily accept it but it should also gross you out and repel you.

"I figure the real trick with explaining what's going on is that Willie isn't going to believe me. You will, but he won't. I've been watching his face and he is trying very hard to be the doubting Thomas, the rational sceptic.

"Your desire to be a rational man is admirable, Willie. If more people would commit themselves to such a position the world would be a much better place. The problem is that you are so rational you can't admit something miraculous might happen now and again. You just said it's impossible for Maria to be turning Samoan and yet I'm sitting here admiring her and thinking she sure seems to be doing a good job of it so far."

The doctor shifts in his chair. "Maria, what's your favourite Romni swear word, the one you use to describe someone you really hate?"

"Mleccha!" she swears.

"Ever hear it before you became a gypsy?"

"Well, as a matter of fact, I think I heard my father say it under his breath, when he was really mad."

"Know what it means?"

"Not exactly, Grandma Nose said it meant the offspring of a pig and a human."

"It's *rajasthan* for the unclean, it's how the *rajput* aristocracy described the Afghan-Turks," the doctor says. "Let me move along more quickly, I do want to get to my eureka moment. Some people believe the Rom originated in India, many centuries ago. They might have been slaves in Afghanistan for as much as three hundred years. Once the conquest of India was over, in 1192, there wasn't much need for the few tattered slaves out in the desert and they were allowed to wander away. Some of these pre-Rom wandered back toward India.

"The rest wandered westward, ending up, eventually, those that survived, in Tabriz. Tabriz in the years of the thirteenth century was one of the most dynamic and cultured cities in the world, a hub port in an expanding world of trade and commerce, firmly in the control of the Caliphs. Shortly after the arrival of the gypsies the city was cut of from the rest of the Caliphs' empire by the arrival of the hordes of Ghengis Khan. The gypsies, most theories agree, were likely trapped in Tabriz for a hundred years or more, unable to continue their migration, and it is probably there that the final version of the gypsies as we know them developed. As the Mongol threat subsided the gypsies continued their migration into Turkey and eventually Constantinople. From there they spread to Greece, and possibly Egypt. When they arrived in Paris, they claimed to have come from Egypt, thus the term gypsies.

"The reception that the Rom got in Europe varied very much from country to country. In France at first they were welcomed like nobility — exotic, fortune-telling nobility. In Romania, they were hunted for sport."

Dr. Dempster pauses and smiles. "What sort of gypsies were the people you lived with in England, Maria? Bayash?"

"No. We called ourselves Romanitchels."

"Your husband's family are Kalderash I assume?"

"Yes."

"And do they practise coppersmithing?"

"Only when it suits them, as something to tell the police, or welfare. But their father did. His sons are useless, anything that might be work is beyond them."

"What has all this got to do with Maria's problem?" Willie asks, feeling a little bewildered.

"Well, the only way to fully account for the oral histories of these people is to assume that some of them, somehow, escaped from Turkish captivity very early in the process of the Muslim conquest of India. Most scholars think these people intended to return to India, but as we discussed, they were now unclean. Some stragglers probably got swept up by the Mongols and ended up in China and Mongolia. Some appear to have spent the turbulent years of the Mongol invasions in Tibet, before working their way back into India through the back door as it were, Nepal, and Bangladesh.

"But the most adventurous of them took to the seas, settling in various locations throughout the Indian Ocean, the Maldives possibly, various islands in Malaysia and Indonesia. The farthest their great migration is supposed to have taken them is Samoa."

Willie sputters. "No offence, doctor, but you are out of your mind. And we are out of here." He stands up and starts to drag Maria to her feet.

"No. I want to hear what he has to say," Maria commands, her voice pitched high. Willie settles back into his chair with a deflated sound.

"Willie, isn't it true that Samoans believe they are the people of travel, children of the wind?" Dr. Dempster asks.

"Yes we do, " Willie sighs. "The fact is that we respect those who travel, take great pride in how far they've gone. But that doesn't make us gypsies."

"Now, no offence to either you or Maria, but isn't it true that Samoans look on everything and anything as communal property? That they are, um, great thieves?"

"I guess I'd have to admit that some are. But so what?"

"Maria, what do the gypsies call themselves, to themselves?"

"Children of the wind."

"Do the Rom believe everything is communal property?"

"Yes."

"Are they thieves?"

"Yes."

The doctor slaps his desk. "I put forward the following hypothesis, Willie. The Maslets gave rise to the gypsies who gave rise to the Samoans. Thus, there is no genetic reason why Maria can't make the transition from Maslet to gypsy to Samoan."

Maria sticks her tongue out at Willie.

"But just because something could theoretically happen," he continues, "it doesn't mean it will. So what was the trigger? What's the underlying psychology? The biochemistry? I don't believe it's simply Maria's karma to, in one lifetime, recapitulate the travels of the Rom, any more than I believe that Maria is trying to get big so she can rape men."

Dr. Dempster stops, looking a little deflated. "Maria, I want you to think about what I said, the questions I asked, and see if you can't figure out for yourself the psychology involved in your transformation. I think you know what is going on if you'll just admit it. Come back in a day or two and we can talk about it more. Meanwhile I'll do some further research into the possible triggers and biochemistry, so that we can satisfy Willie's rational mind." He ushers them out before either Willie or Maria can ask any questions.

CHAPTER · 26

That afternoon, while Willie is obsessing over the doctor's theory, his own thesis, and Maria's metamorphosis, he decides to go to the farm. He thinks maybe a change of scenery might help him. Maria begs off, claiming she feels like she has a summer cold coming on.

Once Willie is safely on his way to the farm, Maria makes a long distance call. It's a number she's gotten out of Willie's desk. It rings four times, then someone picks up but doesn't say anything.

"Maam, you don't know me, my name is Maria and I'm a friend of your son Willie."

"I know you," a husky male voice says. "You're the gypsy girl Willie is in love with, the one that wants to be a Samoan. I'm Willie's uncle, Duncan. You can call me Dunk."

"How did you know all that? Has Willie told his mom about me?"

"No."

"Did you see me in a vision?"

"I'm sure you are a vision, and I sure wish I'd seen you in a vision, but sadly, no I did not. Whenever Betty, that's Willie's mom, whenever Betty doesn't hear from Willie for a few days she phones up Dingo and checks to make sure Willie is all right. That man can't seem to keep a secret. Well neither can Betty, so I know all about you. I was just flaked out on her couch, getting over the jet sag. I flew in last night, and the phone woke me. Betty's out in the garden, do you want to talk to her?"

"Actually, it's you I want to talk to, but first tell me please what jet sag is?"

"Well, most people when they fly, their internal clock gets all out of whack. Right now I think it's yesterday in Samoa. These people they drag their butts around for some days after flying, trying to re-set their clock, the docs they call that jet lag. Me, I'm a medicine man, I can reset my own clock, no problem. It's the air on those planes gets to me, it's so damn dry it sucks all the tropical moisture right out of me. Then my skin starts to sag, and I have to say I do have a fair amount of skin to sag. If I'm flying somewhere else wet it's okay, I step off the plane and suck up the moisture and re-inflate. But here in Salt Lake City their idea of wet is being licked by a cat so I stay all shrivelled up for a few days, lie around on the couch and drink soda pop by the carton until I plump back up. I call it jet sag. So why do you want to talk to an old Samoan medicine man?"

"Willie has a problem, Dunk. He's working on his Ph.D. thesis. Now I'm not sure why but getting it done is really important to him. He isn't getting it done. He can't figure out what to write about. I guess I can say this to you, I learned how to be a gypsy medicine woman, I know some powerful magic. I used a bit of it to find out what Willie should be writing about. Turns out the answer to his problem lies in his talking to his dead ancestors. Which says you'd know how to do, but he won't. I thought maybe you could help convince him to try it, help him do it."

"I'd like to, I've wanted Willie to follow in my footsteps ever since I realized he had the gift. He sort of knows how. He's even seen me talk with the old ones. My favourite is my cousin John, he was a serious romantic, never met a woman he didn't fall in love with. The problem was he slept with all of them, at least any he could seduce and he was one mighty charming man. If their husbands, boyfriends, or fathers found out, John could talk his way out of it, he had what we call corned beef tongue, that John did. Never bothered to smooth the waves of discontent that rose up when one of his women found out about another. Well all those waves gathered up together and became a tidal wave. The girls, that's what he called them, the girls got together, plotted and planned, hit him on the head one night when he was a little drunk, and castrated him. He lived a lot of years after that, still trying to seduce women, still a romantic. And guess what?"

"I give up, what?" Maria asks.

"He was more successful than ever with the women, even some of the ones what cut his balls off. Got hit by a falling coconut tree, in a big storm. He's the ancestor I go to if I need to know anything about women. Now there is a point to my telling you about John. John, he'd tell me that helping you with Willie isn't good for my health, unless somehow I get Betty to agree to my doing this thing. You know Willie is scared of his Maam?"

"Yes, he's made that clear."

"Well he ain't half as scared of Betty as I am. She's got what you'd probably call the evil eye. She look at you wrong and you start having the kind of luck leads to a palm tree falling on you. Anyway, Betty, when she was just a slip of a girl, Betty she falls head over heels in love with John, doesn't realize he isn't entire. You with me?"

"I think so."

"Well, Betty, she is none too pleased with John when she finds out. Gives him that look, and a coconut palm falls on the guy. Next time I see that look she is mad at Willie's dad, madder than I've ever seen her, no idea what about, and the next day a mountain fell on him. I don't need no looks thanks very much. But I think I know how to get her to go along, think it's her idea maybe."

"How?" Maria asks.

"That Dingo he doesn't miss much, and like I say he's got a big mouth and a loose tongue. He says you and Willie aren't doing it, and it isn't that you aren't trying to get Willie to do it. Long time ago Betty went to a fortune-teller in Los Angeles. Even then, Willie would have been maybe eighteen, she's think about grandkids, has a bit of a thing about it, ever since she tried to convince poor Willie he was a girl. She's worried that Willie will get himself killed before he has any children. He was some wild boy I tell you. This was while he was in and out of jail and always in some sort of fight, though I think mostly kids picked on him, thought it was funny when he went nuts, *musu*. You know what *musu* is?"

"Yes, Willie explained it to me."

"This fortune-teller told Betty there was nothing to worry about. Willie, he'd get over his problems, become a fine man. But grandchildren, that was a different story. Only way she'd have grandkids is if Willie married a woman who could do magic, fertility magic. Dingo pretty much has Betty convinced that you're the one can do this. Of course conception isn't very likely if you aren't having sex.

"I think I can convince her that the only way to get Willie to have sex with you is to have a *kava* rite. I mean ever since Betty learned about you she's been going to the tabernacle of them Late Day Christians and who knows what mumble jumble doing there but at home she's saying *novenas* and lighting candles trying to get you pregnant. Always believed in maximizing her options, that Betty. None of this is working so now she's maybe ready to try the old ways. Add another option."

"Yeah, well, we'd have to find a way to get Willie to go along as well," Maria says. "I don't think just because his Maam says it's okay he's suddenly going to embrace the idea."

"I'm sure you're right. But a few months ago Willie called me wanting help to get Dingo to sober up. I sent him some *kava*. The idea was he'd do a simple *kava* rite and get Dingo to help him. Once Dingo tried *kava* beer, which isn't actually alcoholic at all, he'd never go back to real booze. It's worked great in Australia amongst the Aboriginals. I've never heard from him so I guess he didn't get around to doing it.

"Anyway, we get Dingo to pretend to go on a bender and get Willie all het up and then I'll show up to help Willie do a *kava* rite with Dingo. The worst that can happen is that Dingo gets off booze. Maybe your magic is the real thing and Willie gets his thesis topic and you get laid. Who knows, maybe even Betty gets what she wants. What do you say, shall I shove Betty in the Volvo and truck on up there?"

"Yeah, I think maybe you should," Maria says, thinking that maybe she's not the only one that needs a little help turning Samoan.

Later that day Willie comes back from the farm and picks up Maria and they head into town. When they get to International Investigations Dingo and Roger are waiting for them.

"So where do we go next?" Dingo asks.

"I think we have to intensify our coverage," Willie says.

"In English," Roger says.

"Willie is saying we have to start tailing Bob every minute of every day," Dingo says.

"But doesn't that make it more likely he's going to spot us?" Maria asks.

"Yes, no matter how good we are, how careful, he may make us," Dingo says, "but that isn't necessarily a bad thing."

"Why not?" Roger asks.

"He's planning a scam. We all think so, but none of us can figure out how it's supposed to work. So right now he's in command. We are waiting on him. By tailing him all the time, two good things can happen. First, he doesn't make us and we learn what he's up to, who he's working with," Willie says.

"And the second?" Roger asks.

"He makes us but we still stick on his butt. The pressure starts to get to him," Dingo says. "And he makes a foolish mistake."

"Can I help tail him?" Maria asks.

"You ever watch detective shows on TV, Maria?" Dingo asks.

"Only since I met you guys, now I watch Simon and Simon, Rockford Files, and Magnum, PI," Maria says.

"Reruns," Willie explains.

"And Snoops, I used to watch Snoops, until it got cancelled," Maria says.

"Don't forget VIP, Maria," Willie says.

"Okay, VIP," Maria says.

"The problem with all those shows is none of them had a clue how you tail someone. Magnum does it in a Ferrari for God sake, a red one to boot. Guess how many red Ferraris there are in the state of Hawaii, I checked vehicle registrations, there are five. Phoned the owners, only two are roadworthy at the moment. Like someone isn't going to notice being tailed by a six-foot-five guy who looks like a movie star and drives a bright red Ferrari. Simon and Simon's better, at least AJ looks like he could tail someone, he drives a no-name sedan, wears a simple suit, could be a banker, a lawyer, an accountant, or he wears a windbreaker and slacks or a disguise. Rick he'd be made in a minute, the trademark hat, the monster truck.

"What I'm trying to say is that to successfully follow someone you have to be Joe or Jane average, a blender, wear a suit when you're working downtown, cowboy boots and a Stetson during the Calgary Stampede. You can't be physically odd. That was Rockford's problem, his car wasn't that unusual, but when he got out of it and continued on foot he limped noticeably, and even if you aren't watching for a tail and aren't consciously aware, you do notice things like a limp. You and Willie won't be much help in a close-up tailing job."

"If he makes you, then can I help?" Maria asks.

"Then you and Willie can play," Dingo says. "You know it seems to me this guy is making everything too complicated. I wish he'd just contact Roger and open negotiations. Roger has to be the mark, the intended victim. But instead he keeps stalling. I wonder why?"

"I say we tail him and find out!" Maria offers.

"I agree," Roger says.

"You all know that our tail is just window dressing," Willie says.

"Window dressing?" Roger raises an eyebrow.

"A distraction. Maria is going to do the real damage."

"Me?" Maria asks.

"You. We are going to use your considerable skills as a pickpocket and a close-up magician to put a bug right on him," Willie says.

"You really have lost your mind," Dingo says.

"No I haven't, boss. It's going to be right behind his ear, we'll hear whatever Bob hears and whatever he says. The beauty of it is that while he probably checks his phone and his office, if he has one, and his home, and confederates and strangers for wires and bugs he will never dream of searching himself," Willie says.

"We're going to put a bug in his glasses," Maria says as she finally figures out what Willie intends.

"Does he wear glasses?" Roger asks.

"He's been wearing them every time we saw him," Dingo says.

"I spent my morning checking," Willie says. "He has to have them to read or drive."

"What about contacts? Maybe he wears contacts when he's in a criminal mood," Dingo says.

"I checked that as well, boss. He doesn't, his eyes are so bent out of shape that he can't. That's what his optometrist says," Willie says.

"How did you get this optometrist to tell you anything?" Dingo asks.

"He thought I was a research assistant at Bausch and Lomb looking for subjects to try an experimental type of contact lens. Thinks he'll get a nice little fee for each of his clients that we use in our study."

"You can't possibly think that you can take his glasses off his face and put a bug in them and put them back on him without Bob noticing," Roger says.

"I can't but Maria can. She bumps into him, manages to knock his glasses off, catches them before they hit the ground, hands them back to him. Except they aren't his glasses. He just bought new ones, which makes it much easier, what happens is Maria palms his glasses gives him back exact replicas, except these ones have a bug."

"Is there really a bug that small, won't he notice the weight difference?" Dingo asks.

"Yes, they aren't cheap but they really come that small, and he wears these really heavy tortoiseshell monsters that look like they are from the fifties. I can't believe that you never noticed them, Roger," Willie says.

"I'm not much of a noticer or much of a looker. I'm much more interested in things than people. I mean we'd met twice before I realized that Willie had tattoos all over."

Dingo chuckles. "Yesterday, Roger is at my trailer, I'm making him supper and I ask him to go into the pantry and get some chili pepper. He's gone a long time, three, four minutes. I go looking for him and he's in there tearing the shelves apart looking for the chili pepper. Which is right on the shelf in front of him, at eye level, with a big label on it saying chili pepper," Dingo shakes his head. "I guess your plan is sound if Maria can pull it off."

"I can, no problem. I could steal his underwear without him knowing it if I wanted," Maria boasts. "But what would I do with them?"

CHAPTER · 27

Average Bob turns out to be more than average hard to tail.

"It's that he drives so damn slow," Dingo says. Dingo and Roger are following Average Bob in his bright red SUV down 70th Avenue headed toward 111 Street. "He's like an old lady. It's so much easier to tail a speed demon."

"Why?"

"Try driving slow and then try speeding. When you are zigging and zagging in and out of traffic, watching for photo radar and cop cars, or checking your radar detector to see if it's working, and dodging pedestrians, you don't have much time to check whether someone is tailing you."

Dingo talks with his hands. He's driving his gunmetal grey Chrysler New Yorker. No matter how hard he tries he keeps ending up almost riding on the Explorer's bumper. It's that Bob keeps stopping suddenly, for no reason.

"If I have to do something aggressive to keep the tail intact, like run a red light or squeal around a corner, chances are the speed demon doesn't think that's weird because he does it all the time himself."

It's like Bob is listening, he turns sharply at the last moment on 108th Ave, races off down the street. As Roger and Dingo round the corner, they see Bob turning into an alley half a block ahead. Dingo guns it and the Chrysler slipslides as he turns into the alley. He knows it's a short alley and that if Bob gets to the end of it before he has visual again he could well vanish.

Dingo never stops talking.

"Grannies are notoriously difficult to tail because they creep along and are terrified of being in an accident. They've read all about car insurance scams and so they are always checking their rear view mirrors looking for suspicious cars."

Dingo actually turns his head to demonstrate. That's when they plow into Bob's rear bumper. He's stopped for some children leaving a playground.

"Be calm," Dingo tells the clearly agitated Roger.

Roger isn't listening. He's leapt out of the car and is screaming at Bob's side window. "You did that on purpose."

By the time Dingo gets out of the New Yorker the two men are into it big time. The invective is flying. Dingo lets them go at it and examines the hood of his priceless New Yorker. The damage looks pretty superficial.

"I'll need to see your insurance," Bob says to Dingo as he walks up. The two combatants are standing beside the open door of the SUV. "Maybe I should call the police," he says picking his cell phone up from the seat of the Explorer.

"We don't have to report this, surely," Roger says.

"Not enough damage that we have to get the police involved."

"You were driving recklessly, perhaps you've been drinking," Bob says. "I think the police are a good idea. I'm not sure I want you on the road. Though you could make it worth my while not to call."

"You want a bribe?" Roger screams and lunges at Bob.

"Take it easy mate," Dingo says catching Roger easily by his belt.

"I don't have any money on me," Dingo says. With his free hand he reaches into his pants and pulls out his wallet. He opens the inner flap and it's true, he has no money.

"He must have some," Bob says pointing at Roger.

Roger splutters, then reaches into his pocket and pulls out his wallet, "I'll give you a hundred."

"Look at my bumper, does it look like a hundred dollars will fix that?" Bob asks.

"There isn't a mark on it," Roger yells. "Or anywhere else."

"A thousand. That's my deductible."

"I don't think he has a thousand dollars," Dingo says.

"I'll take what he's got." It turns out to be six hundred and eight dollars. Once the money has changed hands Bob says, "And I'll still need your insurance."

"We just paid you to forget the whole thing," Roger fumes.

"No, you just paid me not to call the cops. But what if my frame is bent, or my brakes don't work. Hidden damage, might be thousands of dollars of hidden damage. And my neck, I think my neck is starting to hurt. Whiplash can be expensive."

Dingo happily hands over his insurance. Bob writes down the pertinent information and then, with a wide grin, drives off. Roger is boiling over and so is the Chrysler's radiator. "Puncture," Dingo says. "What an unfortunate accident."

"Accident! Are you out of your mind? The guy set us up so we rear-end him. He gets all of my money, he gets a claim he can make against your insurance company and he gets rid of the tail. All in one easy step."

"We are going to have to take some steps of our own," Dingo agrees.

"What steps?" Roger asks.

"First we're going to go to a rental car place, I like the south-side Hertz, and we are going to get a better car."

"What's wrong with this one?" Roger asks.

"It's a grey Chrysler New Yorker," Dingo says. "It's new and it's clean."

"That's bad?"

"Yes, that's bad."

"Why?" Roger asks.

"It doesn't look like the kind of car a cautious driver would own. We want a more common model in a more common colour, we want it a little dirty and maybe a bit used looking."

"What's a more common colour?"

"The best would be blue. In a perfect world I want a blue Taurus with a little grunge."

They spend the rest of the day looking for the perfect rental car. Hertz doesn't have a blue Taurus, any blue cars. They have a red Taurus.

"Wrong colour," Dingo says.

Tilden hasn't got any Tauruses. They have a blue sedan. It's mid-range blue.

"Good colour, wrong car," Dingo says.

Avis has a blue Taurus. But it's a station wagon.

"Right car, wrong model," Dingo says.

Alamo has a blue Taurus sedan. It's dirty. It's perfect. Until they try to check it out.

Dingo reaches into his pocket and takes out a wallet.

"That's not your wallet," Roger says.

"Sure it is," Dingo says.

"Is this your wallet or not?" The clerk, a tall young man with a pronounced cranium and a shaved skull, asks.

"Certainly is, look at my driver's license. That's me. My social insurance card. VISA. Master Card. That's even my money."

"You gave him fake insurance, you made me pay the bribe," Roger says.

"What's this about fake insurance, we frown on that sort of thing."

"He's just trying to give me a hard time, ignore him."

"Okay," the clerk shrugs. "We're already to go, just sign there. And initial here. I hope you aren't planning to let him be an extra driver. We find it's always the pranksters that bring the car back with damage," the clerk says.

"I'm not a prankster," Roger says.

"It's not the big stuff you know," the clerk says in a conspiratorial tone to Dingo. "It's the coffee stains, the rock chips, the broken windshield wipers. How do you break a windshield wiper?"

Roger sighs. "I'd never damage your priceless car. But you're worried about renting to me. Instead you're going to rent to a drunk."

"You have to admire his persistence," the clerk says.

"He never gives up," Dingo agrees, signing the rental agreement and passing it back across the counter to the clerk.

"It'll be about ten minutes," the clerk says.

"Why?" Dingo asks. "The car is right out there." He can see it through the window.

"We have to wash it first," the clerk says.

"I want it dirty."

"I can't let you drive a dirty car. It's against company policy," the clerk explains.

"I'll pay extra."

"No. It makes no difference. An Alamo car is a clean car. If you won't let me clean it, you can't have it."

"How about a bribe?" Roger asks.

"An Alamo employee is a honest employee," the clerk says, offended.

"We'll wait while you clean the car," Dingo says.

"You're just going to take it out and get it dirty aren't you?"

"What difference does it make?" Roger asks. "That one is already dirty."

"But I'm going to clean that one. And an Alamo employee never rents a car to anybody they know intends to willfully damage it."

"We aren't going to damage it," Dingo says, "we are just going to dirty it up, run it through a mud puddle or two."

"Let me check my manual," the clerk says. Some time passes. The clerk goes line by line through the manual.

"Does that book have an index?" Roger asks.

"Yes."

"So you can't look up dirt in the index?"

"No."

"Why not?" Roger asks.

"Because a good Alamo employee always reads the entire manual to make sure that they fully understand the rules. And here it is. No employee shall, under any circumstances, rent a vehicle to anyone who, to the clerk's knowledge, intends to expose the car to conditions that might be detrimental to the vehicle's operation. So that's it. I can't rent to you."

"Why?" Dingo asks.

"The mud might get in the gas. Maybe gunk up the plugs or points. Corrode the battery terminals."

"Christ, man, we aren't planning to race it off-road."

"How do I know that? You don't seem very trustworthy and I know you like to get your cars dirty. Plus look at that car you are driving. It looks like you've been running it in the demolition derby. Go to Tilden."

Later that day Willie recounts a somewhat similar experience to Maria.

"He's a sitter."

"A sitter?" Maria asks.

"I follow him to the University and he goes to the Rutherford Library, goes into the North building, goes to the fourth floor, grabs a bunch of books,

190

finds an empty carrel and sits down. Then he digs out a notebook. For the next five hours he sits there reading and taking notes. Doesn't even go to the bathroom. The only good thing is they have some new books on Mark Twain in the library so at least I didn't waste my time."

"What kind of books was he reading so intently?" Maria asks.

"Gaming theory, some stuff on gambling, particularly on strategies for playing twenty-one."

"How did you find that out?"

"He left them behind when he was through at the library."

"You took time to read them? Weren't you supposed to be following him?" Maria asks.

"Yes, but I got curious."

"But if you don't follow him isn't that going to mess up the plan?"

"Not really. First off, the fun doesn't really start until we have the glasses ready to use. Did you manage to get the exact same pair?"

"Yes, but I'll tell you the woman at Shopper's Optical really didn't make it easy. She was some certain that I couldn't buy glasses for my husband as a surprise present even if I did know his prescription, and what model I wanted. She kept trying to upgrade me to a "better class of frames." I told her my husband liked retro, that big, ugly frames are in fashion. But I finally got them. Now what are we going to do with them?"

"I'll tell you that in a second. The thing is, you should know that Dingo used to be the best tail in the business. Then he started drinking. You probably can't tell but he's sort of perma-soused. He's a little drunk all the time these days, though he hasn't been on a real bender since Roger showed up. I'm hoping that in order to prove me wrong, show me that he can still tail anyone, anywhere, Dingo will sober up. He has to sober up before I can help him."

"I'm confused, help him what?" Maria asks.

"I want to cure his alcoholism."

"Cure it, I thought there wasn't no cure."

"My Uncle Dunk gave me this powder from the roots of a shrub that grows in the South Pacific…"

"*Kava-kava.*"

"Yes, how did you know that?"

"I read about it in a magazine."

"Well Uncle Dunk swears that if I can get Dingo mostly dried out and then get him to drink some *kava* that he'll be cured, or rather he'll prefer *kava* to booze and it's a hell of a lot better for him and even improves mental performance. The problem was I couldn't figure out how to get him sober. Now, of course, I can't think how I'll get him to try the *kava*."

"Oh Willie, leave that to me. I can get him to do it no problem. Now what do I do with these glasses?"

"You are going to deliver them to this TV repair place on Whyte Avenue, Acme Appliances. Ask for Eugene, you can't miss him, he'll be the drooling badger. Eugene knows what I want done. When he's through, you won't be able to tell the glasses were ever touched but the bug will be safely nestled inside and transmitting everything it hears. While you are there, you should get Eugene to show you all his other toys, not that you can probably stop him. Eugene loves his products."

CHAPTER · 28

The next day Maria visits Acme Appliances while Willie resumes his surveillance of Average Bob. Acme is located in an old Pizza Hut building at the east end of Whyte Avenue. The interior is neat and clean but somehow decrepit.

Eugene is multi-tasking when Maria arrives. He's talking on the phone to a customer while helping another customer over the Internet. To Maria the stuff in the shop looks like junk. Portable junk. Portable junk with price tags in the thousands. She can't help it, her fingers start to itch. She tries putting her hands in her pockets but that just makes everything worse.

It starts with just a single little transmitter. But soon she's using all her tricks. And merchandise is disappearing. Eugene isn't paying any attention. Finally he gets off the phone and out of the computer.

"You're Willie's girlfriend, right? Maria," he says.

"What's this?" Maria asks holding up an odd little device that looks rather like a silicon and metal caterpillar.

"Oh you'd love that. It's a telephone hold monitor. You attach that to your phone. It lets you place a caller on faux hold. You know what I mean. No, I can see you don't. It disconnects your microphone, the part you speak through. The person on the other end hears that typical dead phone sound you get when you're on hold. I can even sell you a model that plays music to keep the person entertained. The thing is you can still hear them. You'd be amazed the things people say while they think they are on hold.

"This one you have here," Eugene says, reaching into Maria's purse, "is the Cadillac of telephone hold monitors, it's worth $800.

"This one's neat," Eugene says, going through the other goodies he's unloaded from her purse.

"Isn't it just a phone number decoder? Willie has one on his phone," Maria says, stroking a little black box with an LED display.

"Yes and no. Lots of people have telephone number decoders, they let you see who phoned you even if they didn't leave a message. Telus even sells packages along with their caller ID plan. However, not everyone wants you to know who they are so they use scrambling devices, people like telephone solicitors and boiler room prize scam artists, they don't want to be traceable. This particular decoder also descrambles so no one can phone you and remain anonymous. That tape recorder over there turns the decoder into a lethal weapon."

"What does it do?" Maria asks picking up the tape recorder and peering into it. "Looks pretty innocent to me."

"Let's say you hate phone solicitors, I sure do. So you take a call from one. Even though you are talking the decoder still traces the number. The tape recorder hooks to your phone, you hit play and it autodials the last number from the decoder and when it gets an answer it plays a long series of beeps, hums and whistles which not only fry the phone that answers but any software or hardware that's hooked up to that phone. It's vicious, but if everyone owned one there wouldn't be anymore phone solicitors and that would be a very good thing."

Eugene holds up a silver metal box, a cable jack hangs from one end, the other looks a bit like the grill from a fancy sports car. The box is half as thick as a cigarette pack but otherwise the same dimensions. "Speaking of telephone toys, I bet you can't guess what this is. It's designed to fit inside your telephone. It nestles in there snug as a bug in a rug. Now you can phone home from any touchtone phone in the world and punch in a code and this box turns into a microphone and you can hear anything said within thirty feet. It's a great way to spy on your staff."

Eugene starts returning the pilfered goods to their boxes. "Would you like to know how I got into the business?"

"Sure, I guess," Maria says.

"Well, as a kid I loved James Bond. You know who he is?"

"I lived in Britain for years, I've seen every Bond film."

"Me too. Well, before the film there were books by a guy called Ian Fleming, right? Well, he actually had once been a sort of spy, during and after the Second World War. He actually worked for a bit designing spy gadgets. His writing so impressed the British intelligence establishment that they even tried building some of the toys he described in the books. I met him not long before his death."

"No shit."

"No shit. I was studying at Cambridge, electronics, and he wandered into the lab one day looking for ideas for his next book. I showed him some of the things I was working on and I guess he took a shine to me because he asked me all kinds of questions, trying to find out if some of his more outlandish ideas would work. One of those ideas changed my life. Credit cards were just becoming common then and he had the idea for a credit card bug. It would work just like any other credit card and you would carry it around unsuspectingly and it would record everything you said.

"The first one I made looked like this," Eugene reaches into the pockets of Maria's sweater. He holds up a credit card sized piece of chipboard. It's covered in transistors and diode and geegaws. "This transmits in the UHF range. You stick it in the pocket of your toddler and you can hear them and anything anyone says to them up to about three hundred feet away. I licensed the technology to a Japanese firm.

"Then came this," he holds up an actual credit card he's retrieved from the waistband of Maria's pants. "This transmits on UHF, but you give it to your unsuspecting teenager, comes in MasterCard, VISA, and American Express. Now if you are within three hundred feet you can eavesdrop. Many of my clients found having to follow an erratic teenager around and keep them within that radius a big pain the butt, plus the signal was pretty garbled, so there wasn't much market for it, but then I figured out how to build in a recording function. I also improved the microphone and got much better quality sound. Now parents can give their unsuspecting teenagers a credit card and it will record everything they say and hear, then the next time they pass through the house to grab a bite or create dirty laundry the parents can download the recording and listen to it at their convenience. The same Japanese firm that did my tot card wants the rights to this baby."

He stops. "But you aren't here to listen to me ramble. Let's see what I can do with these glasses."

He's gone ten minutes, deep into the back of the shop. Where he doesn't invite Maria. When he returns he has the glasses in his hand. Maria takes them and can't notice any difference. She wonders if her leg is being jerked.

"Willie told me to give you these four bugs as well," Eugene says. "These are also Japanese, and I know what you're thinking, they look like leftover gum you'd find stuck under a theatre seat. They are sticky and you should be careful that they don't stick to you or your clothes because this sticky gunk can be real hard to get off wool. Embedded in that glue are the most powerful bugs currently available in Canada. Each unit has a microphone and a transmitter that will send a signal almost a mile. It also has built-in memory and is voice activated. If there is no noise it won't be broadcasting, which saves the power source. In a busy office these things will work for about eight weeks."

"Doesn't Willie have to have some sort of special earphones or radio or something to pick up the signal?" Maria asks.

"Sure he does, but he's already got it. I modified a cell phone for the purpose a couple of years ago. These are pre-set to that frequency," Eugene says.

"How much do I owe you?" Maria asks.

"Nothing, Willie and Dingo run a tab. Will you come back and see me sometime, Maria? I'd like to show you my other treasures. I think you might really get into them."

"I'd love to come back," Maria says and turns to go.

"By the way, would you like me to do a full body search or shall I just charge all the rest of the merchandise to Willie's account?"

Sheepishly, Maria begins to hand Eugene back all his stolen goods. The first batch comes from her hair. Eugene just waits, holding out a box. Maria digs around in her bra and produces several thousand dollars worth of tiny microphones. Eugene is still standing there. Out of her panties Maria extracts a variety of pinhole cameras. That's still not enough for Eugene. He searches her socks and shoes and finds a collection of ninja fighting stars. He can't even remember stocking such a thing. Finally he pries open her mouth, digs around in her cheeks, and finds a small global positioning transmitter, as well as a couple of diodes from his parts bins.

Maria finally gets away from Eugene and heads off to join Willie. It's only once she leaves the shop that he realizes she's stolen his computer mouse.

It's Maria's turn to follow Average Bob. She guilts Willie into helping her, complaining, explaining, how Eugene humiliated her. The plan is that working together they'll try to get close enough to Bob to switch glasses.

Tailing Average Bob turns out to very easy and exceedingly boring. He goes to the bank they already know he has an account at. He takes out money and heads to the grocery store they already know he shops at. He's impossible to miss in his big bright red SUV. At the grocery store he buys all the things they already know he buys. He takes the groceries home. He takes the dogs for a walk. Then he heads to the gym they already know he's a member at and works out.

Finally he heads out dancing.

It's one in the morning when Willie and Maria arrive back at the office of International Investigations. They've spent an agonizing evening trying to get close enough to Bob to plant the glasses. The agonizing part is where he's taken them. Turns out Bob is a fan of loud, bad, poorly played rock music and he's been doing a tour of every club on Whyte Avenue. At least every one where loud rock bands play bad music poorly.

Bob drinks orange juice, cruises the single women. Has considerable success. Dances with them. Jokes around and then says goodnight. Willie can't figure if he's trying, unsuccessfully, to pick them up, or shopping, looking for the one he wants for the night. But he goes home alone in any event.

By then Willie and Maria are yelling at each other. Not because they are angry, though Maria is a little uptight. It's because they can't hear. Coming in late, staying well behind Bob, they haven't always been able to pick where they wanted to sit, or stand. Several times they've been right beside the amplifiers, awash in mind-numbing back beat.

Roger and Dingo are waiting for them. Dingo is clearly drunk. He listens impatiently to Willie and Maria's story. To Maria's apology for not being able to get close enough to Bob to switch glasses.

"Waste of time," he says. "Waste of time, not important. Time of waste. Of waste time. Waste to time, time to waste."

"I suppose something important happened here, while you were drinking," Willie says.

"Big doings," Dingo says. His speech is slurred. He is sitting on a ergonomic chair, on coasters. As he speaks he paws the hardwood floor with his feet until the chair is in motion, rolling across the office. Once he is in motion he starts spinning around and around in the chair.

"Whee!" Dingo says as he plows into the far wall.

"We got an invitation!" he exclaims as he comes flying back across the room.

"An invitation to what?" Willie asks.

"A party," Dingo says, spinning back the other way.

"A poker game," Roger explains.

"*The* poker game!" Dingo qualifies as he heads back towards Willie. Willie reached out and grabs the chair, bringing it, and Dingo, to a standstill.

"Could you perhaps explain a bit more thoroughly?" Willie asks.

"Just after noon today we got a courier package from Mr. Average Bob. It was an invitation to a high stakes poker game at the poker lounge in Casino Edmonton," Roger says.

"Who got this invitation?" Maria asks, just before Willie can. They both really want to know the answer.

"I did, as it happens," Roger says.

"It was addressed to you?" Willie asks.

"It was, indeed," Roger answers.

"It came from Average Bob?" Maria asks.

"I can't say for certain. It came by Western Dispatch courier, no sender indicated, but I surmise it must have been he," Roger says.

"And you surmise this why?" Willie asks.

"Minimum buy-in is a million large, you've got to buy a million dollars worth of chips. Certain items of Kennedy assassination memorabilia will be offered in lieu of a million dollars, to wit Kennedy's brain, by the organizers of said match. It's winner take all, by invitation only. I'm supposed to invite anyone I know might be interested. If there aren't at least six players, plus the organizer, it's a no-go."

Willie is briefly distracted and Dingo takes off again. He wheels and spins around the room, eluding Willie's attempts to corral him, laughing maniacally.

"There can't be too many conspiracy nuts with more money than brains that play poker," Willie says.

"Oh the idea isn't that we will play ourselves. We can have someone play on our behalf. I've phoned seven of the people I thought I might sell the brain to, eventually. I've invited them, four said yes right away, two phoned back later to confirm. Apparently in the intervening hours they recruited top professional players to represent them," Roger says.

"Who are you going to have represent you?" Willie asks.

"My plan is to have Maria represent me," Roger answers.

"How much money will we be playing for, six times a million that's..." Maria asks.

"Six million dollars," Roger says.

Maria blanches. "Six million dollars," she squeaks out.

"Six million dollars and Kennedy's brain."

"When is this event supposed to happen?"

"A week from today. If I can get all the players lined up. I'm still waiting to hear from the Smithsonian and the National Archives."

"Hey, I bet you could get the CIA to play," Willie laughs.

"I need a drink," Maria says.

"I second that," Dingo screams as he careens across the office.

"Don't you think you've had enough?" Willie's meaning is clear.

"My dear boy, as Roger would say, there is no such thing as enough."

"I don't like this," Maria says. "Roger could lose a million dollars. It could all be some sort of set-up."

"But we've got to go ahead anyway," Willie says.

"Why?" Maria asks. "Why don't we just walk away?"

"Because you are going to win six million dollars for us. I don't know how we are going to split it, but you are going to win it," Willie replies.

"Listen, I'm good and I can cheat with the best of them but this game is going to draw all the best players. They'll outplay me and match me cheat for cheat, or boot me the first time they catch me. I know my limitations, there is no way I can win."

"Yes, there is."

"How?"

"With magic — magic and a little help," Willie says, spinning Dingo in his chair.

CHAPTER · 29

Later, alone in the trailer, Maria tries again to convince Willie to walk away.

"I've got to finish the game," Willie says. "Play it out to the end."

"I thought you were just doing this for fun. Or maybe for me."

Willie smiles gently.

"Bastard. Then why?"

"Lots of reasons. My friend, my best friend, is in the clutches of a sado-masochistic creep. He's also deep in the bottle. No matter how good *kava* is, it isn't going to pull him out of the bottle, not if he's nurturing a broken heart."

"I'm not sure I'm with you," Maria says.

"Well, I'd guess you were right: Dingo is gay. He's fallen big-time for Roger. If I pull the plug on this whole thing, poker game and all, then I'd bet Roger is out the door so fast Dingo's pants will be on backwards. So first I have to get him sober, then I can drop the whole thing. I'm not sure I have time to get Dingo sober and secure before the poker game."

"I see what you mean," Maria says, slipping up against Willie on the couch. She lays her head in his lap as he strokes her hair. "Are all Samoans such good people as you?"

"I'm not a good person, Maria."

"You really care about Dingo, maybe even about me, right?"

"Yes. Very much."

"Then you're a good person," Maria says.

"It's that simple, is it?" Willie asks. "This being a good person."

Maria thinks. "No, I guess not," she says. "But you'd never hurt anyone else deliberately, would you?"

"Of course I would," Willie answers.

"No, you wouldn't," Maria says. "Well, maybe if they were hurting someone you cared about. Or committing a crime. But not out of sheer badness. Just for the joy of it."

"No. I guess you are right about that. But surely that isn't enough. What about honesty, for example?"

"Honesty is highly over-rated," Maria says.

"Oh. How do you figure that?" Willie asks. "Would you like it if I lied when I said I loved you?"

"You never said you loved me," Maria points out.

"It's a hypothetical, a what if, what if I'd said I loved you and lied?" Willie asks again.

"Okay. Let's say lying is misunderstood. There are lies you tell with your heart and with your mouth. The first are very bad. Like saying you love me when you don't. The other kind, they aren't so bad. You might even have good intentions."

"You mean a white lie."

"Exactly, Mr. Willie. Is someone a bad person because they tell white lies?"

"On Falemusu, they didn't think of lies like we do here. A lie is nothing or it's dangerous. Some lies, they become the truth as soon as you say them and they can really come back to haunt you. Other lies they just deceive the listener and they are okay. No problem to tell one of those."

"How do you tell the difference?" Maria asks.

"That's the problem. You can't," Willie says.

"Tell me what would make a good person in Falemusu."

Willie wraps a strand of Maria's hair around his finger. "Look after your family. Help out around the village. Pay attention to your ancestors. Be generous. It's so much simpler there."

"And here. What do you think it takes to be a good person here?"

"The same things, but more. You've got to truthful, trustworthy, dependable, polite, respectful, devout, sincere, clean. Give me a moment and I can probably think of a whole bunch more."

"You think too much."

"I know I do. I've thought about this a lot. In Sunday school the nuns taught us there are two kinds of sins, venal and mortal. Venal you can be forgiven for, mortal you can't. I've committed quite a few of both."

"Give me some examples," Maria demands.

"I've committed adultery."

"This the kind that's in your head, or the kind that uses this?" Maria says running her hand down over Willie's groin.

"The real kind," Willie says, adroitly blocking Maria's hand before it gets too frisky.

"I didn't know you were married," Maria says, more than a little surprised.

"I wasn't," Willie says.

"Then how could you commit adultery?" Maria asks.

"I guess technically I wasn't, but the woman I was with certainly was," Willie says.

"Yeah, but that's her problem, not yours."

"I've stolen."

"That's a mortal sin?" Maria asks, surprised.

"One of the seven major sins," Willie assures her.

"I'm in big trouble, Mr. Willie. But how does God expect you to make a living if you can't steal?"

"Probably figures you will marry a rich man," Willie says.

"But I'd have to steal him from his current wife. Probably commit some adultery along the way. Plus wouldn't I be guilty of coveting? I'm only marrying him because he's rich. I'm just not sure I can lead a sin-free life, Willie."

"Well then, we'll have to find a religion that allows us to be forgiven our sins at the last minute, just before we die. That way we can go on being bad and not worry about things like mortal and venal sins."

"Sounds good to me," Maria yawns, her eyes starting to close.

Once Maria is asleep, Willie slips out. He gets into Truck and heads into the city. He needs the solace of his rock.

In Capilano Park he hides Truck behind some high bushes. Then he heads over to the three rocks. It's a silent, cool night, lit brilliantly by stars and moon in a clear sky. In the brush around him Willie can hear scratches and scurrying animals. He hopes it's just birds and squirrels.

After stretching and jogging in place to get warm, Willie turns all his attention to the rock. He rests his back against it. He's nearly in the sitting position. Then he tries to straighten up. For years nothing has happened. Thousands of times he's done this and nothing has happened.

This time the rock moves. It tilts away from him, quite sharply. Willie spins around and catches the rock as it tries to roll back into place. Now he has his hands under it, at the base of it, and with one mighty coordinated shove of his chest, his back, his arms, and his legs he sends it right over on its side.

The next part will be easy. Rolling it down the slight slope to where he's parked Truck is nowhere near as difficult as rolling cars or big truck tires. He's done both in strong man competitions.

He and the rock arrive, exhausted but none the worse for wear, after about twenty minutes. Willie has been entertaining himself wondering what he'd say if some policeman came along and asked him where he thought he was going with the rock. Well officer, you see this rock holds the spirit of my father entombed within in it. And if I'm going to free him I've got to liberate it. That wasn't my question, the policeman says, I just want to know where you're going with it? I'm taking it to my truck. Is that its final destination? No. I thought if I can get it on my truck and the truck can stand the weight of the load I'd take it out to my farm. I'm sorry but that doesn't make any sense. Farmers want rocks off their land, especially rocks like this one, that could eat a combine. Well it isn't exactly a farm. What is it then. It's more like a swamp. That makes far more sense then, taking the rock I mean. But what are you going to do with it when you get it there? What is he going to do with it when he gets it there? Willie hasn't got the faintest clue.

He is still resting from rolling the rock when a voice whispers "Boo" in his ear. He nearly jumps over the rock. It's Maria.

Once his heart has returned to normal he asks: "How did you get here?"

"Hitched a ride in the back of Truck. What can I do to help?"

"Help?"

"You don't think I'm going to let you risk your immortal soul without me do you?"

It takes every ounce of ingenuity, perseverance, patience, and teamwork to finally get the rock into Truck. Truck sags, dragging its butt on the ground, but not impossibly so. They don't drive out to the farm. They crawl. Any sort of speed and Truck's mighty engine begins to whine, and beg. Any sort of bump and the chassis hits the ground.

Somewhere around the outskirts of the city Willie begins to fear for Truck's future. By the time they get to the farm he is in a full scale panic. Willie stops Truck fifty feet up the sloping driveway that leads from the road. The remaining thirty feet, the steepest thirty feet, would be too much for Truck.

It's down to manpower. Willie is determined he can move the rock by himself.

He's done it once before, and this time the rock is already on a bit of a grade caused by the driveway and Truck's slumping springs. But it just isn't happening. He's too agitated to concentrate. Willie can't remember ever having felt so excited, confused, and fearful. He's in tears when Maria climbs up in to the truck bed with him.

"Some mortal sins are just harder to commit than others," Maria says. Then she squeezes his shoulder. "Let's try with both of us pushing at the same time."

Together, leaning their backs into the rock and pushing off Truck's cab they are able to get the rock to roll once. However, neither of them has thought of how to stop it. Once in motion the rock remains in motion, begins to pick up speed. It rolls out of the truck bed. Begins rolling back down the driveway toward the road.

Willie jumps out of Truck and goes racing after it. Trying to get it ahead of it. Like he plans to jump in front of it and stop it with his bare hands. Maria is sure that's a dumb idea. She grabs a small stone and fires it at Willie's head. She is right on target. Willie comes to a halt, grabs at his head.

That's just enough to let the boulder get away. Half way down the driveway it bounces off the road and begins crashing through the aspen forest and underbrush. It plows over some rosebushes and breaks through a saskatoon thicket, finally coming to rest in a small clearing.

Maria catches up with Willie just about the time the rock stops rolling. She reaches up and pulls his head down towards her. She checks carefully for any sign she hurt him. Finding none she apologizes.

"I'm sorry. But I was afraid you'd jump in front of that rock. Get hurt."

"Don't worry about it," Willie says. "I have a very hard head. Where did you learn to throw like that?"

"You won't believe me if I tell you."

"Sure I will."

"Playing cricket."

"You're right, I don't believe you."

"Told you," Maria says.

"Come help me figure out how to get that hunk of rock back up to the trailer," Willie says.

When they step through the saskatoons into the clearing they know that won't be easy. The ground is soft and boggy. Wet, even. Covered in peat moss. The boulder has already settled more than a foot into the moss.

"I'll have to winch it out," Willie says.

"Don't," Maria responds.

"Why not?" Willie asks.

"Think about this, that rock could have rolled here, it could have rolled there. Down the driveway to the road. Off the road the other way and there would have been nothing to stop if from rolling into the lake. It chose to come to rest here, right here. If your dad really is inside maybe he has his reasons.

"It's like that cross. We've been aimlessly moving rocks and dumping them. What we got was a cross. Now we got us a giant rock in our saskatoon batch," Maria concludes.

"I'd like to believe you," Willie says.

"But you don't. Here's something for you to think about. You know I've been reading all about Samoa and the south Pacific?" Maria asks.

"I've noticed. I don't think it'll help you become Samoan, knowing so much about it."

"One of the things I learned," she says, "is about worship rocks and flat temples."

"Worship rocks and flat temples?"

"You seem to have forgotten some pretty important things. There is this big mystery about strange rock platforms that are found throughout the south Pacific. Somebody, some people have gone to a lot of trouble to haul small to mid-size stones, sometimes they've even shaped bigger rocks so they'll be flat, but whatever, they've piled those rocks in flat mounds, small, shaped hills. Some of them are rectangular when viewed from above, some are square, others are star shaped, or round. A few even appear to be crosses. They are anywhere from a foot to twenty feet high," Maria explains.

"Nobody has any idea what they are for or when they were built?" Willie asks. He's interested despite himself and his frustration with his father's boulder.

"Seems not. There is no sign they were ever used for anything. Maybe they were purely decorative."

"Okay, so what are worship rocks?"

"The reason they think the mounds might be some sort of temple, modern archaeologists think, is because nearby is often found a huge boulder, clearly moved great distances, and around that rock there is evidence of religious ceremonies taking place. Or perhaps important meetings or even trials. I'm thinking maybe your Samoan part knows something. First you build a temple mound, them you get yourself a worship rock."

"I hate my Samoan side."

"No, you don't. You hate being out of control. This time, I think maybe you're under a higher control."

Willie can't decide if Maria is jerking him around or means it.

"Thank you," he says, finally, his hand resting on the giant rock. Then he bends down and kisses her forehead. "Let's go back to the trailer and get some sleep."

CHAPTER · 30

The next morning Willie and Maria have just got back from training. There is a nip in the air, and wet dew coats car windows. They are anxious to jump into the shower. Then the doorbell rings. Willie goes to answer it.

On the doorstep is a truly monstrous Samoan man. Willie blinks. The monster grabs him in a bear hug and lifts him off the ground like he was a child.

"Uncle Dunk!"

"Surprise!" Dunk says. "Thought I'd stop by and see how you were doing. And look who I brought."

"Maam. Maam." Willie starts to cry as he hugs his mom. It's a little awkward, the reunion, because Willie's feet still aren't touching the ground as Dunk carries him in one arm like a baby.

"Dunk, put me down."

"Oops sorry. There you go. Now where is this gypsy girl you won't sleep with."

Maria steps nervously forward. Dunk reaches down and lifts her hand. Then he gently kisses the back of her hand.

"Try to forget I'm a cannibal," he says as he gives her hand back.

"You know I wouldn't have believed it if I hadn't seen it with my own eyes," Maam says looking at Maria. "Come here and let me have a proper look."

After a careful scrutiny she says, "Girl, you look just like Wilma Wash."

"Who's Wilma Wash?" Maria asks, puzzled.

Dunk giggles. "When Betty and I were growing up there was a girl we went to school with, Wilma Wash. Her dad was Samoan, her mom was a white nurse who went native. Well, a little more than native. She ran around stark naked, screwing any island man that sat still for half a second. So we never did know who Wilma's dad was. When Wilma was six her mom put on her clothes, got on a boat, and left. Every family in the village took turns raising Wilma. Of course we all expected Wilma to go insane one day, just like her mom. Except it never happened, she went away and got to be a nurse like her mom, then a nurse practitioner, got married, has a family, works on Guam for the U.S. Army."

"That's more than the poor girl needs to know," Maam says. "My point was that Wilma was the first mulatto I ever saw and I thought she was beautiful. When I found out I was pregnant with Willie I thought that was what he'd turn out like. Instead he's plug ugly. I guess you can just never tell. When I heard you were trying to turn Samoan I figured that with Willie as your model you'd be a regular pig. Quelle surprise. And he still won't have sex with you. Even as a baby he was some stupid."

Willie and Maria run through the shower. More accurately Willie drags Maria through the shower. Maria likes to luxuriate and normally Willie lets her. Not today.

"Why are we in such a hurry?" Maria asks.

"You don't want to leave my uncle in the room alone. Not one that has food in it."

By the time they emerge Maam and Dunk are sitting down to eat.

"Just a little snack," Dunk says. Every bit of food Willie has in his trailer is on the table.

"Some sandwiches," Dunk says. He's assembling one that is made of an entire loaf of Calabrese bread. Lettuce and tomatoes are topped with onions and bell peppers and hot peppers. Over top of that are provolone cheese, cheddar cheese, mozzarella, and American. The whole thing drips with mustard, mayo, horseradish, and hot sauce. It disappears in three monstrous bites. Even as he's devouring the first sandwich Dunk is assembling a second.

Maam is hoarding ingredients out of Dunk's reach. "I thought I'd make us a nice salad. If I can keep Dunk from eating the salad bowl. We'd have been here early but this bozo had to stop and eat every couple of hours, of course it takes him a couple of hours to eat, so our progress was slowed."

"So why are you here?" Willie grins. "Really?"

"It's Dingo," Maam says. "We got a call from him a couple of days ago. He's drunk as a skunk. I don't think this slimy guy he's hanging out with is good for him. His new mate, what's his name?"

"Roger," Willie says. "My Maam is in love with Dingo, won't admit it of course, but she is," Willie says to Maria, as an explanation and a warning not to say anything to his mother about Maria's idea that Dingo is gay.

"I'm not. He's a lovely man who has been really good to my only son and right now he's clearly having some sort of crisis."

"So we've come to fix him," Dunk says.

"Fix him," Willie says.

"Cure his alcoholism," Dunk says.

"Uncle, are you sure we should be talking about this now?"

"You mean because I disapprove of your uncle's medical practices?" Maam asks.

"Maam, you don't just disapprove, you think they're a load of hokum," Willie says.

"Now that's not true. I admit I'm opposed to them, I don't think they're Christian. Or at least I didn't use to."

"Something happened to change your mind?" Willie asks.

"Lately I've been having the rheumatoid. Oh, I ache something fierce. Then Katherine suggested I try a little old time healing."

Willie explains to Maria: "Katherine is Maam's next door neighbour, she must be well over eighty. She likes to be called Sister Percival. She belongs to a breakaway splinter of the Church of Jesus Christ of the Latter Day Saints. Every time I see her she's trying to lay her hands on me, to fix what's wrong with me. She's never any too specific about what that is, of course."

Maam nods. "Katherine took me to a tent meeting. Boy, that was something. Praying and dancing and speaking in tongues, all under this huge big top set up out in the middle of the desert. Katherine dragged me into a lineup and one of the ministers touched my head and it was like I was struck by lightning. Next thing I know I'm getting up off the ground, and blessed Jesus, the pains are gone.

"Later on the minister, he's quite a young man, he comes along to check and see how I'm doing. We get to talking and he asks me about religious healing in Samoa. I tell him about Dunk and his brothers and he's fascinated, wants to know more. I say he can't possibly believe in all that malarkey and he says, 'Betty, the Lord works in mysterious ways.'

"I thought about that a lot, and I had to admit, much as I find the idea preposterous, that God would have such bad judgment, maybe Dunk is doing the Lord's work and just doesn't know it. I know for a fact that the one thing Dunk can cure is alcoholism."

"How do you know that?" Willie asks.

"I was with him in Australia when he cured an entire town of Aboriginals of drink. They didn't all drink, but those that did, when Dunk was through with them, they stopped. I heard from some missionaries from the church that they haven't taken it back up — the Aboriginals, not the missionaries. The missionaries they never did drink.

"Dingo needs help and Dunk is just the guy to provide it."

"Your talking about doing a *kava* rite aren't you?" Willie says.

"I am," Dunk says around a mouthful of his third sandwich.

"The only problem is that there is no way on this earth you are going to get Dingo to agree."

"You think he might be a bit resistant?" Maam asks.

"Like a rebar in concrete," Willie says.

"That will make my work a bit tricky. He does have to agree voluntarily. Not to say that he needs to know the truth, that we are trying to cure his drinking. We can tell him, and it's the truth, that we need extra men to make the rite work. That is if we can convince him that it's one of us that needs the help."

"You could say your helping makes me Samoan," Maria volunteers.

"I don't think so. I wouldn't want to tamper with your success. I might get it wrong and reverse the process. Not to mention you're a girl," Dunk says.

"What's that got to do with it?"

"Only men do the rite. You can help us, in fact we will need you, but you can't actually take part," Dunk says.

"That isn't fair," Maria pouts.

"It isn't, but they're men and they have to have their mumbo jumbo and toys or they get really cranky and they don't want any girls playing with them neither," Maam says.

"Well then, how about we tell Dingo that Willie needs to do this rite in order to get past his writer's block and finish his thesis," Maria says.

"That's preposterous. He'd never believe that," Willie says.

"I think he just might," Maam says. "He is awfully fond of you. I say we try it. If we can just get him to take part we can cure his alcoholism and maybe it'll break whatever spell this weirdo Roger has over him."

They walk over to Dingo's trailer. Dingo is lying on the front lawn in his clothes, sputtering snores into quiet morning air. Everyone shakes their head at the same time which has the weird effect of bringing Dingo to consciousness. Seeing three and a half giant Samoans staring down at him sobers Dingo.

"Have you eaten yet?" he asks solicitously.

Much to Willie's amazement it takes Maria just a few minutes to convince Dingo to take part in the cure. But he insists on inviting Roger, which leaves Maam more than a little put out.

"It's okay," Dunk says. "It'll give me a chance to get inside his head and mess with him a bit. By the time I'm through with him he'll want to run screaming back to whatever rock he crawled out from under."

"Aren't you guys being just a little hard on Roger?" Maria asks. "You've never even met him."

"I listened to Dingo talk about him on the phone and I got one of my feelings. He's slime, that's what I thought," Maam says.

"Betty's feelings are never wrong. Of course she thinks it's Christ talking to her and I think it's her rocks. She has this marvelous rock garden in front of her house. They talk to me," Dunk says.

"Those rocks were there when I bought the place. I keep telling you that."

"Yeah, they told you to buy the place. Of course, they were there first. You see, Maria, every Samoan person with the gift, they have a special rock. It's all set before they ever get born, these people, that this is their rock. When they meet their rock they become whole. Betty walked over this rock garden and ever since she's been having feelings."

"What if you don't find your rock?" Maria asks.

"If you don't find it, the rock finds you," Dunk answers.

"Willie, do you still have the *kava* I sent you?"

"Nope, I used it."

"You used it?"

"Yes. I wanted to make sure that before I used it with Dingo I had some idea what it was going to do."

"That was one great whack of *kava*, Willie," Dunk says. "Good thing I brought more with me. Never leave home without it."

That night they have a *kava* rite in a clearing in the forest not far from Willie's building site. Willie, Roger, Dunk, and Dingo, are going to take part in the actual rite. Maria is there to chew. Maam is there to keep her company and offer instruction.

It begins with Dunk taking some root, it doesn't look much different from any other root to Maria, from a burlap bag. It's dirty and Dunk washes it with distilled water he found in Willie's pantry. Once it's reasonably clean he takes a large hunting knife and begins hacking away at the root. He manages to make chunks of various sizes. These he tosses in a wooden salad bowl. At least that's what it looks like to Maria. Once he's through chopping up the root he turns to Maria and nods.

"Okay dear, take some of that distilled water and rinse out your mouth two or three times," Maam says. Maria does that.

"Now put the smallest piece of that root you can find in your mouth and start chewing. Don't, whatever you do, swallow. When your mouth builds up with saliva spit it into that bowl Dunk is holding." The bowl is not as large as the salad bowl and rests on a base made up of four little corpulent pigs. The wood is hard and black as night.

Maria begins to chew. It's like gnawing on a tree. Now Maria knows how beavers feel. Slowly saliva builds up in her mouth and she spits it out. As she chews the taste just keeps getting worse and worse.

Maria gropes around in her brain for some similar taste she's experienced and survived. As a kid she ate the dirt walls of the hut her family lived in. That was infinitely better. In England she ate haggis and tripe, but at least that was food and when you couldn't handle the taste you could force it down your gullet. Grandma Nose's cure for the ague. That's the only thing she can remember that tasted this bad.

By the time she's worked that out, the taste is gone. In fact it doesn't feel anywhere near so much like gnawing wood. That's because she can't feel much of anything in her mouth. She has to focus with all her might not to chew her tongue off and spit that out.

"It's okay darling," Maam says, "your mouth is supposed to go numb. Just keep chewing and spitting, a couple more times with that piece and then start on the next one."

Time stops for Maria. That's what it feels like. It may be taking her days to chew or mere seconds. It all feels the same. Soon she can't focus her eyes, everything is a blur.

"That's enough," Dunk says. Then he takes the cup from Maria, it's nearly full to overflowing with a murky white liquid, only slightly thicker than water. He pours some of the liquid into a smaller cup, made from the same wood but very plain.

He drinks from that smaller cup and spits. He spits to the north, to the south, to the east, and to the west. Then he hands the cup to Willie on his right. Willie repeats the process, as do Roger and Dingo. The little cup is now empty.

Dunk refills it and takes a hearty drink from it, which he swallows. Then he hands the cup to Willie.

"Come on, Maria. It's time for us to leave and let the men play their silly games." Maam pulls Maria to her feet. Maria can't remember ever having sat down, so this is somewhat disconcerting to her. What's worse is her legs are numb and she can't walk too well.

"Don't worry sweetie, the numbness will wear off in just a few minutes. Let's go home." They find their way to Truck and Maam hops in and starts driving. As they drive back to the trailer park Maria curls up against the large woman and falls asleep.

When Maria wakes up they are home and she's lying on the couch. She wiggles her toes cautiously. They move. She tries moving her jaw, first with her hand and then on its own. It seems functional, if a little sore. Then ever so slowly she opens her eyes. Everything is not only in focus, it's super bright and right up close. She slams her eyes shut. There is an awful ticking in her brain. It's going to explode, she just knows it.

"That's the wall clock you're hearing," Maam says, yelling in Maria's ear, "and actually I'm whispering. You've been out for several hours. Once the numbness starts to wear off all your senses are more acute. You hear, see, and smell things like dogs see, hear and smell things. My mother called chewing *kava*, doing the dog."

"Ip...is...it...ik...iz...spizzle."

"Your tongue is the last thing to return to normal. Here, drink some of this coffee, it's iced so you won't burn yourself. It's really strong and it will help, trust me."

"Thas besser. Will the mep be life thus?"

"The men will be much, much worse. And it will last a lot longer. Now you know why I told you not to swallow. A *kava* intoxication can go on for several days. We'll go check on them in a little while, once you're fully yourself. Make sure no animal has eaten them or anything. Maybe wrap them up in blankets so they don't get too cold."

"Will them see vissons?"

"It doesn't work exactly like that. You get paralyzed, at least with that wicked stuff Dunk uses. Then you get all mellow, time slows down, becomes not important. Then sometimes, if you believe, your ancestors, they come and talk to you. It's like they're in your head all the time and the *kava* just lets them out."

"You sound like you know all this first hand."

"Ah! I see you get your talkability back."

"Yes. I think I half, short of. Thought women weren't supposed to use *kava*."

"Oh men, if women did what men tell them to, the world would have come to an end a long time ago. My friends and I, after we'd chewed *kava* we'd slip away and make some brew ourselves and get blitzed."

"You bad girl!"

"Yeah, but if I wasn't a bad girl I'd have never gotten Willie's dad inside of me. You think you're having problems with Willie, his dad was worse, I swear. I knew he wanted me from the first time I ever saw him and I sure wanted him. He was so pale, nothing I'd ever seen was that pale. So I did what island girls do."

"What?"

"I tossed my hair. I brought him food. I cleaned the grass hut where he lived. I moved in, looked after him. Sound familiar?"

"Yes."

"Then I took him swimming in the lagoon. I figured that we'd both get naked and let nature take its course. No luck. He didn't even get hard.

"I started taking baths with him. I'd climb into bed with him at night. I'd massage him, eventually got really bold and tried to rub his man thing. He'd just slap my hand away like I was a fly."

"So how did you get him?"

"He saved me," Maam says.

"Saved you?"

"Yes. I was attacked by some boys from another island. They had evil intentions, he stumbled on us. He was so masterful, driving them off. He got a black eye, a cut lip, and some bruises. I tried to take him back to his hut. We only got a few feet before he attacked me. It was wonderful. I'd been with other guys but never anyone like him, not since either. I still miss it, and I still miss him.

"Of course it took me years to finish repaying all the favours I owed my cousins."

"Cousins?"

"My cousins from the main island agreed to help me stage the entire thing. We had a big party afterwards."

"Was Willie's dad there?"

"Oh yes."

"Wasn't he mad?"

"He thought it was funny. Now let's go see how the men are doing. Grab those blankets, I'll get some newspapers to help start a fire."

The men are resting peacefully. Dunk is propped against a tree, sitting up. Roger is sleeping on his stomach on a mossy patch. Dingo is flat on his back, his arms and his legs stretched out so he forms a star, in the middle of the clearing. Maam bends down and wraps him in a blanket. Them she gives him two kisses, the first on his forehead, the second on the lips. Standing, she shakes her head and comes over to where Maria is standing, looking down at Willie.

He's curled up in a ball sucking his thumb.

"He looks positively angelic, doesn't he?" Maam asks. "He was the cutest baby. It's hard to believe what he's capable of, watching him now."

"What do you mean?" Maria asks.

"He was always a scalawag, even when he was little. He was a great kid for minding other people's business. He'd sneak around listening to other people's conversations, watch who was making out with who. Then he'd use what he knew to make trouble. Let it slip that some miscreant husband was sleeping with his sister-in-law or that the priest was stealing chickens.

"He just loved to make mischief. What a tongue he had on him, knew exactly the thing to say to make my blood boil, other people too. He'd get under everyone's skin. It was only when we moved to Los Angeles that he got really wild. And that wasn't his fault exactly.

"There were these kids who kept teasing him. Well, maybe it was closer to terrorizing him. They were mean through and through, especially for Samoan kids. The only person who seemed to scare them was this little runt of a track coach. He carried around a machine pistol in his jacket and he must have known like a dozen kinds of martial arts, and he worked with throwers, huge kids with ugly tempers who'd do whatever he told them."

Maam frowns. "At first I thought he was some kind of chicken hawk, so I tried him out. He was definitely not interested in little boys. Second best I ever had. Anyway, to be protected Willie did track. I kept thinking he'd get tough, like my big brothers, no one in there right mind would mess with Dunk, or any of my other brothers. But Willie, he was a pussycat when it came to violence.

"But he kept right on making trouble. He found out which gangs were fighting for drug control in the neighbourhood and then he set them against each other. He'd tip the police, claiming to be from first one gang and then the other. I only learned all this later. He got free sex from the teenage prostitutes that worked on the edge of our neighbourhood by tracking down their Johns and figuring out who they were, at least the regulars, then he kind of made sure the girls all knew that he knew. That's all it took. None of their pimps said boo. They all thought he belonged to the same Samoan street gang that was terrorizing him.

"Then one day this kid, Woo-woo Fat they called him, trapped Willie. Woo-woo had all his cronies in tow for protection. I don't know what was said between them, but Willie went *musu*. He says he's never been able to remember anything about the entire incident.

"I saw the end of it. That was just a fluke. I was coming home from working the till at the Superfoods. Looked down this alley and there was Willie.

"He's got a hold of the feet of this much larger kid and he's spinning him around. Woo-woo's head is just off the pavement. At first I thought they were just playing but Willie keeps spinning faster and faster. All Woo-woo's friends are just standing around, dumbstruck.

"Finally Willie let's go of Woo-woo's feet. And he comes flying down the alley towards me but about ten feet above my head. I can hear him screaming woo woo, over and over. He goes flying out into the main street and is hit by an ice cream truck. His face is impaled in the wind screen.

"Later I measured how far he'd flown and it was ninety feet to impact. Broke his skull in three places, his cheek in five and his jaw in a dozen. He had his jaw wired shut for eighteen months. Couldn't eat anything but ice cream and milk shakes. Lost a hundred and sixty pounds. He eventually gained it all back. But by then the kids had all started calling him Woo-woo Airplane. Willie was their new leader."

Maam sighs. "I had to get him out of there. When he got out of prison I moved us to Salt Lake City. Dumb move."

"Why?"

"Them Mormon kids, they were way worse than the Samoan street punks."

"How's that?"

"They were always praying at him, telling him that his immortal soul was in danger. Eventually, I guess he started to believe them. He became the most uptight kid, obsessive-compulsive the doctor called him. Still is all kind of frozen up, can't move on with his life, or can't enjoy the one he's got. He thinks he is, but he's not, trust me."

"That's your job, to free him up."

"But he's terrified that if he lets go the Samoan part of him will get him nothing but trouble."

"The Samoan part?" Maam asks. "He thinks it's his Samoan part that causes trouble?" She is doubled over laughing.

"It's not?"

"Lordy, no. It's his dad. That man was pure mischief. There were times I wondered if he wasn't the devil's own child. One time he doctored the still in the village. All the men pissed purple for a week. Another time he switched a bunch of kids around the island. Claimed we all paid so little attention to our children we'd never notice the difference. Gave the kids gold coins to go along, to call their new parents Mom and Dad. Near to drove some people over the edge."

"What about *musu*, he's scared he'll go *musu* all the time."

"Boy has only gone *musu* once and Woo-woo, that kid had it coming to him."

Maria looks down at Willie and smiles. "What do you suppose he's dreaming?"

 **CHAPTER · 31**

"Wake up, William."

A tall, sandy-haired man is inside Willie's brain.

"Dad," Willie says.

"Son. I'm glad to see you're well."

"You look great, Dad."

"For a dead guy."

"There is that," Willie agrees.

"I have to say this place, whatever it is, agrees with me. Have you been following my advice?"

"I've been trying, Dad. God, it's hard."

"William, if you want this girl to be passionate about you and with you, then you have to hold out. Nothing makes a woman more enthusiastic and lusty than a chaste man. When she's climbing all over you think about this: is she giving you her heart and mind, or just her body?"

"How will I know when the time is right?"

"God will give you a sign, son. You will know, believe me. There is someone I'd like you to meet. I think the two of you might have a great deal to talk about. I'll be right back."

He returns leading an older man. The older man has white hair, waves of white hair, and a handlebar mustache.

"William, this is your great-grandfather. Sam, this is Willie. I've told you about him."

The older man smiles crookedly. "I understand you are trying to write about me. Not having much luck either, so I'm told. Come on lad, brighten up. You know who I am, right? No, I can see you don't. I hope you're brighter than this when you aren't imbibing of the intoxicating pepper. I'm Sam Clemens."

Willie tries to close his gaping mouth. "Mark Twain was my great-grandfather?"

"No, of course not. I was your great-grandfather. I suppose people today may assume that Mark and I were one person. I told enough people that hooey about taking Mark as a pen name when I started out as a journalist.

"People like an easy truth to believe. Like to believe what it pleases them to believe. I was apparently a harmless old coot, with a heart of gold. Perhaps over-fond of telling tall tales, but for the most part without guile.

"Mark was a complete person. Made up of flesh and blood, and with his own demons and desires. For fifty years, for the most part, I liked him better than I liked myself. I was an angry man. Before that, I was an angry boy. A boy who couldn't get his father to love him. I couldn't pilot a steamer up and down the Mississippi. Nobody would read my scribblings. I was a clay shell, without spirit."

"So you invented Mark Twain?"

"No, Of course not. He was always there, even before he had a name. He craved attention, always. I was sad, the circumstances of life made me feel guilty. Mark seized opportunities, engaged in hedonistic pleasures, smoked and chewed tobacco and cussed. He struck out in anger when I whimpered.

"Father wouldn't pay me any attention. He was a distant, hollow man. But he was fascinated by fire; volunteer fireman, deputy chief, chief. If there was a fire, Father was there. In those days, on the edge of civilization fire was everywhere. At least everywhere Mark was."

"You're saying that Mark Twain was an arsonist?"

"Well, my first auto-erotic exuberance was at Mark's first fire. He burnt this old, abandoned farmstead. Watching the fire consume the farmhouse, spread to the grass, and race towards town excited me. Listening to the bells on the fire wagon as it rolled out to meet the flames, knowing my father was on it, might be burnt, imagining his fat candling, I committed the sin of Onan for the first time, scattering my seed on the scorched earth.

"Mark was always a daring lad. We had wild times, the two of us."

"Tell me about those."

"You have a particularly prurient curiosity, young man."

"There isn't much point in having dirty little secrets if you can't share them with someone." Willie suggests hopefully.

"You don't give me much credit. None of my dirty secrets are to be found in the diminutive. If I share them with you, are you going to write about them?"

"Of course."

"You are a man after my own heart. Try this one then, William. You know my father hated the idea of slaves?"

"Yes."

"And you know it tore him apart when he had to punish them."

"Yes."

"He was trapped by his age. He had to be a white man. Once he had to beat the Duchess. You know who I mean?"

"The maid."

"Nursemaid, maid, nanny, cook, teacher, aunt. All that and more. Mark heard Father tell Mother, 'She thinks she's a Duchess. I won't have it. Not in my house.' The name stuck.

"I never did know what she did. My biographers say she sassed Mother, but I don't believe that for a moment. Father took Duchess into the sitting room and drew the doors, shutting out the family. Mark and I were hiding in the closet. We saw the entire thing.

"'Take off your clothes,' Father said. The Duchess removed each garment slowly, seductively, saying nothing.

"'Turn around and put your hands on that chair. Push it forward.' Then Father took his belt off. I'd been the recipient of punishments delivered by that belt and I wanted to cry out for the Duchess but Mark held his hand over my mouth.

"I don't think I was ever given a beating like that. Father was in a frenzy. He lashed her back, her buttocks, her legs. Finally he was spent. 'Turn around girl. Stand up and face me,' he said. She stood there, unashamed, defiant.

"'Now tell me, do you know your place?' Father asked, barely able to breathe.

"'No,' she said. One simple word.

"'I want you off the property tomorrow! Now go to your room.' Duchess gathered up her clothes and proudly strode from the room, carrying her things under her arm. My mother and brother must have seen her, seen the welts, the violence, her nakedness.

"My father stood there for a long time, sobbing. Mark couldn't help noticing the bulge in the front of his pants and took great delight in pointing it out to me. I found the whole thing...unsettling. It wasn't that I hadn't ever seen a naked woman before. I'd taken a good long look at the dead girl in the cave. You know about her?"

Willie shrugs. "I'm still not sure how she came to be there, but I know that a lot of young boys took the opportunity to see a naked girl. Even if she was dead, which kind of freaked them all out."

"Mark went further than just looking. He had the nerve to explore the corpse. Prod it with his fingers, even kissed her. That experience left Mark, and I must admit me as well, with a fascination with naked women, which we found remarkably easy to satisfy. You see, it could be a damnably hot country. A moist heat that lasted well into the night. Even the most prim and proper lady could reasonably be expected to shed their ridiculously stifling foundation garments and cool themselves in the breezes produced by open windows.

"Many, presumably, felt safe behind their flimsy curtains. But those barriers lost what little power they had to conceal as they fluttered in those self-same breezes. Others never bothered to draw their curtains, if indeed they had such a thing. The twins across the road were of that latter persuasion. Over a number of summers, Mark and I watched in awe as curly red hair sprouted between their legs and their breasts ballooned. As they grew a physical affection grew between them, a positive friskiness. They were to be Mark's second and third, or third and second women since the events were mostly simultaneous and the players on one side of the field indistinguishable. Of course, I maintained we were going to hell. I was a great fire and brimstone spewer.

"Now you're thinking I'm a caricature, the dirty old man, telling stories. But I was a deviant from a young age and believe that I shouldn't be required to change now that I'm dead. There is more to the Duchess story, would you like to hear the rest?"

"Please," Willie says.

"Well, once Father left the room Mark and I snuck out. We found a bottle of salve and crept on catty toes to Duchess's room. She lay face down, still naked, on that bed, in that little box of a room. We could hear her sobbing softly. When she finally realized someone was standing there watching her, she turned her head a fraction.

"'Oh! It's you Sam. You shouldn't be here.'

"'I brought salve.'

"'That's downright kind of you Sam, but I can't be reaching these wounds, least not most of them.'

"'I'll do it for you, Duchess.'

"'Sam, I wish you wouldn't call me that. And I canst be letting you rub that salve on me, much as I'd be real grateful. It just ain't a proper job for a young boy to be doing.'

"'You can be proper and in pain or let me relieve your suffering. You know me, Duchess. I'm not much of a one for proper behaviour.'

"'Well, that's a true fact for sure, Sam. Let's say I let you rub me, you won't be telling, will you?'

"'Ever know me to tattle about anything?'

"'No. Maybe you could just sort of start and we'll see how it goes.'"

Willie isn't just listening to Sam's voice lovingly delivering one of his famous stories. He's feeling it, seeing it, touching it, tasting it. He has begun at last to realize why *kava* is such a popular agent with shaman and medicine men throughout the south Pacific.

"Mark started at her shoulder and worked down," Sam continued. "Her skin wasn't anything like the dead girl's. It was soft and warm and gave against the slightest pressure. She winced every time salve came in contact with a cut or bruise, but clearly it was working some good. She'd stopped sobbing. When Mark worked down to her buttocks I thought she'd tell him to stop but she didn't.

"The worst of the welts were on her legs, the belt had curled around and licked the inside of her thighs. By that point in the beating, Father, in his madness, had turned the belt around so the buckle was lashing Duchess. Mark couldn't help his hands brushing her most improper areas as he applied salve to what were clearly painful wounds.

"'Did Father beat you there?' He asked touching her.

"'God, boy you shouldn't be touching me there. It's not proper. It feels good boy, but it's not right.'

"'So why is it wet, if Father never beat you there?'

"'It's wet because if feels so good, you're rubbing it boy. It would feel even better,' she said reaching behind her and guiding Mark's hand, 'if you reached in here, and rubbed here, all kind of at the same time.'

"I'll never know why a grown woman, I think she was maybe forty, shared her body with Mark and me. Maybe she was getting even with my father or wishing we were our father. Perhaps being beaten just made her aware of herself.

"I've got to go now, time gets short. Do the right thing, son." And with that Sam is gone.

"Sam said to tell you he hopes you'll come back so he can tell you more stories," Willie's dad says as he enters Willie's brain through some unseen door.

"Was Sam Clemens really my great-grandfather?" Willie asks.

"Yes, I swear. Ask your mother, she knows all the details. She was always good with stuff like that, genealogy and what all. I was always so busy chasing my last disaster, my next obscure disease, I never had time for family. I ask myself now, often, what sort of man spends his life praying for other people's misery."

"Are you guys really in my brain? Am I hallucinating?"

"Of course you're not hallucinating. *Kava* is a hypnotic, not a hallucinogen. Do Sam and I really exist? No. We are what you might call a collaborative venture. In some weird way we are floating out there, somewhere, Sam and I, waiting. When you take *kava* you invite us in, but we get altered as we cross into your brain from wherever we've been. In part you create us out of memories, things you've read, things you've heard. And it's all coloured by what is going on your life right now.

"Ask yourself why Sam told you that story and not about the young Chinese girls, the Native American women, the prostitutes, the drugs, or his various boyfriends. All of which would have been equally salacious, I'm sure. The worst part of being a prude is I'm stuck in eternity with the most libertine man of his generation. And now he can indulge his passion for dirty stories. I know somewhere you've read about how he hated having to edit his stories of their more exuberant details. Now he has no one to please but himself."

When Willie wakes, Maam and Maria are waiting anxiously.

"Did you see anything?" Maria asks.

"Are you all right?" Maam asks.

Willie stretches and grins. "I am better than all right. I'm the wonderfully marvelous marshmallow man from bugle company B. And by the by, little sort of Samoan female, I know why Sam Clemens created Mark Twain. I've got my thesis topic. Samuel Clemens was an arsonist. But he was a good boy and he couldn't reconcile the two. That's what split him apart. I'm going to call it *Firebug: Confessions of a Storyteller*. Now all I need is some paper."

"I think you'd better sit down here on the nice safe ground and drink some of this coffee while your brain figures out what it has done with your body," Maam says. "Meanwhile I and the little sort of Samoan female are going to go over there and finish a perfectly lovely conversation we were having when you interrupted us by waking up."

Once they are across the lake and out of even *kava*-invigorated hearing range Maria says, "I'm completely serious. That's how I picked Willie."

"You are lying in the road, sort of daydreaming, trying to will yourself to get big. A truck almost runs you over. A huge, ugly man, gets out and bends over you, and you decide he's there to show you how to get to be Samoan. Fliffle!"

"That's only part of the story. Just a little part, the rest is just like I told you."

"I'm not completely dumb. You tell me you picked him because he has money. I'd believe you, that is a pretty damn fine reason for picking a man. Only problem is my son, he's allergic to money, or it's allergic to him."

"I swear to you Maam, he's going to be rich. That morning I could see it clear as I was looking through a picture window. Willie with more money than I've ever seen in my life."

"You do have some confidence in your fortune-telling skill, don't you. So you've latched on to my boy 'cause he's a going to be rich. Fair enough. But then he starts messing with your head. Won't sleep with you, leads you on being all romantic. Ever occur to you that he's on to your game? Knows you are just after his money, that money he ain't got yet. But like you, maybe he knows he's going to be getting it. So he's messing with you. That's just the sort of thing he'd do. Or would have done before he got religion."

"He's not that smart," Maria suggests.

"One of his professors said once that the really frightening thing about Willie is his brain is proportional to the rest of him."

"You mean maybe he's scammed me. I'm hanging around waiting for this money. Money maybe he knows when it's going to show up. And he's using the time to make me love him."

"Deviousness does run in the family. You know Mark Twain was Willie's great-granddaddy?"

"Mmm."

"Four square. As a little boy Willie carried around a small notebook he filled with quotes from Twain. One day he said he'd found his mission in life. I asked him what it was and he showed me this quote from his book: 'An experienced, industrious, ambitious, and often picturesque liar.' That's what my boy aspired to be."

CHAPTER · 32

Maria starts the morning of the great poker match for Kennedy's brain by going for her second appointment with Dr. Dempster. Willie is off running some secret errand. He's taken a cab, and left her Truck.

"Have you figured out why you are turning Samoan yet?" Dr. Dempster asks, once they've gotten through the usual hand-kissing and other pleasantries.

"I've thought about it and thought about it," Maria shrugs. "I don't know why."

The doctor nods. "This phenomenon has been dealt with by Haverlock Ellis. Ellis said that if our boundaries are violated enormously we have two choices. We can split apart, go mad. Or we can expand our boundaries and that can include our physical boundaries. It's not uncommon that rape victims gain weight, try to make themselves physically unattractive."

"You think I was the victim of some sort of horrible boundary violation."

"Yes."

"And I'm turning Samoan so I can build boundaries that can physically include what was done to me."

"And make sure it isn't done again," Dr. Dempster says.

"You think I was gang raped, or something similar?"

"Not necessarily, the boundary violation doesn't need to be sexual, or even physical. I know a guy who fell seven thousand feet down a mountain and survived, pretty much unharmed. But it changed his life forever. He stopped climbing. No thrill in it anymore. He became risk neutral. He became the most relaxed person I've ever met. Cancer survivors often undergo something similar. Start taking chances. Living life on their terms.

Opening their hearts to love in a way they never imagined was possible. And yes, changing physically. Getting fit, getting fat, becoming stronger."

Maria frowns. "So you have no idea what happened to me?"

"I'm pretty sure I know exactly what happened to you," Dr. Dempster says.

"What?"

"Dislocation anxiety," Dr. Dempster says as if this explains everything.

"Okay. What's dislocation anxiety?" Maria asks.

"If you get moved from one place to another, one culture to another, it can make you very upset. If it happens to you again and again then you can become really mentally ill. The difference in culture and geography is a kind of boundary violation."

"You're saying that because I got forcibly removed from India, thrown out of the *kumpania*, ran away from my husband and his family to live with Willie, I'm turning Samoan?"

"Precisely. It is classic acting out. People who are acting out dislocation anxiety desperately need to belong somewhere, they need to feel accepted, and secure. But it needs to be a place, a culture, a person of their choosing, not something that's forced upon them."

The doctor leans forward. "Think about it. What happened is you need to belong so badly that you've actually altered your body to fit into the group you've chosen to join. But that isn't all."

"It isn't," Maria says.

"In order to change your body you first had to change your mind."

"How?"

"Do you mean how did it happen or in what way has it changed?" Dr. Dempster asks.

"Both, I guess," Maria says.

"I can't really answer either one. I'd guess you just thought about being Samoan so much that you changed some of the wiring in your head."

"We have wires in our head?" Maria asks, puzzled.

"Not exactly, but we have specialized cells that carry electric current just like wires, and the electric signals coming from your brain tell your body what to do. You managed to will yourself into this change, you altered the way those cells connect to each other. The result is your body started getting a very different signal. Instead of telling it to be Maslet, your brain started telling your body to be Samoan. But in the process you probably changed your brain in a lot of other ways. You may well think differently, feel things differently, value new things, and so on."

"My brain has changed, so maybe now I think like a Samoan," Maria says pensively.

"I'd doubt that."

"Why?" Maria asks.

"None of the other cases I've be able to find report a brain change anywhere near as dramatic as the changes to their body. They are more subtle. Much more subtle."

"But you think I'll stay Samoan?" Maria asks.

"If by that you mean big and brown, then yes. I don't think you'll ever revert."

"And you don't think I'm mentally ill?" Maria asks.

"Not anymore. I think by undergoing this transformation you overcame your dislocation anxiety. You now know, beyond any shadow of a doubt, how totally in control of your own life you are."

Maria can't wheedle anymore out of Dr. Dempster. In his mind he's explained her and cured her. Or rather diagnosed her as having cured herself.

Back at the trailer Maria takes a shower. Standing under the pulsing hot water she marvels at how her brain could make her body change so much. But how does she get her mind to turn Samoan?

The phone interrupts her thoughts. Dripping wet, she runs to answer it.

"Hi, is Willie there?"

No, who is this please?"

"Maria, it's Bob Struter."

"How are you?"

"Good, Maria. You?"

"Good, but I was sort of in the middle of something."

"I won't keep you. Can you tell Willie I got his fax with the thesis outline. It's brilliant. Now all he's got to do is write the thing. Fast."

"I don't think it will be a problem, Bob."

"Neither do I, Maria. Bye."

Maria climbs back into the shower. Maybe if her brain could tell her body to change then her body can tell her brain to change. She stands under the shower until she runs out of hot water, trying to figure out how to get her body to talk to her brain.

Maria is just about to get dressed when the doorbell rings. It's the Raklos: Draj, Marko, and Yannis. They are looking for Maria. They don't realize they are looking at her.

Maria stares at them. They stare back. She knows they don't know her. The lack of recognition she sees in Draj's eyes does something to her. The anger, the dislocation caused by her body's rapid changes rush through her bloodstream.

Standing there on Willie's stoop, in a too-small towel, confronting her ex-husband, Maria goes *musu*. She reaches out and grabs Draj by the throat with both hands. Then she twists and tears. Her attack is so sudden, so unexpected, that Draj can only clutch at her arms trying to pull her hands away.

Marko and Yannis are a little slow to react but when they do, they put their entire souls into the effort to save their older brother. Yannis grabs at Maria's towel. Tearing it off has no effect. Hitting her with it is even more useless.

Marko picks up a rock, a fairly hefty one, the biggest nearby, and whacks Maria upside the head. No response. Draj is beginning to turn blue. Marko summons up all his strength and smashes the rock into the side of Maria's skull. *Musu* is *musu*, she doesn't respond.

Yannis jumps on Maria's back and tries to add his strength to Draj's weakening battle to remove Maria's hands. Marko dashes past Maria looking for something else to attack her with. In the entranceway there is an umbrella. Not much of a weapon but all he has. He tries to ram it up Maria's ass. That causes her to swing around like an angry bear attacking a pack of dogs. Draj, his feet of the ground, swings with her. She uses Draj as a tool to shoo Marko away.

Yannis is digging his heels into Maria like he was riding a horse. When that has no effect he tries to stick his fingers into her eyes. She ducks her head, defeating his purpose. Her movement unseats Yannis and he starts to slide over Maria's head. All that stops him falling off is that Maria catches his right ear in her mouth and starts to bite it off.

Marko returns from a search for weapons with a frying pan he found in the kitchen. It's a large, cast iron skillet. He takes careful aim and nails Maria on the back of her skull. The force of the impact travels from her head to the frying pan to Marko's hand, arm, and shoulder. He drops the frying pan. It has a substantial dent in it.

Maria slowly releases Draj. He collapses, falling backward off the stoop and onto the ground at the base of the trailer. He is sputtering, coughing, and clutching his throat. Her mouth opens and Yannis is free. He falls to the floor at her feet.

Maria kneels down. At first Marko thinks he's succeeded in knocking her out. Then she finds the handle of the frying pan and lifts it as she rises back up, obviously in pain, and turns to confront her attacker. Marko bolts past her, grabs Yannis by the neck and pulls him to his feet. The two of them drag Draj toward the van they all came in. It races away moments later.

Maria spits out what she assumes is a piece of Yannis' ear. No one ever tells you that part of the agony of a concussion is that ideas, random ideas, hard beams, get set adrift and bash into your brain wall as it sloshes around inside your skull. "I don't like bacon anymore. I should never have got the Raklos involved in this. I've got to get to the casino. I'll make Willie suck my big toe." Then she collapses.

CHAPTER · 33

It's a Tuesday night. The date has been chosen carefully. Tuesday is cheap movie night. All the theatres in town have movies for half price or less. This keeps the crowds at the casinos light.

At Casino Edmonton the players are starting to gather around 8:00 P.M. There are seven bidders for Kennedy's brain. Roger is one, he'll be represented at the large table in the poker lounge by Maria. The other six bidders aren't present. They've each sent experts to represent them. Most have sent a team of three. One is handling the money. A second is there to check out the brain. The third is there to play poker, serious, high stakes poker. The bidders know if they walk away with the brain they also walk away with six million dollars. A million dollars from each unsuccessful bidder.

The brain is in a locked room in the back of the casino. The experts are escorted in, one at a time, to examine it. They find it in a glass case. A case they aren't allowed to open, which troubles most of them.

On the other hand they can't say it isn't Kennedy's brain. It's male, the right size, bears the marks of a gunshot wound, and a subsequent autopsy. Everything fits. Nothing counter-indicates. Their employers have been most specific, if there is any chance it is the brain, play cards.

All seven bidders have been offered the same guarantee by Average Bob. If the winner isn't one hundred percent happy with the brain he gets to keep two million dollars and the rest is returned to the unsuccessful bidders. If Bob wins, the brain goes to the Smithsonian. If it isn't Kennedy's brain, then the bidders get all their money back.

It seems foolproof. To Bob.

Each team carries the million dollar entry fee in the exact same suitcase. Samsonite, molded grey plastic and bright steel, with a lock. The suitcases have been chosen to allow space to carry not only the million dollars but an extra six million dollars and the brain.

The entry fees are turned over to the casino manager inside the money cage. There are extra security guards everywhere, most of them off-duty police officers. One at a time the teams pass through the security checkpoint. Inside the cage they open the suitcases and the cage clerk takes the money and counts it, feels it, smells it, and confirms the amount and authenticity. She then replaces the money in the suitcase and the team relocks it. The suitcases are then placed in the vault. The manager gives each team a million dollars worth of chips, their choice of denomination. It is a time-consuming process but reassures everyone. Roger, Dingo and Willie are the last team through. Willie has been stalling, waiting for Maria.

Once they have all completed the deposits the teams make their way from the cage to the poker lounge. It is a separate room, almost a separate building. For the evening it's been stripped down to one table. The public is allowed in but can't play poker. The casino will be raking off three percent of the pot in return for providing the dealers, the cards, the table, and the space. As well as handling the money. Two hundred and ten thousand dollars. For that you get the red carpet treatment.

"What are we going to do?" Roger asks nervously.

"Dingo plays," Willie says.

"I'm not sure I'm up to it," Dingo says.

"We don't have any other choice, Dingo. I'm a terrible poker player, Roger is too excitable. You're it until Maria shows up."

Everyone has agreed to a thousand dollar ante, and a minimum bet of a thousand. Even playing with ten grand in the pot, minimum, it's going to be a long night. The first few hands settle nothing except everyone's nerves. Bob takes the first, a pro named John Chance, from Austin, Texas, takes the second. The third goes to Dingo. They are playing straight five card stud. With the cigars lit and the whiskey flowing, it is like a re-enactment of a poker game from the old West.

The game is well under way when the Raklos arrive. They'd finally gotten patched up at the hospital, after a three and a half hour wait. X-rays showed there was no lasting damage to Draj's throat, some inflammation of the vocal cords is all. The doctor hopes it will go away. Yannis's ear they sewed back together, what of it they had. He is swathed and thinking he looks remarkably like Vincent van Gogh as the three of them walk into the Casino.

The Raklo boys don't jump right in. They wander the casino playing a little roulette, some slots. Even when they finally join the craps game it's not all at once and there doesn't seem to be any sense of urgency. Marko's in first. Playing conservatively he is up almost five hundred dollars after a half hour of playing, mostly betting on the house. Then he gets the dice and gets on a roll, in no time he's up five thousand dollars. He's drinking like a fish, garrulous, tipping his waitress far too generously.

Once Marko finally loses, Draj enters the game. They both play heavy on the house line, betting against the other players. Luck is with them. They are both up substantially when Yannis returns from the poker lounge and joins the game. Yannis bets big and well, but Draj still hasn't put the rigged dice in the game. Marko has another long winning streak, with Yannis betting with him and Draj against him as they hedge their bets.

Meanwhile, in the poker lounge, Dingo is remaining sober and giving some awfully good poker players a run for their money. He has held even, about a thousand dollars up after twenty five hands. With a dealer change under way Willie massages his shoulders and brings him a Coke.

"Looking good," Willie says.

"Not feeling good, I'm starting to be all trembly. Can't concentrate," Dingo says.

"Stick with it. Everything will be okay. I think maybe you're going to win this thing."

"Really," Dingo says.

"Really," Willie says.

"You're a true mate." Roger is nowhere to be seen. The pressure clearly got to him early and he's been wandering in and out every five or six hands. In between he's outside chain smoking.

Yannis can't believe what is happening. Sure he knows the stories about people beating craps fair and square, betting mostly with the house, and against it in large amounts at exactly the right time. But in this case an entire table has gone nuts. Draj has had a run of eleven consecutive points made,

Marko has done fourteen, and had a run of five straight sevens off the pass, doubling down each time. In that little mini-streak he's won eleven thousand, two hundred dollars.

But the Raklos haven't held the dice the longest, there have been two streaks of fifteen rolls and one of nineteen. With runs like that every one of the thirteen players crowded around the table is betting against the house much of the time, betting big, and winning. Yannis works out that the table must be down almost a million dollars in the three hours since Marko joined the game. At least three hundred thousand dollars of it is in Yannis's pockets. Out of his last hundred bets, each five thousand dollars, he's won eighty.

The casino has tried everything to stop the run. They've put in new dice four times. The casino manager forced his way into the game. When the dice got to the security guy Yannis places major bets with the shooter, against the house. And the boss cost the house thirty-eight thousand dollars before he was smart enough to pass the dice on to Yannis. Up until then Yannis had been passing the dice. This time he takes them and runs off six points in a row, including four tens, before passing. A furious conversation is going on between the head of security and the manager of the casino. The manager is standing, off and on, right behind Yannis. A little psychological warfare, ruined by the fact that Yannis is amused by the man's name plate. Mr. Stubby. And he is, short, and fat. Stubby.

The first player is eliminated from the poker match at the four hour mark. It is pretty clear that the battle is between John Chance, Average Bob, and maybe Dingo. Dingo is up two hundred thousand dollars, not more than a million like Bob and John Chance. But they are the only three in positive territory. The loser, Jolly James from Kansas City, is bitching and whining about all the racket as spectators scurry back and forth between the craps table and the poker match. How it made it impossible for him to concentrate. "Couldn't hear myself think."

A remarkable thing is happening at the craps table. The Raklos are walking away, cashing their chips and walking away. They looked at each other, nodded, and walked away. A cohesive team for the first time in their lives. At the money cage they turn in three hundred and ninety seven thousand dollars worth of chips. The security chief makes a terrible mistake. He lets them get the money before he challenges them.

They are in the hallway that joins the casino and the poker lounge, headed out into the night rich men, when the security detail stops them. The team closes in on the Raklos, demanding to search them, which is within their power, possibly. Yannis isn't worried. It's been a great night, other than his ear just hurts worse and worse. He's taken the fixed dice from Draj, the ones they didn't ever need, and casually dropped them in the garbage, using his body to block the security camera's view. He used a napkin, no prints, so even if the casino finds the dice they'll never be able to prove the Raklos had anything to do with them.

The head of security is very impressed by the young man. That's when it hits him.

"How old are you, son?" He asks.

"Twenty-one, why?" Yannis asks. He isn't sure what the legal age for gambling in Alberta is. One fact he didn't check. So he's hedging his bets. The problem is he doesn't look that old.

"I think maybe you're underage, that's why. Got any proof of that?"

"I'll tell you what, Mr. Yankowich, is that how you say your name?" Yannis asks, reading his name plate.

"Just Yankowich," the man says.

Yannis makes good eye contact with the older, bigger man. He is learning to read people and this Yankowich is two kinds of trouble, sour and clever. The sour part means he doesn't want anyone else to be happy, walk away ahead, particularly not anyone he thinks cheated. The clever part has him calculating how to prevent it from happening. But Yannis, pure of heart, is way ahead of him.

"I give you back the money I won. You give me a receipt. I go get proof that I'm of legal age. My passport. You can use the time to figure out how I cheated. When I get back you give me my money."

"How about I just arrest the three of you and call the police."

"Fine idea," Yannis says. "The police they come and first think they ask, 'How did they cheat?' and you say, 'I don't know.' Not a good place you got yourself in. I'm demanding a lawyer, threatening to call the police, making lots of drama. Maybe the police impound the money as evidence while they look into the way things really are. More likely they give it to me and send me on my way. Tell you and your bosses that you are lucky I'm not suing your asses off, pressing criminal charges."

"Suing us, what for? Criminal charges, you're crazy," Yankowich says boldly.

"False arrest. Only way you get this money you arrest us. Only way you search us is if you arrest us. Then you find nothing. And I promise you won't. No proof of any wrongdoing besides that we won, which isn't going to look good in the paper or in court. If you tried to take money from me and my brothers and you had no reason to believe we committed a crime, then you stole from us.

"My way, we walk out of here unchallenged. You get back your three hundred thousand dollars that I won. My brothers keep what they won. Your damage is limited to less than a hundred grand."

"How do you figure that?" Yankowich asks, beginning to see an out as a crowd gathers. "You come back with proof of age and I'm out another three hundred thousand dollars. But if I search you now and find some illegal dice then I get to keep it all and you go to jail."

"If I come back, and I will, with proof of my age we both know you aren't going to give me that money without a fight. You're a clever guy, by then you will have thought of some new argument. Then you and me can spend the next hundred years in court fighting over that loot.

"As for searching us I think maybe you'll have a riot if you try." He's hoping that this stupid man will just give in and he can get out of there. He doesn't feel well. His ear is throbbing. He's starting to sweat.

Yankowich knows Yannis is right. Security is picking on a winner. In front of a group of losers. Who hope some day to win. The situation is growing ugly. But Yannis's sudden attack of the sweats is just the proof Yankowich was looking for that Yannis's is guilty. Which is when the manager arrives. From a distance he appraises the scene. Yankowich is saying silently, "Call the bastards' bluff, call it."

Mr. Stubby, with nerves of steel and razor-sharp mind, draws his hand across his neck in a sawing motion. He's telling Yankowich to let them go, with all the money. He's sure they've been cheating and he doesn't care enough to make a scene. It's a big night for the casino and he doesn't want to ruin that. Plus Mr. Stubby has been watching the formerly red hot craps table go stone cold. He knows, years of experience, that the punters around that table are going to chase good money with bad until the casino earns back more than it's lost to the Raklos.

The problem is that Draj misinterprets the signal. Thinks he's being threatened. He pulls an automatic pistol out of his sports coat. The guards dive for cover and the crowd scatters as he fires a volley into the ceiling. Then he and Marko flee into the night. With the money.

It is a testimony to the intense concentration of first-class poker players that none of them even blinks when automatic weapon fire shatters the silence of the lounge. Up until that moment Dingo's luck had been getting better and better. When he loses the pot is small, when he wins the pot is big. At the moment of Draj's assault on the ceiling he wins a four hundred thousand dollar pot with just two pair when Bob bluffs everyone else out of the pot while holding a pair of jacks.

Draj hasn't lost his mind. He has a problem. He's never liked Yannis's dice. They don't win fast enough, big enough. He's carrying a second set. A better set. He's been slipping them in and out of the game all night. Right under the noses of the security people. Fooling even Marko and that know-it-all Yannis. When Yannis asks for the dice, no way Draj is giving him the lucky ones, he gives him the dice he expects, the pitiful ones he expects Draj to use. Now he has to get far ahead of his pursuers so he can ditch the dice.

He also knows full well that possession is nine-tenths of the law. If he and his brothers get off the casino grounds with the money Marko is carrying in a satchel then the casino isn't ever going to get the courts to give it back. Not when they can't prove any illegal act was committed. He figures he can argue in court that having won all that money when approached by men with guns he assumed they planned to rob him and defended himself. Him being a foreigner and all, and born and raised in a very violent country, he will sweet-chat the judge into six months suspended.

Marko, first out of the casino, only makes it a few feet. Then his brain kicks into gear and he stops, turns, drops the bag, and turns to smile at his pursuers as Draj races past him. "Why me run?" He asks himself. He isn't underage. He didn't start shooting up a casino. Plus he's got the money and he is pretty sure he can find a lawyer who will work damn hard at helping him keep it.

Turning to face his pursuers causes them to come to a sudden halt, frozen by the idea Marko might also have a weapon. His immobile pursuers are a major barrier for those chasing Draj. That's when Marko realizes Draj has grabbed the satchel. The bass tart.

Draj gets just far enough ahead to toss the dice, the evidence, unseen, out into the dark night. Yannis has told him often about fingerprints. He makes sure there are none of those on the dice before he makes his throw.

Having got rid of the evidence Draj just needs to get off the property and he'll skate completely.

He doesn't trust the security guards. He isn't sure they won't shoot at him. He weaves in and out of the cars, trucks, and minivans in the parking lot. He's almost off the grounds when he encounters a large brown woman getting out of a taxi.

Looking at her in just the right light, the truth dawns on him.

"Maria," he says. "Maria, how could you?" Then he raises the gun and points it at her.

The next thing he knows Draj is flying through the air, semi-conscious. His gun goes flying one way, the satchel the other. He scrambles after the gun on all fours. Has his hands on it, when a massive foot steps on the gun, making sure Draj can't get it off the ground.

"I don't think you should be playing with that," Draj looks up, way up, and there is Willie.

"What you hit me with?" Draj asks. "A car?"

"My hand," Willie says. "Be glad I didn't kick you."

Yankowich is right behind Willie. Attempted murder, unlawful possession of a firearm, disturbing the peace, he's still thinking up charges as he drags Draj, now handcuffed, to his feet, and discovers the two dice Draj has fallen on. "Now what have we here," he says. Draj begins to cry.

When Draj first started shooting, Yannis couldn't figure out what was going on. All he knew was it made his ear hurt even badder, all that noise. He runs on instinct, like a greyhound at the track chasing the rabbit. But outside, for the first time in his life, he turns away from his brothers. One guy's got the money. One guy has the gun. One guy is missing an ear and weaving like a drunk. The security people chase after the first two. Yannis runs like hell at first but has a hard time standing up. He keeps falling, getting up, running a few steps, falling.

Behind the casino the property is fenced, a fence he isn't up to climbing. His ear seems to be infected. It's making him dizzy, awkward, and disoriented. He has to go around the front again. By the time he gets there he is crawling. Hearing Draj's voice he crawls towards it. And gets hit in the face by the satchel. No one stops him, notices him, as he crawls out of the parking lot, behind the damn fence and into the night carrying the satchel in his teeth. In agony, on his way to freedom, he keeps having the same thought, I need new partners.

It's only later they come looking for the satchel. Accusations fly fast and furious. Yannis is oblivious. He is asleep in a dumpster, clutching the money to his chest.

CHAPTER · 34

By the time Willie gets back, the poker game has begun to shake itself out. It is down to three players: Average Bob, John Chance, and Dingo. As each player exits they leave behind, in the pot, the keys to their suitcases. Of the seven million dollars, Bob has four million and change, Dingo has two million, and Chance is just short of a million. The stakes rise to a twenty-five thousand dollar ante and fifty thousand dollar minimum bet.

Chance is getting fatigued. They all are. But unlike Dingo and Bob he doesn't have the resources to be able to afford the stupid mistakes that fatigue causes. He's broke in less than two hours. Most of his worst losses have been to Dingo. He and Bob have roughly equal piles of chips by the time it's just the two of them.

"How about one hand takes all?" Bob asks.

"Let me consult," Dingo says. He's exhausted. He isn't sure he even has one more hand in him. But he figures that this is where Bob's going to go for the kill. All the money.

Everyone huddles. "Go for it," Willie says. Roger, back from his latest anxious tour of the casino and its bathrooms gives Dingo's shoulder a squeeze. Turning to face Bob again, Dingo nods his agreement. It's a struggle just to get his head back to the upright position.

Bob gets three queens in the deal. He draws another queen. Dingo has zip: five little cards, no pairs. Dingo realizes his only hope is a miracle. He keeps the two, three, and six of hearts. Dingo draws the four and five of hearts. Inside straight. He can't believe it. With a sigh, Dingo lays down first.

Bob gets up and storms out of the casino. His discarded hand lies face up on the table. The crowd goes nuts. Willie and Dingo embrace. Dingo's dancing now, his fatigue forgotten. He grabs Roger and they waltz around the poker lounge.

"I did it, I did it. God, what were the odds?" Dingo yells.

"Just good enough I guess," Willie says.

"Willie, where is Maria?" Dingo asks.

"I don't know," Willie says. "I haven't seen her since last night."

The three men go to the money cage. In their presence and with the assistance of the manager, the cage clerk counts out the money from each suitcase, takes the casino's two hundred and ten thousand dollars and stacks the remaining six million, seven hundred and ninety thousand dollars in Roger's Samsonite case. Roger opens the glass container that holds the brain. Extracts a smaller glass jar. Unscrews its lid, peers at the brain intently. Nodding, clearly satisfied, Roger takes a handful of money and hands it to Dingo.

"That should be twenty-five thousand dollars," he says. "A bonus. Send me the bill for your regular services. Now, can you gentlemen give me a ride to the airport?"

"You're not leaving," Dingo says.

"I have to. Soon as word leaks out I've got this money I'm a target for every lowlife scum in the underworld. And the brain," Roger says, nestling the glass jar into a special compartment he's had built into his suitcase, "when the wrong people find out I've got the brain, I will have to run far and fast."

"But where are you going?" Dingo asks.

"I'll decide that at the last moment, harder to find me, that way," Roger says.

Willie carries the suitcase to the minivan Roger has rented.

"You can keep the van, turn it in tomorrow. It's all prepaid on my credit card."

The trip to the airport is very quiet. Once there Roger buys a ticket on the next flight to the U.S., into Denver on Northwest, leaving at 5:35 A.M.

That leaves eight minutes until boarding. Roger gets on the plane. He's paid extra to allow the suitcase to fly as a passenger. Willie's been hauling it around the airport, now he surrenders it to a steward.

"Let me come with you," Dingo pleads with Roger.

"I can't ask you to do that," Roger says as he gives Dingo one final hug. Then he's gone up the gangway on to the plane.

Willie stares at Dingo. "Let's go get some breakfast."

He drags Dingo to Arby's. Willie stocks up on pancakes and syrup, four orders, and six orange juice. He manages to force a cup of coffee on Dingo.

"The ungrateful, uncaring jerk. Twenty-five thousand dollars. That's all I get for winning him his dreams. That and a broken heart," Dingo says.

"Want to listen to the uncaring jerk's parting words?" Willie asks, pulling a small tape recorder from his cargo pants.

"You planted a bug on Roger," Dingo says, shaking his head.

"Yup," Willie says. "Shall we listen to it?" He turns it on, and there surrounded by sleepy diners and bathed in the perfume of smoking grease the two men learn just what serious treachery they've been confronting.

The first voice they hear is Roger's.

"Kick me in the teeth, it worked, it actually worked."

"Just like Maria planned it," Bob says. "She's a one hundred percent, certifiable genius. What did you say she told you at the casino?"

"She comes up to me outside, just as we're loading the money. I didn't want to let that big Samoan bastard out of my sight for a minute. Not with almost seven million dollars."

"Six. Don't forget our portion was funny money. Ran it off on the printer myself," Bob says. They both sound like they've been drinking.

"She threw a stone at me, damn thing hurt, got my attention. Told me she still had a few loose ends to take care of and she'd catch up with us in Baja," Roger says.

"You made sure the money was okay?" Bob sounds a little nervous.

"Don't worry. He was only out of my sight for a minute. The case is a combination lock, he's not good with locks. And I checked. All the money is there, and the brain."

"I'll always thank the heavens for the day I met Maria outside that theatre," Bob says. "But part of me sort of hopes she never makes it to Baja. More for you and me, Roger. More for me and you."

"I can't believe how well Dingo played. When Maria didn't show up, I thought we were done like dinner," Roger says.

"Yeah, that was always the weakness in the plan," Bob says. "We mark all those decks, and sure that gives us a competitive advantage, but if I'd won we'd have bought no end of trouble. I'm certain the sore losers would have made sure the brain went off to the Smithsonian by overnight courier. They were gathered around the table like vultures near the end, just waiting to swoop down and make me keep my promise. Probably would have kidnapped us and waited for the results."

They clink glasses.

"Maria was right, though," Bob continues. "If she won, then you could just announce you'd had the brain authenticated and it was genuine, we keep the money and some day we can find a sucker and sell the brain. No one is ever the wiser. I look like the big loser."

Roger laughs. "But Dingo was even better. So much more believable. I think by the end everyone was rooting for him."

"I figure I should get a bonus for controlling all those early pots to make sure that when Dingo lost he didn't lose big and that when he did win, he won big. I couldn't believe it when he finally got on a roll. Imagine drawing to a low straight flush like that."

"What were you going to do if he didn't?" Roger asks.

"I had this plan. I was going to take my whiskey and pour it on my cards and use my lighter to set them on fire. Then I was going to get up and walk away from the table. Let everyone assume that Dingo won with crap in his hand."

Willie shuts the transmitter off and goes back to eating pancakes.

"Hey, leave that on," Dingo says. "Maybe they'll say where they're going in Baja."

"Trust me," Willie says. "You don't want to know. In fact, all you need to know about Roger is that Mark Twain described him perfectly. 'If you pick up a stray dog and make him prosperous, he will not bite you. This is the difference between a dog and a man.'"

"But he's getting away with a six million dollar scam," Dingo protests.

"Mark Twain had an expression for that too: 'He is now fast rising from affluence to poverty,'" Willie says.

"Which means what?"

"Wherever they are going they are going to present almost six million dollars of counterfeit money to some bank. It's pretty good counterfeit. Eugene knocked it off for me."

"You switched suitcases," Dingo says. "We are sitting here eating breakfast and out there in the parking lot is six million dollars." He shakes his head. "But where did you hide the suitcase? There was no place in the minivan, Roger would have seen it."

"I shoved it under the truck parked next to us."

"We've got to go get it," Dingo says, jumping up.

"Don't worry, Dingo, it was only there for a couple of seconds," Maria says, sitting down beside Willie. She's carrying a Samsonite case. "Were you beginning to worry I wouldn't show up, Mr. Willie?"

"Nope."

"You are way too sure of yourself."

Dingo stares at the case. "You've known it was a scam for a very long time, haven't you?"

"I knew I was being had the day that Maria showed up at my trailer. I didn't know how. Then Roger shows up and I knew we were both being set up. It was all just too coincidental. Then they kept trying to blind us with sex. If they weren't doing it with us, or trying to seduce us, they were telling us dirty stories. Sex is important, but these people were obsessed. Sex was moondust in our eyes."

"What about the brain? Did you take the brain as well?" Dingo asks.

"I didn't have much choice. I had to take the entire suitcase. So ours has a brain in it, in a typical glass autopsy jar, just like theirs. It's the right size, has a gunshot wound, some sections."

"So we have Kennedy's brain?"

"Of course not," Willie says.

"How do you know?" Dingo asks.

"That brain, the one everyone was supposedly playing high stakes poker for, it was packed in formalin. Kennedy's brain was placed in formaldehyde after the autopsy. That brain, just like the one I replaced it with, had never been anywhere near formaldehyde," Willie says.

"How can you know that?" Dingo asks.

"I went to med school. I know the difference between formaldehyde and formalin when I smell them."

"But how could you have known how to package your dummy brain?" Dingo demands.

Maria turns to Dingo. "So you agree with me that Willie has a dummy brain?"

"Maybe it was a lucky guess," Willie says to Dingo, ignoring Maria.

"I doubt that somehow," Dingo says.

"I figured out where Bob was hiding his brain, broke back into his house, it was much easier the second time, and had a good look at the brain," Willie says.

"Where was he hiding it?" Dingo asks.

"In a large bag of President's Choice Premium dog food," Willie says. "I went back and forth over all that data Mary Beth generated from the marketers and discovered Bob always bought Eukenuba for his dogs, but I remembered seeing a bag of President's Choice. Which made me really curious about the bag. No one who fed Eukenuba would ever feed that lower end stuff to his dogs. That's all there was to it."

"Part of it was dumb luck," Maria says. "Bob, brilliant Bob, he hid the counterfeit money in the same place. Which gave Willie the idea for the switch."

"Where did you get the brain?" Dingo asks.

"Liberated it from the path lab at the U of A. We'll put this one back in its place," Willie says, pointing at the case.

Silence settles over the breakfast table. Maria takes a deep breath.

"So you guys are going to return that money, right?"

Dingo and Willie just look at each other.

"Maybe I'll have some breakfast after all," Dingo says.

"You have to give it back," Maria insists.

"Why?" Willie asks. "We won it fair and square. We didn't cheat."

"You let Roger lure those people there with a brain that you knew wasn't real. Then you let them play cards with Bob knowing he was planning to cheat."

"You and he together," Willie points out.

"Two wrongs don't make a right."

"You are not convincing me," Willie says.

"Okay. It's not Samoan," Maria says. "It's devious and unkind. If we are going to be good Samoans, you and me, we have to give the money back."

"You are not Samoan," Willie pronounces. "And I'm only half Samoan."

"You got that wrong. I'm Samoan, know why?"

"Why?"

"Because you can't prove I'm not, not anymore. I just found out that individual humans are more alike genetically than any other mammal. There just isn't any way of knowing what genes make someone Samoan and what genes make them Maslet."

"Where did you hear that?" Willie asks.

"On the radio driving over here. I look Samoan, I think Samoan, that's all that matters. Which means there are one and a half Samoans at this table and we all vote to return the money."

Dingo pulls a flask out of his pocket, stares at it, then puts it back. "Not to get in the middle of your fight, children, but as the white guy at the table I have to point out that half of us are white and doesn't our vote count equally?"

"Yeah," Willie says to Maria. "Fifty-fifty."

"But the Samoan fifty percent is way bigger than the white fifty percent and might makes right," Maria says, giving Dingo a dark look.

"What are you going to do to me if I don't give the money back?" Willie asks.

"I'll never have sex with you again."

"You haven't had sex with me before, so that's hardly a threat."

Maria grins. "But if I don't have sex with you ever, then you'll never know what you've been missing all this time."

EPILOGUE

From Willie's trailer it took one cab, three airplanes, two ferries, and fifty hours to reach Falemusu. At each stop, as they got ever closer to Willie's birthplace, Maria fought the impulse to ask him, "Do you feel more Samoan yet?" She felt like she was going home.

Uncle Dunk had told them they could use the palm-thatched hut on the edge of the village during their stay. When he was home, it was his office. Patients came from all over the islands to consult with him. But it had a bed — Dunk liked to sleep on the job, helped him get in touch with the spirits — and a good solid roof.

The bed was a mattress of palm fronds and canvas. It was raised a foot off the ground by a very sturdy looking iron frame.

"Why is it raised up like this?" Maria asked.

"Dunk doesn't like the rats running over his face while he's sleeping. He's afraid he'll choke on one," Willie said.

They spent their first twenty hours on the island sleeping. While they slept Willie's aunts crept in and out, singularly and in groups. Each time they left something, ripe mangoes, a sarong for Maria, a baseball cap for Willie, something.

It was late on a glorious blue morning when they woke. They explored the village and beach. It didn't take long. Most of Falemusu is straight up and down. Willie hadn't prepared Maria for the towering mountains that seemed to hang over the huts. Of course, he hadn't co-operated much right from the time Maria suggested the trip. She'd had to make all of the arrangements.

All she'd wanted, she thought, was for Willie to be happy. In order to be happy he had to be more spontaneous, less didactic. Maybe in Samoa, where he'd grown up, he could find his inner child. Maria had taken to reading self-help books, and soon learned she was trying to replace her need for sex with books, food, wine, chocolate, soap operas....

They took a picnic lunch and hiked through the palm forest to the lagoon where Willie swam as a child. The sun beat down, the sand was a fiery orange, the palms throwing puddles of shade, the mountains so close it seemed like you should be able to reach out and touch them. Maria realized it was Willie's future, the one she'd seen that first day. What a frightening thought, to be stuck on that small island, seeing the same people, doing the same things, day after day, forever. The idea made her shiver.

Gradually the gentle breeze, the moist air, and a bottle and a half of some sweet dessert wine, no label, relaxed Maria. At which point Maria remembered her original purpose in suggesting the trip. She climbed onto Willie's lap, raising her sarong up over her hips.

"Not yet," Willie said.

"Why not?" Maria asked.

"Listen," he said.

She heard the wind in the trees, and grunting.

"What's that?" She asked.

"Well it could be pigs. But I'd bet it's my aunts pretending to be pigs. Let's go back to the hut and get this over with."

Maria thought Willie meant let's get the sex over with, which was fine with her, if a little unromantic. In the hut she began sucking on his face.

"Not yet," Willie said.

"Why not?" She asked.

"You'll see. Just sit here like a good girl and wait for my aunts."

Maria had met the aunts when the ferry docked. Eight gigantic brown women with big smiles and knowing looks. But she couldn't have said which one was which.

Aunt Germaine was first, Uncle Dunk's wife.

"Damn," she said, sneaking into the hut without knocking. "Dunk said you'd be all over each other like Spam on bread. I should know never to listen to him."

Aunt Alexia was next. Ten minutes had passed. She made a pretense of knocking. Gentle little taps, like light rain.

"Girl, don't you know that sex is women's work," she said, before she stormed out, pouting.

"That's two," Willie said.

Mabel, Martha, and Sheila were next. After Sheila left, Maria could hear women's voices raised in anger outside the hut. "I tell you the boy is only interested in books, that's the problem with so much education, shrivels the balls," she heard Sheila say. "Boys," one of the other women said. "Boys and books," Germaine said.

Beatrice, Annie, and Nell dropped by over the next half hour. Just to chat. Willie was downright anti-social. The women all recognized *musu* coming on and cut their visits short.

"Now can we do it?" Maria asked. She could still hear the women's voices outside. She was not going to let these women intimidate her out of having sex. "Not yet," Willie said. "But soon."

The voices settled down. Then there was a polite knock on the side of the hut. A clearing of the throat.

"Come in, Aunt Germaine," Willie said.

She came in and quickly squatted down across from Willie and Maria.

"The girls and I have been talking and we've decided you should have sex Samoan style. Just in case you haven't done it before. It's best not to try anything too exotic the first time. Stick with the basics. Boy meets girl, kaboom."

"Thanks for the advice Auntie, now beat it, all of you. Before I do go *musu.*"

Once Germaine had left Maria asked, "What's been going on?"

"My aunts have a little pool going. They all tossed in their shopping money and the one who catches us having sex first gets the jackpot. My aunts are compulsive gamblers. And they've always been fascinated by my sexual orientation."

"So what's Samoan-style sex?" Maria asked.

"Who knows? Aunt Germaine is jerking our chain. No that's not right. What is it Dunk told me? It's been years.

"Wait, I've got it. Okay, take off your clothes," Willie said, tossing his sarong aside.

Maria did as she was told, for once. She'd never been so proud of her body before. She was fabulously round and dark.

"Now I'm going to lie down on the bed," he lay down on his back, "you lie facing me." They formed a perfect X.

"Shouldn't we kiss first or something?" Maria asked, a little panicked, looking at the enormity of Willie.

"Samoans don't believe in foreplay. Just relax. The idea is for you to be like the sea, washing in and out.

"Hold me up against you, then slide down on to me, a little bit at a time."

"Oh...my...God," Maria said.

"Now slide up and down, you set the pace," Willie said.

"This is a little awkward, Willie," Maria said. "Can't we try a different position?"

"Like this, I can go on forever, getting bigger and bigger. That's what Dunk taught me. Pretty soon you won't care how uncomfortable it is."

"Willie, women aren't men. We do care about comfort."

"Here, put this pillow under your head. You mean to tell me you've never had sex all scrunched up in the back seat of a car? In a hay loft? What's the most uncomfortable place you've ever had sex?"

"In Provence, in a grape crushing shed. It was late in the harvest, horribly hot, the shed was metal, the floor was cement covered in grape skins. Sticky, red grape skins, a little juice. How about you?" Maria asked.

"Inside a coffin," Willie said.

"A coffin?"

"It was while I was locked up in Lompoc. They'd send us out to work. Cheap labour. I had a month-long job making coffins outside San Luis Obispo. It was a co-ed project, supposed to teach us how to get along with the opposite sex. Obviously didn't work in my case. Actually, we mainly spent our time trying to figure out where we could have sex without being caught.

"After the coffins were nailed together they went along a conveyor belt to a separate building to have the plush interiors installed. We did it in the roughed-in shell of the coffin while it worked its way down the belt. We'd have gotten away with it too, except I got a little too aggressive, and the lid came down on us and locked in place. We were in there for an hour, packed like two sardines, until the workers opened the casket to put in the lining."

"Speaking of aggressive, maybe this would work better if you tried to meet me halfway. Thrust back against me as I come forward," Maria said.

"I'm afraid I'll hurt you," Willie said.

"You are certainly the biggest, and the strongest man I've ever been with. But if you aren't going to use that in bed, then what's the point? No, not like that, you really aren't very good at this are you?" Maria said, her frustration finally getting the better of her.

That's when Maria saw that strange look in Willie's eyes that any Samoan woman can instantly recognize as *musu*. Willie rolled out of bed suddenly, tossing Maria on to the floor on her butt. He reached down and grabbed her, lifted her up and onto his shoulder. He carried her out of the hut. The aunts were still there, waiting to see what was going to happen next.

Willie carried Maria, kicking and screaming, like a sack of potatoes over his shoulder and marched down majestically to the lagoon. The entire village came running, alerted by the aunts. Willie waded partway out into the lagoon. Then he heaved Maria as far as he could out into the water.

She came up sputtering, just in time to see Willie dive under the water. A minute later he surged past where she was standing on tiptoes in the water. As he went by he bit her ass. Not much of a bite, but enough to get her attention. A few feet away he surfaced and blew a mouthful of water at her.

Maria began to swim away. Willie dove again. Maria wasn't making much forward progress, turning around and around trying to spot Willie. Occasionally she saw a big, brown bum break the surface like a shark's dorsal fin. Next thing she knew his head was surging up between her legs and he was tugging at her labia with his teeth, pulling her under the water.

Slapping at Willie, Maria managed to break free, to reach the surface again. Before she could swim away, Willie grabbed her ankle and began to tow her out towards the reef. A few feet short of the surging tide and the razor-sharp reef Willie slowed and pulled Maria up to him.

"Know what time it is?" he yelled over the ocean. "Coming up on high tide."

Willie rolled on his back and began to float, his penis sticking up like a mast pole. He was bobbing up and down in the surge.

"Climb up on me," he said.

"You'll sink."

"Not a chance. I'm a Samoan, we're completely unsinkable."

Sitting, straddling Willie, Maria could hear the villagers clapping and cheering. She put Willie, wet with the sea, inside her. Then she tried her best to drown him by thrusting down. The harder she pushed down the higher he bounced up, coming right up out of the water, like a cork.

Maria thought a gypsy thought, there on the Samoan sea. It's like breaking a stallion, you want to leave a little bit of him wild.

Her stallion began to smile, and laugh. Laugh so hard he shook. Willie's trembling body was the last straw and Maria lost herself in orgasm.

She saw a whole new future for them. Being Samoan, American, Rom, or Maslet was the past, the foundation. Now, recognizing who they were, together they could become...